Spritzer Vallier is the manager of a large commercial jug winery in Northern California. The new owner, Spritzer's great-aunt Del, wants to make a quality champagne as well as the cheap wine that is the bedrock of their business. Being a down-to-earth, no-nonsense guy, Spritzer resists Del's fantastic idea. However, she insists and hires Michel, a French champagne master, to direct the setup of the new venture for four years until Spritzer can take over the running the winery by himself.

Spritzer and Michel must work closely together and right from the beginning it is clear there will be fireworks. Michel tends towards arrogance and control. Spritzer resents Michel's authority and demands, and is a bit of a stubborn hot-head.

Keeping the two in check is Del—steady, caring, and wise, she directs the two toward the accomplishment of her dream.

Storms, accidents, and money problems plague the progress of the new winery, but eventually Michel and Spritzer work their way towards a successful conclusion to their efforts. But fate seems to have another destination for them as well, as they begin to fall in love with each other.

Spritzer must deal with his girlfriend, Kan, and the fact that Michel will be returning to France at the end of his contract. Michel must deal with the fear of loving and committing to another. How will they find a solution to their conundrum?

Published by
NineStar Press
PO Box 91792
Albuquerque, New Mexico, 87199
www.ninestarpress.com

Print ISBN # 978-1-945952-80-7
Cover by Natasha Snow
Edited by Elizabeth Coldwell

SPRITZER

A Sparkling Gay Romance

Jon McDonald

PROLOGUE

2012

Spritzer Vallier stood in contemplation, gazing at the strange sight before him—a couple of dozen or more folks, dressed mostly in black, standing at the crest of a hill overlooking a Sonoma vineyard. It stretched out below them as far as one could see in every direction; rows and rows of cultivated grape vines, marching neatly in their straight lines. The early morning mists slowly evaporated in the warmth of the climbing morning sun.

Spritzer ran a hand through his dark, curly, unkempt hair, distracted from the immediacy of the memorial service for his recently departed great-uncle Tom, as his mind wandered to the urgent need to be harvesting the glowing, ripe grapes spread out before him. There is a moment when the grapes' sugars are at their peak, and any delay might harm a season's harvest. Spritzer had checked the sugar levels in the grapes just yesterday afternoon and decided that they should start the harvest today. But Aunt Del, Tom's sister, had already arranged for the memorial service to be held this very morning.

He shook himself free from those thoughts and turned his attention back to the droning priest. Spritzer was standing between his great-aunt Del—short for Deloris—and his childhood buddy, and occasional girlfriend, Kan. He turned to his aunt and squeezed her arm, as the priest extolled her brother's many virtues.

"Are you holding up all right?" Spritzer asked gently.

Del looked over and smiled. "It's still hard to believe he's gone."

"I know."

Kan—blonde, lean, and tomboyish—leaned into Spritzer and whispered, "Nice service, don't you think?"

Spritzer turned to her and said, "Yeah, yeah. But look at all those fuckin' grapes. The old man would kick off just when I need to start the harvest, right?"

Just then, a biplane approached from behind the gathering, flew low over the heads of the crowd, and began to spray the vineyard.

Kan looked puzzled. "Isn't this an odd time to be spraying insecticide, for Christ's sake?"

"That's not insecticide, that's Uncle Tom," Spritzer answered, with a flash of his quirky grin. Kan looked at him questioningly. "Some people want their ashes at sea. Uncle Tom..." He gestured toward the vineyard.

"Yuck. It's going all over the grapes. What's that going to do to the wine?"

Spritzer thought about that for a moment, then answered. "Probably make the horrid supermarket plonk we produce a hell of a lot better than it was when he was alive."

Kan laughed and turned back to the service.

PART ONE

CHAPTER ONE

All was inky black, tempered by only the faintest violet bruise of dawn on the eastern horizon. The night mists continued to huddle between the rows in the lowest contours of the vineyard. The dew-diamond grapes were plump, ripe, and ready to be squandered in the ancient art of winemaking. Not even the earliest birds were yet stirring, and the valley rested in stillness and an almost heartbreaking silence.

Then, from far away, an imperceptible rumble began to grow. On the western horizon, the bounce of headlights betrayed the advance of several armies of flatbeds loaded with stacked tubs for collecting the grapes, harvesting machines, and pickups filled with sleepy-eyed workers. It was the commencement of the Vallier Winery harvest. Spritzer was driving the lead truck. He pulled off the road and down the embankment to the staging area for the harvest. He parked and then began directing the various vehicles to their proper destinations.

The harvest of a vineyard of this magnitude was not a haphazard affair. Every square meter of vines was accounted for, and strategies for the most efficient harvest were planned for weeks in advance. These strategies varied from year to year, depending on the conditions of the grapes. Each year, the variations in weather determined which section of the vineyard would ripen first, and the ripest grapes were always the first picked. It was Spritzer's job, as the new manager, to oversee this year's harvest, and he was totally prepared.

Even as the dawn progressed, the large harvest machines were already at work, straddling the rows of vines and extracting the grapes in the most efficient manner. This was not a boutique vineyard where the grapes were carefully hand-harvested in order to leave them unbruised. It did not matter in the slightest with jug wine. Efficiency and expediency were of primary importance here. Volume. Volume. Get the grapes off the vines and into the tubs—onto the trucks—to the crusher destemmer—and then get the juice into the waiting stainless-steel fermentation vats.

Once the harvest was well under way, Spritzer turned the operation over to Francisco Delgado, his deputy, and Francisco's son, Lorne, and headed back to the winery to oversee the arrival of the first grapes.

Francisco was a short, tough, wiry, and weathered man in his early sixties, whose family went back many generations to the very early days of Spanish California. Spritzer's father, Brian, and Francisco had worked closely together their whole working lives, and they considered themselves best friends. Spritzer had complete faith in Francisco's abilities and knew that he could always count on him to make the right decision. He saw Francisco as his second father, and knew that, even though he was now the boss at the relatively young age of twenty-six, Francisco knew much more than he did, so he relied heavily on Francisco's experience, knowledge, and wise decisions.

Lorne and Spritzer had grown up together. They'd been best friends, just like their fathers, until Spritzer went off to UC Davis to study viticulture and they'd drifted apart over time, even though Lorne still worked with his father at the vineyard.

Vallier Winery was a vast operation, housed in a massive series of warehouses, situated in a level section of the upper valley not far from the Russian River. The operation was equipped with all the latest, sophisticated high-tech equipment. A large control room was situated high in the first warehouse, with a commanding view of the arriving trucks where the tubs were emptied into the processing machine that destemmed and crushed the grapes before the juice was extracted and sent to the vats for fermentation. The entire process could be observed from the control room.

Spritzer stood at the control panel with his clipboard while the operator supervised and directed the arrival of the trucks and the distribution of the grape juice.

A call came in on Spritzer's walkie-talkie.

"Spritzer, this is Francisco. Do you read me?"

"Read ya," Spritzer responded.

"Five more trucks leaving number ten. Should be there in twenty. Over."

"Roger, ten-four."

Spritzer turned to the control panel operator. "Let me know as soon as number eight's clean. Looks like we'll need it today."

"Yeah. Sure thing."

Spritzer left the control room and strode along the catwalk above the fermentation tanks, checking to see that each tank was filled to its capacity, before opening up the next one.

* * *

Outside the winery there was a line of trucks waiting to be emptied. It was strange to see a stretch limo tooling along beside this row of trucks. The limo drove over to the entrance of the winery and parked. And even stranger was to see half a dozen tourists get out of the limo holding glasses of champagne. They were followed by the appearance of Nelson Wayland, Spritzer's cousin. He looked around his surroundings, and was oblivious to, or unaffected by, the exigent activity of the harvest swirling around him. Nelson was dressed very smoothly in a white linen suit. He was in his midthirties, but looked a little older, with his receding hairline and his plumping waist. He was holding a small white Maltese dog. "Oo need go pee-pee?" he cooed to the wee one. He set the dog on the ground, and she ran to the weeds to relieve herself and then began stalking grasshoppers.

Nelson turned to his guests. "Well, here we are, my dears—the familial chateau. Home and origin of the most god-awful supermarket jug swill you have *ever* tasted—red and white. Cheap and lethal. But I promise you a good laugh, and then we'll be on our merry way to sample some of the really good stuff farther down the road."

"Why bother, Mr. Wayland?" one of his guests inquired.

"I have a little business with my aunt during your picnic lunch at those darling tables on the patio over there. I shan't be long, I promise."

"Is there a tasting room?" another guest asked.

"Afraid not. Public poisoning is not good for business."

The guests had a hearty laugh at that.

Nelson looked around the property. He called his dog, picked her up, and turned back to his guests. "Let me see if I can find my cousin, Stevie. He runs this place. Maybe he can show you how this witch's brew is made, if you insist on knowing. It is a state-of-the-art commercial operation and should hold some interest for you. Come, follow me."

Nelson led the group from the limo into the warehouse, through the entrance where the trucks were unloading their tubs of grapes. There was a great deal of noise and activity, with workers tipping the tubs into the crusher, the empty tubs being loaded onto forklifts, trucks departing, and more forklifts loading cartons of wine into a semitrailer for delivery.

The visitors were curious and wandered around the warehouse indiscriminately, oblivious to the obstructions they were causing.

Forklifts had to stop or go around them where they stood clumped together. Workers had to stop what they were doing to answer questions.

There was so much noise from the trucks and machinery the visitors could not hear as Nelson tried to round the group up and move them along.

Finally, a supervisor, noticing the commotion, called Spritzer on his walkie-talkie. "Spritzer, you read me? This is Chuck."

Spritzer, still up on the catwalk above the vats, answered. "I read ya. What's up?"

"We got a group of civilians screwing around on the floor down here. Did you authorize a tour or something?"

"Not me."

"Well, they're causing a hell of a mess. You might want to check on it."

"Be right down. Ten-four."

Nelson finally rounded up his flock and led them to an area where cartons were stacked on pallets ready to be shipped. Nelson put down his dog, ripped open a carton, took out a jug of red, unscrewed the cap, and began pouring it into the tourists' champagne flutes.

Nelson began mockingly, "Notice the distinctive, full-bodied aroma. The heady, yet substantial, undercurrent that suggests both the fruit and the floral. A bold, presumptive, sassy, semiclassic. Wouldn't you say?"

Spritzer was down from the catwalk and came charging over to the group.

"Nelson, you are so full of shit. What the fuck are you doing here?"

"Ah, coz—sampling this foxy little Bacchanalian delight. Vino for the masses. Proud tribute to the Vallier heritage and name..."

Spritzer reached over, took the jug from Nelson, and proceeded to pour it over his head.

"It also has a quite delicate, yet persuasive way of silencing loudmouths." Spritzer turned to the tourists. "Ladies. Gentlemen. Now it's time to get the hell out of here. This is a place of business, and we are very busy with the harvest, and I don't want to have to pull any of your mangled bodies out of the stemmer-crusher after you fall in. Good day."

The tourists scattered back to the limo like mice before a cat. Nelson was rendered momentarily speechless, his hands fluttering as he tried to get out his words of indignation while blotting his face with his handkerchief. But all he could do was sputter. He picked up his dog, turned to Spritzer, and finally spit out, "Aunt Del is going to hear about this."

"I'm sure she will. And she'll have your ass for disrupting our operation and endangering your guests during harvest."

* * *

Nestled in rolling hills at the far end of the vineyard, secluded and quiet, the Vallier family home was a classic California hacienda-style house that had expanded, grown, and wandered its way across the property over many decades. When the vineyard was first established in the 1850s, the house was a simple, single dwelling for a modest Spanish family that spent whatever funds they had buying more land and putting in more vines. There was little thought to how the house looked. But over time, and as the vineyard and winery prospered, succeeding generations began to expand and improve the humble dwelling. When the Vallier family acquired the property in the 1920s, they named it Coeur du Chêne—Heart of the Oak—and made more improvements, with particular attention to the kitchen and the master bedroom wing.

Currently, the large adobe brick and stucco building rambled around a central patio with lush plantings of hibiscus, birds of paradise, night-blooming jasmine, and bougainvillea in various brilliant shades of orange, red, and purple—all surrounding a central fountain that spilled gently into a pool with the soothing sounds of falling water on a still summer's night.

The house was U-shaped. The central wing had a large, welcoming entrance that led directly into a vast living room, with two fireplaces—one at each end. French doors filed along the wall leading to the patio. Even on the hottest summer afternoon, with the doors and windows open, and with the thick adobe walls providing insulation from the summer heat, a light breeze could waft through the living room, keeping the occupants pleasantly cool. In the winter, again the adobe walls insulated the room, and with cheery fires in each fireplace, the room was warm and comforting. One could sit on the sofa, a standing lamp over one's shoulder, lit candles on the coffee table before the sofa, reading a book, and look out through the patio doors and see the snow falling, piling up on the edges of the fountain, making a delightful sculpture on the patio.

The floors of the house were hardwood oak or polished Saltillo tiles. Rich carpets from around the world softened one's step in the living room or the bedrooms. The walls were the rich, deep colors of burnished ochre, deep wine red, or persimmon orange. The library, which served as a meeting room for the winery's staff from time to time, was a lush forest green.

The left wing of the house had the dining room and the spacious kitchen. In the center of the kitchen was a sturdy pine table, made by the first owners of the house. There was a fireplace with a spit that still roasted meats, a wood-fired brick oven for baking, and a variety of essential modern appliances—a six-burner gas stove, a refrigerator, and a freezer to store the fruit and vegetable surpluses in the autumn. There was also a pantry filled with jams, jellies, and preserved fruits from the orchard that one could see from the open side of the U. Also surrounding the house were well-established trees giving abundant shade—large cottonwoods, eucalyptus trees, and a few evergreens.

Lastly, the third wing contained the library, the bedrooms, and the bathrooms. The master bedroom was at the very end of the hall. It was surrounded by windows on three sides. It had its own fireplace, a large, canopied bed, and an area for sitting, a room for dressing, and a master bath. The other bedrooms were modest but comfortable.

* * *

Del lived alone in this vast, rambling hacienda. She was helped by Clara, Francisco's wife and Lorne's mother, who managed the house and cooked Del's meals. Clara was not only Del's housekeeper and companion, but also her dearest friend—trusted and indispensable. Spritzer had taken his own apartment in town some years ago, preferring to establish his independence at an early age.

Del's pottery studio was in an outbuilding, not far from the kitchen wing, which she'd had constructed when she first moved back to California from France to be with her brother, Tom. It was a comfortable, cozy studio with shelving units covering every wall space that didn't have a window or door. She'd constructed an outdoor kiln, and had her potter's wheel set up in the center of the studio next to a large worktable where she did her glazing.

Del was still sprightly at eighty-three. She was unusually tall but well proportioned. She wore her reddish-gray hair piled up on the top of her head, held in place with tortoiseshell combs. She had bright, smiling eyes, and though she suffered from minor arthritis, she continued to work with her hands at the wheel like an eighteen-year-old.

Del went to France in the early 1950s on a student exchange program and never left—not until Tom's wife died and he'd asked her to come home to help out with the winery. She was enchanted with the bohemian lifestyle in Paris and became a modern dancer until she discovered ceramics. She studied briefly with Raoul Lachenal, late in his life, and became renowned for her richly colored volcanic glazes. She'd had a studio just outside Paris and became celebrated and widely collected in museums and by individual collectors. When she returned to California, she continued her work, but now her output was more restricted because of her advancing age. But her prices continued to soar along with her reputation.

This morning, Del was sitting at her potter's wheel working on a series of large bowls. She was covered in slip and looked like she had just stepped out of a clay pit. There was a rapid pounding at her door, and Nelson came storming in, covered in red wine, and carrying his dog and a briefcase.

Del let out a hoot of laughter. "What the hell happened to you?"

Nelson paced and sputtered, finally putting the dog down, which then raced around the studio like a windup toy.

"I've never been so outraged in all my life!" he said, with a great deal of personal indignation.

"Aww...what happened, sweetie?" But she was having a hard time being sympathetic when all she wanted to do was continue laughing.

"Stevie...Stevie..." Nelson chuffed.

"Here—come give us a kiss," Del insisted. Nelson leaned over, and she gave him a kiss, and then slapped his behind with a towel. "Do you want to take a shower?"

"No, I'm fine. The wine-in-the-face look is all the rage this season."

"Nelson, have you been a bad boy?" she asked.

"Me? Me? What about that...that...barbarian? He poured wine all over me."

"Tsk-tsk. Well, you were probably in his way and asking for it. He's running a business, you know, not a cocktail party. I know all about you and your 'wine discovery tours.'"

"That's no excuse. He could be civil. I am, after all, one of California's major wine brokers, and I happen to be leading a tour with some *very* distinguished wine connoisseurs."

"Well then, hon, what are you doing *here*? I can't imagine our jug winery is high on your list of Sonoma must-sees."

"This is our visit to a *commercial* winery. We've just come from some of the more *select* of the Napa vineyards. I forgot how cheap and nasty this wine really was.

"Yes, honey, but it sells."

"Maybe, but to whom?"

"Nelson, you are *such* a snob."

"But surely, it wasn't always this bad, was it? I remember when I was a child the winery turned out a fairly decent reserve cabernet. Is that not so?"

"Yes, Papa had great plans for the vineyard. His dream, you know, was to produce fine champagne like our family did in France all those many decades ago. But Tom, who was running the winery by then, discontinued the select cabernet when he got the supermarket contracts. The good stuff took too much time and money to produce properly, he said."

Nelson picked up the pooch and squeezed her to him. "Well, he should be ashamed." He stopped. "Sorry. I forgot he's gone. Shouldn't say bad things about the recently departed."

Del nodded. "I forget too, sometimes."

"Was the memorial service nice? Sorry, I couldn't make it yesterday. I have this tour for a week."

"It was as he wanted it," Del answered.

Nelson hesitated a moment, then said, "Well, Del, now that you are the new owner, I'd like to suggest..."

"What?"

"You've got a good facility here. And a good enough vineyard for a really fine select label. A lot of big commercial wineries are now developing quality lines. There's plenty of money to be made with those there these days. The California select wine market is booming. The good wines are bringing excellent prices, and they add a lot of prestige to the name. Now that this is all yours, you really should consider doing something like that too."

Del thought about what he'd said. "You really think I could?"

"You've got the soil, you've got the perfect exposure, and you've got an established facility. All you'd need now is the will—and some high-quality expertise."

Nelson reached down and took some papers out of his briefcase. "But that's not the real reason I'm here. I don't know how much you know about Tom's personal affairs, but I'm afraid I have some bad news, which could certainly affect your decision about what you might want to do next."

* * *

At the end of the first day of harvest, Spritzer was exhausted. He'd forgotten how demanding the work was, and he'd always had his uncle to work with before. He slumped at his desk in his dingy, cramped office. He was studying a pile of papers he needed to deal with, but just couldn't muster the energy, or the will, to do anything more this evening.

Kan leaned in the door. She was dressed in work clothes and looked a bit tired herself.

"Hey, kiddo, lighten up a little, huh? You look as beat as I feel." She went over and gave Spritzer a kiss on the back of his neck.

"Hey..."

She pulled up a chair, swung it around, and straddled it, resting her arms on the back and facing Spritzer.

"Wanna drink?" he asked. "I could sure use one."

"You bet. Bitch of a day, but Dad and I got most of the harvest in. And I think it's time to do a little cel-a-brating, don't you?"

"Oh yeah." He went over to a small fridge, poured a glass of Vallier white wine for Kan, and fixed a white-wine spritzer for himself.

"Bushed?" she asked.

"Yeah, but a good first day for me. First time all by myself, directing the whole operation. But I do miss Uncle Tom."

Kan nodded. "Yeah, I bet you do." She started to laugh. "Hey, I heard about that little episode with Nelson. Wish I'd seen that."

"Yeah. Son of a bitch..."

"O-o-o-o, touchy, touchy. So, did he impugn the quality of your *cuvée*?"

Spritzer laughed and handed Kan her wine.

Francisco knocked at the doorframe. "Hi, Kan."

"Hi there..."

Francisco addressed Spritzer. "Del wants to see you before you go, okay?"

Spritzer groaned.

"See you tomorrow, bright and early," Francisco tossed off as he was leaving. "Got another killer day tomorrow."

"Say hi to Clara," Spritzer shouted to the retreating Francisco. He then turned to Kan. "What's the time?"

"Little after seven."

"Hey, we'd better split. I'm starved. Never had time for lunch today."

"How 'bout I pick up a pizza and meet you at your place?"

"Okay, but it's got to be an early night. It's going to be another bitch of a day tomorrow. And I've still got to check in on Del before I leave." Spritzer got up from his desk.

"Sure, but make it quick, okay. I'm beat and starved too."

"Okay, see ya soon."

* * *

"Did you want to see me?" Spritzer asked, as he came into Del's studio.

"Uh-huh."

"It's late. Why aren't you in the house? You must be exhausted. You shouldn't be working this long," Spritzer scolded her.

"Oh my dear, it's what I do. You should know that about me by now."

Del was cleaning up at the work sink after an afternoon of glazing. He stood waiting for her to speak again, which she didn't for a moment or two. Del finished at the sink, dried her hands, and then turned to Spritzer.

"Nelson came to see me today," she informed him, smiling slightly.

Spritzer laughed. "Yes, I bet he did. Do I have to go stand in the corner without any supper?"

Del smiled. "No. I expect he deserved it. Though it *was* amusing to see his pink, wine-stained pooch. Seems she caught some of the splash."

Del continued to tidy up the studio and wipe down the potter's wheel.

Finally, Spritzer said, "Listen, hon, I know you want to talk, but I'm really bushed and hungry, and I've got another big day tomorrow."

Del turned toward him, came over, and pinched his cheek. "Now, don't be in such a hurry. Humor the old broad a little, will ya?"

Spritzer sat down at her worktable. "Okay, okay."

Del then gave Spritzer her full attention. "Did you know Tom played the horses?"

"I had a suspicion or two. But we never discussed it. None of my business."

"Well, I didn't. Seems he lost tens of thousands. He mortgaged pretty near everything here to Nelson, who's been keeping him afloat for some time."

"Oh shit."

"Yeah. Oh shit. It's all come as rather a shock to me too. I'm sorry to lay this on you right now, but I need your advice. Nelson has offered to buy me out. His family has the money of Croesus, and I think he fancies a new plaything."

"Nelson! Good God, no! He knows nothing about running a winery."

"But you do. And I'm sure he'd want to keep you on, unless you totally alienate him with your shenanigans."

"Are you kidding? I couldn't work for him. No way! You mustn't sell to him, Del. There's got to be another way. I'll do whatever I can to help you through this."

"Well, that depends…"

"On what?"

"Just a minute." She walked over to a shelf and brought over one of her finest, beautifully flared, shallow bowls. She handed it to him. "Do you know how many years I've needed to make pots to get a work like that?"

He looked up to her as he ran his hands over the surface of the bowl. It was a deep stone color with subtle variations of pockmarked gray and black, sprinkled with dots of bamboo green.

"Forty-seven. And let me tell you, with all modesty, that there's a really good piece—maybe even great. I'm proud of that, and when I'm gone, it will still be here, and people will remember."

"I'm sure they will."

"Yes, but I'd like to make something that special here at the vineyard as well."

"What are you getting at?"

She went to the sink, and came back with a mass-produced cereal bowl, and put it down next to her work of fine art. She pointed to the cereal bowl. "The winery makes plenty of this." She then pointed to her bowl. "But now I want us to make some of that."

Del sat down at the table and took Spritzer's hands. "My papa had a dream. When Tom and I were growing up, all he wanted to do was to make champagne like the family used to do in France. However, at that time, in this country, there wasn't the technology, or the sophistication in the grapes, that we have now. Papa settled instead on making a fine cabernet with the resources he had. But when Papa died, Tom, being the eldest, inherited the winery, discontinued the cabernet, and chose to make this mass-produced piss we sell now."

"But it keeps us going pretty well. It's a good business."

"I know that. But humor me a moment, please. I was the rebel in the family. I went to Paris where I danced with the Paris Opera Ballet, modeled for Picasso, Cocteau, and van Dongen, and then finally discovered my ceramics. I lived and worked there for nearly thirty years and loved every minute of it. But when Tom needed me, I came home. And it wasn't my place to tell him what to do with his winery. But, in my heart, I have always kept our papa's dream alive. Stevie, you are a vital part of this family and this winery. And both you and Nelson are my heirs."

"Del..."

"I've decided I don't want to sell the vineyard to Nelson so he gets it all. I've got some capital of my own, and I want to invest it in the winery and set up operations to make the very best champagne in California— not your supermarket, shortcut, carbonated fizzy, but using the traditional *Méthode Champenoise,* which makes the finest champagne."

Spritzer got up from his chair and began pacing. "What? Do you know what that would cost? It's not just a matter of changing the label on our bottles, you know. It's going to take lots of committed time and money. It would take at least several years before we could release the first bottle, and that's if we started today."

Del sighed. "I'm aware of the expense and the time. But look, I'm eighty-three. What else have I got to do with my money?"

"Okay then, but you know I know nothing about making champagne. It's a very specialized procedure. And it's a full-time job just running the winery as it is now."

"Fine. Then let's find the very best person to make this champagne and hire him. This is something I want to do."

"Sounds crazy, Del."

"Maybe. But it comes down to this—and believe me, I'm serious. Either you help me make champagne and we keep this winery going together, or I sell it to Nelson and he gets it all right now."

"That's blackmail!"

Del smiled and nodded. Spritzer sat down again and leaned back in the chair, flabbergasted. He shook his head as he tried to assimilate the impact of this new venture. Del leaned in closer and held up her bowl to him.

"I don't know. I just don't know," he said.

"It's true we'll never get this quality without a lot of time and effort. But it's worth it. Don't give up on me, Stevie. I'm willing to risk it if you are. Stretch yourself. Promise me you'll think about it."

Spritzer suddenly pulled himself together, leaned forward, and kissed her on the forehead.

"I do need to think about it."

Del stood. "Good. Meanwhile, I'm going to contact the *Chefs de Cave* I researched, and see who might be interested in working with us on this."

"What the fuck's a *Chef de Cave*?"

"A master champagne maker."

"Hmm."

"Why don't you go away for a few days after the harvest and think about it?" Del suggested.

Spritzer nodded. "Okay, but I still think you're a wacko dingbat."

"Yes, of course, but I'm the wacko dingbat that owns this winery."

He got up from his chair, kissed Del again, and left.

CHAPTER TWO

1987

Clara and Francisco sat in the doctor's office waiting for the test results.

Francisco took Clara's hand. "Are you okay?"

She looked up at him. "I just want this over with." He nodded. "What if...?"

"Not now." He patted her hand.

The doctor came into his office where the two were seated in chairs in front of his desk. "Good morning," he said. Clara and Francisco were too nervous to respond. The doctor sat down and pulled a medical chart from a pile on his desk. He didn't make eye contact with them immediately, but, instead, studied the chart. He cleared his throat and then looked up and nodded a few times before speaking. He addressed Clara first. "Mrs. Delgado, your tests have come back just fine. There is no reason whatsoever why you can't become pregnant."

Clara's face lit up. She turned to Francisco and took his hand. "Oh, thank you, doctor."

"But, of course, at thirty-six time *is* running out, you understand."

She nodded.

The doctor turned to Francisco. He hesitated, but then proceeded. "However, Mr. Delgado, I'm afraid to say your tests are very disappointing. It's difficult for me to have to say this, but, for whatever reason, you are completely sterile. There is no way you can have children as a couple."

Francisco didn't speak but bowed his head.

Finally, Clara asked, "Is there anything you can do for him?"

The doctor shook his head. "I'm afraid there is nothing at this time. I am so sorry. But, of course, there is always artificial insemination or adoption. We can discuss those options if you like."

* * *

2012

Spritzer was *really* ready for a break at the end of harvest. It had been the first time he'd run the harvest solo, and while it had been a success, he'd been exhausted by the stress of his new responsibility. Postharvest was a relatively quiet time at the winery, as the grapes fermented. There was work to be done in the vineyard after the harvest, and at the winery, cleaning up after the pressing, but Spritzer knew he could leave the oversight of all of that in Francisco's very capable hands. Spritzer, with Del's approval, had promoted Francisco to second-in-command after he'd taken over as manager, and he knew all would be well in his absence while he took off for a long weekend. He'd not talked to Del about her proposal since their intense meeting. He'd been thinking about making the champagne, but was still conflicted about the whole setup, and he hoped this weekend away would help him get some clarity on the proposal. He wanted to discuss it with Kan, so that he could make an intelligently informed decision. Uppermost in his mind; however, was that he didn't want Nelson to take over the winery, as there was no way he could work with his cousin as owner.

Spritzer picked up Kan early in the morning at her house, and they set out in his Jeep for a weekend of camping. They had a favorite spot they liked to go to, up in the Sierras, but to reach it required either a long hike in or taking horses. If they took horses, Spritzer had a problem—he was a totally incompetent and inexperienced rider. And Kan was not only comfortable in the saddle, she was a semiprofessional bronc rider on the western rodeo circuit. It seemed unfair, and he didn't like the fact that he was not as good as a girl at anything, but he would just have to bear with it, as they didn't have time to hike in and out if they wanted to spend some quality time at the campsite. Taking the horses was their only practical option.

Kan had friends from the rodeo circuit who had a stable close to where they'd wanted to go, so she'd arranged to rent a couple of horses from them for the weekend.

At the stable, Spritzer was nervous as he mounted the mare with Kan's assistance.

"Are you sure about this?" Spritzer asked nervously. "This horse—is she going to run away with me?"

"Not unless you propose marriage and prove you can support her."

"Ha-ha—very funny," Spritzer grumped. But he did not think riding a horse was at all funny.

Finally, they did get mounted and under way, with Kan leading. It was a spectacular late-September morning, and while it was pleasantly warm now, higher up in the mountains it could be quite chilly in the evenings, with the likelihood of frost by morning. They would have to snuggle up close together in the tent during the night. And Spritzer quietly looked forward to that possibility.

After three hours of winding along the trail, Spritzer's butt was sore and his legs stiff and chafed.

"How much longer?" he shouted forward to Kan.

"We're almost there. Look." She pointed above the trees to the top of a waterfall just coming into view up ahead. "Come on, let's move it."

She spurred her horse into a gallop. Spritzer tried to follow, nudging his horse with the heels of his sneakers, but she didn't respond. He leaned forward and spoke into the animal's ear, "Please, can you go a little faster?" But no response. Then, finally, she seemed to get the idea as the horse ahead of her galloped off. Spritzer did not know how to ride at a gallop and bounced around in the saddle like a spastic dashboard bobblehead, the pots, and pans attached to his saddle clanging frantically.

By the time he reached the campsite, Kan had already dismounted and was unloading her camping gear.

"Slowpoke," she shouted. "What took you so long?"

"Ha-ha..." He dismounted very slowly, and with great effort. Every part of his lower extremities ached. He could barely walk.

"Wanna go swimming?" Kan asked, after she secured the horses.

"Sure." He tried to sound lighthearted as he waddled with his gear to the campsite.

"Race ya." She tossed off her clothes and then dashed toward the lake.

There was absolutely no chance he could race her. He felt it would be all he could do to crawl over to the lake.

But swim they did, even though the water was quite cold this late in the season. It helped Spritzer unwind, and by the time he got out of the water he felt almost normal again.

They proceeded to set up camp, and then took a hike around the lake. As the sun began to set, Kan made a campfire while Spritzer threw together a stew. He was not a great cook, but could call upon a few simple and reliable campfire classics. And, besides, he knew Kan's cooking was even worse.

Later that evening, the two were snuggled around the campfire. She leaned back against him, and he had his arms around her, pulling her tightly against his chest. The crickets serenaded them, and an owl took flight from a nearby tree just as the moon began to rise over the tops of the pine trees.

"That was a pretty good stew, if I do say so myself," Spritzer crowed.

"Yeah. You'll make somebody a wonderful wife someday." Kan chuckled.

Spritzer gave her a poke in the arm.

"Owww. That hurt."

"Sorry." He leaned over and kissed her on top of her head as an apology. They were both silent for a while, just staring into the pulsing embers of the fire. Spritzer tossed another log on the fire. They were going to need the warmth this evening, as it was already starting to get cold, and they'd both donned their down jackets.

"What have you decided about Del's proposal to make champagne?" Kan asked, after they had been silent for a while.

Spritzer rubbed his face. The subject was ever present in his mind, and he'd intended to talk to her about it. But he was feeling too mellow right now, and didn't want to disrupt his serenity.

"Not now, okay?"

Kan said, "Yeah, well...I thought maybe I could help. Sorry if I intruded on your private business."

"It's not that..."

She pulled his arms tighter around her, snuggling closer to him.

"Sometimes you're about as much fun as a Senate hearing on toxic waste." She took a quick look at him. He caught her eye, and she looked away. She paused, then said, "But sometimes you're okay too."

He didn't answer. She looked at him again, then gave him a playful tap on the cheek. They both laughed.

"You're right. I really do need to talk to you about Del's proposal. I'm having a very hard time making up my mind what to do. I've told you all the details—what do you think? I'd like your take on it."

"Well now, let me see if I've got this right. Unless you agree to make a high-quality champagne at the winery, Del will sell the vineyard to Nelson and you will be out of your inheritance and out of a job? What am I missing here? What is there to decide? Seems pretty obvious and straightforward to me, numbskull."

"Yes, but I know nothing about making champagne."

"But Del told you she'd hire someone who does. Is that a problem for you?"

"Well...what if it doesn't work out? It's like having two captains steering a ship. What if we don't agree or don't get along?"

"Sweetie, that's called life. You've got to take each situation as it comes and deal with it as best you can. You're not stupid, Spritz. Look at how successfully you work with, and deal with, dozens of workers, providers, and customers. What is it exactly that's troubling you?"

Spritzer thought about that for a moment. "I think I don't want to have to learn something new. I like what I do. I like what I have, and I don't want to change anything."

"Hmmm. Then you got big problems, kiddo, 'cause life will come along, kick you in the butt, and force you to change—like it or not."

Spritzer thought about what Kan had just advised. She had put the issues very succinctly, and he realized she made a lot of sense.

"You're right. It would be pretty stupid of me if I didn't accept Del's proposal, wouldn't it?"

"I think so."

"Okay, I'll talk to her when I get back."

"Good for you. Smart lad. I see there's still hope for you yet."

"Thanks."

They were both quiet for a few moments, each lost in their own thoughts. Finally, Kan took Spritzer's hand and kissed it.

"And while we're talking about the future, I was wondering what your thoughts were about us."

"How do you mean?" Spritzer asked.

"Well, where are we headed—as a couple? What do you want from our relationship?"

Spritzer *really* did not want to have *this* particular conversation—again. She had brought this question up before but he'd always managed to deflect her line of questioning with some sort of frantic activity. This evening, though, there was no deflection available. He would have to address her concerns.

"Well, we're great friends, aren't we? And I expect we will always be."

She disengaged from his embrace, sat up, and turned to look at him. "Friends? Friends? You see us as just friends?"

Spritzer tried to lighten the mood with a laugh. "Yeah, well, we play around a bit in the sack too. You know—buddy sex."

Now Kan looked really pissed. "Buddy sex! That's it? That's what you think we have?" She stood.

"I thought that's what you wanted. No complications. Just some fun. Pals. Buddies hanging out..."

"Arrr..." Kan seemed too pissed to continue. She charged down to the edge of the lake.

Spritzer poked the fire and put another log on. "Ka-a-an," he called out. "Come on back. It's freezing out there."

"You're a son of a bitch, you know that?" Kan answered.

"I'm sorry, Kan. Really. Just jokin' 'round with ya. Come on back. I put another log on the fire. Come on. I'm really sorry."

Kan held her arms tight around her body and headed back to the campfire. But she didn't cuddle up to Spritzer this time. Instead, she sat on the opposite side of the fire, warming her hands.

Finally, Spritzer said, "Okay then, what is it you want? Tell me. I'm listening."

Kan thought about that and said, "I'm not sure now. I'm all confused. I thought we had something special, but now I can see I was just fooling myself."

"Kan..." Spritzer reached out for her to come back to him.

She hesitated, but then crawled over and snuggled up again.

"You okay now?" he asked.

"Maybe."

"Come on. We've always been close, you and me. Nothing's changed. We'll be fine, won't we?"

"We'll see" was all she would commit to.

Spritzer gave an inward sigh of relief. That was close. But it seemed he'd just dodged another bullet. The old Spritzer charm still ruled.

* * *

Back from his weekend, and refreshed, Spritzer checked in with Francisco, and all was well at the winery.

Spritzer saw Lorne at his locker, hanging up his jacket. He ambled over. "How's it goin', Lorne?"

"Hey, Spritz. You and Kan have a nice break?"

Spritzer nodded. "It was okay. Bit cold, but we snuggled up and kept warm enough."

Lorne smiled. "That's nice. Gotta go. Dad and I are heading out to sector five for some pruning with some of the crew. Catch ya later." He turned and walked away.

"Nice seein' ya…" Spritzer called after him.

Lorne was taller than his father, but slight. He had a fair complexion, and his features were more Caucasian than Hispanic. Some genetic throwback, Spritzer had always surmised. He had particularly nice eyes, which were expressive and lit up when he smiled.

Spritzer watched as Lorne walked away. He suddenly felt a profound sadness, as he realized how far the two of them had drifted apart from their very close childhood days. It was as though Lorne had cut himself completely off from Spritzer. He knew almost nothing about Lorne's life these days. He sensed there was something Lorne wanted to keep hidden. There was nothing left between them now but their superficial daily chitchat at work.

The wine was fermenting quite nicely. Spritzer went to his office and caught up with his e-mail and phone messages. Now it was time to have his conversation with Del.

He drove over to the hacienda. He parked out front and walked toward Del's studio, where he was sure she'd be at this time of the morning. She was an early riser. She'd catch a quick breakfast and then amble over to her studio to start her day's work—often even before the sun was up.

Del had constructed an arbor from the kitchen to the studio, to give her shelter on inclement days. This morning, the wisteria-covered arbor was alive with brightly colored autumn leaves dancing in the morning sun and the light breeze. Spritzer loved his family's wonderful estate, and Del had promised him it would be his when she died. He took great pride in keeping it in good repair for her.

"Del?" he called out, as he entered.

She was at the back of the studio, pulling articles from shelves to be shipped for an upcoming gallery exhibition.

"Stevie? Is that you?" she asked. "How was your weekend?"

She came forward with a beautifully colored sea-green platter and put it on her table with the other works to be shipped.

Spritzer threw himself on her ratty old sofa. "Just great. A bit saddle sore, but I'm sure I'll survive."

"Nelson is going to be here this afternoon. Have you made a decision about what you want to do?"

Spritzer nodded. "I have. I want to help you realize your dream, Del."

She gave a big smile. "I thought you might. I could see the idea of Nelson taking control of the property pissed you off royal."

Spritzer laughed. "Yes. You could say that."

"So...We've got to get ready for the meeting with Nelson. Can you print out copies of the proposal I put together, and any other papers you think he might need to consider my plan?"

"He's going to need your financials. He'll want to see where your capital's coming from."

"They're on my desk in the library."

"I'll get them on my way out and make copies."

"Oh...and by the way, I've found us a *Chef de Cave.*"

"Oh yes?"

"I got confirmation of my offer yesterday afternoon."

"And who is this paragon of champagne?"

"Michel Bast—from Epernay, France. He's accepting a four-year contract. I'm having my attorneys draw up the agreement. He should be here in time for the harvest festival."

"Boy, you didn't waste any time, did you?"

"Stevie, I don't have any time to waste."

* * *

The meeting with Nelson was scheduled for two o'clock. Spritzer went to Del's studio early to go over all the paperwork with her beforehand. This wasn't necessary, as Nelson was half an hour late—as usual. He sauntered in with his prize pooch wrapped in his arm.

"Del...Stevie? Surprised to see you here," Nelson greeted them.

"You're late," Del insisted.

"So sorry. Couldn't tear myself away from the wonderful lunch at Caprice. Such delightful blue crabs. Have you tried them?"

"We're not here to discuss crabs, unless they're the ones you've contracted," Spritzer snidely remarked.

"Okay, you two—enough. We've got serious business to discuss," Del said. "Stevie, will you give Nelson the proposal and financials, please."

Spritzer handed Nelson the papers. Nelson sat at the table after giving the dog a bowl of water. "Okay, let me see what this is all about."

Nelson studied the papers while Del wrapped pots for shipping, and Spritzer paced.

Finally, Nelson looked up and addressed them. "When I suggested you make some quality wine I was thinking of something a little more modest."

"Come, Nelson, where is your spirit of adventure?" Del queried.

"And this is your budget for this folly?"

"It is," Spritzer replied.

Nelson turned to Del. "And do you really have that kind of capital?" Del nodded. "You did all right for yourself then, didn't you, old girl? Have you sold all the jewelry from your Parisian admirers to finance this?"

Del ignored his little dig. "As you can see, I propose to pay you back all the small personal loans Tom borrowed from you. I will carry the rest of your mortgages on the winery from the profits of the Vallier business. And I'll use my own money to finance the new champagne house that I've named Maison Vallier."

Spritzer spoke up. "It might be close, but we can make it work. I'm sure of it. Del and I are one hundred percent committed."

"And who's this Michel Bast?" Nelson asked, studying the proposal further.

Del answered. "The best available *Chef de Cave* from the champagne cellars of France. I received his acceptance to my offer yesterday. He's agreed to a four-year contract, during which time Spritzer will learn the operation so he can take over when Bast leaves."

Nelson carefully considered this proposal. "It seems a bit risky—but very intriguing, I must admit."

"You won't be sorry," Del told him. "I'm planning to announce our new venture at the winery's harvest festival. I want it to be a really grand affair this year so we can introduce our new *Chef de Cave*, who will be with us by then.

"And you're sure you wouldn't rather accept my offer to buy the winery and let me take all of this off your hands? After all, you're not such a spring chicken anymore."

"I think Stevie would have a few objections to that."

"Yeah, just try me," Spritzer stated.

"Well, yes. It does indeed sound intriguing. I'll go along with this as long as this Michel Bast has the final decision in all matters relating to the champagne making. And if you fall behind on any of the mortgage payments, I have the right to buy you out and take over at the price we previously agreed upon."

"Hold on now..." Spritzer's hackles rose.

Del spoke up. "No, no, that's fair, Stevie. And don't worry, Nelson— we'll make sure nothing goes wrong. Okay?"

She held out her hand to Spritzer, who shook it, and then offered to shake with Nelson.

"I guess I have nothing to lose. If it's a success the company makes a lot of money from the champagne. And if it fails I get the whole operation to do with as I please. Either way, I win. Agreed." He finally shook Del's hand.

"Now, you two shake," she insisted.

Spritzer glared at Nelson but went over and took his hand. Nelson shook, but gave Spritzer a mocking grin. It was a good thing Del was going to be in charge, because Spritzer did not know how long he would be able to restrain himself from throttling Nelson whenever he saw his smug mug.

* * *

Spritzer had not seen Kan since their weekend camping trip, nor had they spoken on the phone since then. Spritzer was sitting at his desk late one afternoon going over the agreement with Michel Bast before he submitted it to Del for her signature. He was not great at reading legal documents—too many "the party of the first part" and "whereas the aforementioned..." He realized he could easily nod off to sleep. It was time to stop for the day.

He leaned back in his chair. What did he want to do this evening? He thought about Kan again. He wondered if she would still be pissed at him about his relationship remarks. Time to give her a call.

"Hey. Whatcha up to?"

"Oh..." Kan hesitated. "Hangin' with my dad. We're cleaning the tool shed."

"Well, that sounds like a ton of fun. Wanna go grab a burger at Tony's?"

"Don't see why not. When?"

"Half an hour?"

"Um. Make it forty-five minutes. I gotta finish up here and clean up."

"Okay, pick you up then?"

"No. Let's meet at Tony's. At eight?"

"Right. See ya."

* * *

Spritzer was at the restaurant early and ordered a pitcher of tap. Kan was fifteen minutes late. She spotted him in the booth and came over.

"What's up?" She leaned in and gave him a quick peck on the cheek before sitting down.

For a moment they just stared at each other. "Wanna order?" Spritzer asked, pouring her a glass of beer.

"Sure."

"Del and I are going ahead with the plan to make champagne," Spritzer offered, to break the awkward silence that hung over the evening like the first frost of autumn.

"Glad to hear it," was all Kan coolly responded.

"And what about you? How's your dad?"

"Fine." She wouldn't look him in the eye.

Spritzer stared at her. This was not going well. "Okay, look, I'm sorry about what I said about us last weekend. It was really dumb. I guess I was just surprised by the question. I didn't mean anything by it. Can you forgive me?"

Kan looked at him for a moment. "Do you really mean that?"

"I sure do."

"So then answer the question. Where do you see us going in our relationship, and what are your intentions? And answer me honestly."

This had to be just the right answer. Spritzer thought carefully. "I want to get married, have three children, two dogs, and a cat, and settle down in a wonderful little house with a white picket fence."

Kan jumped up on the table, leaned over, grabbed him by the neck, and gave him a great big sloppy kiss.

Spritzer was surprised and recoiled slightly, wiping his wet mouth. "Kan..."

She scooted back to her seat. "So was that a proposal?" she asked, her eyes shining.

"No-o-o, that was simply a statement of intention, as you requested, not a proposal. I can't think about marriage till we get the champagne making well established and under way."

"And how long is that going to take?" she asked.

"Hmm. I'm guessing at least a year or two."

"Really? That long?"

"Come on, Kan, it's not really that long. We're young. We're together. We're having fun. What does time matter?"

"Well, why not a proposal, then? We could still wait to get married, but at least we'd have the commitment."

Spritzer was not about to be bullied into this. "Kan, that's too much pressure on me right now. Please, be patient with me, okay? I've got plenty else to deal with at the moment."

Kan sighed. "I guess…But let me tell you, if Mr. Hunk or Mr. Hunky-Dory come a-callin' don't think I'm gonna look back."

Spritzer laughed. "You have my full permission. Go for it."

CHAPTER THREE

1988

Clara stood at her kitchen sink staring out of the window into the backyard, imagining a swing set and sandbox. She had washed, and now needed to rinse, a glass, but she just stood at the sink, frozen in her reverie.

Francisco came into the kitchen. Seeing her, once again lost in thought, he went over to her and put his hands on her shoulders. He leaned in and whispered, as he nuzzled her ear, "There's a solution to this, you know. You don't need to suffer so much."

She turned to him and put her arms around him with her head on his shoulder. "There's got to be another way."

"But it's done all the time, my love, with great success."

"I don't trust them."

"But, honey, it's totally controlled. You can read all about each donor and what their physical characteristics are."

"I know. But I can't meet them personally. I can't get a sense of who they *really* are. I can't know who they are from some meaningless printout."

"But you do want a child, yes?"

She just nodded with her head still on his shoulder.

"Okay, okay..." He patted her back and stared out of the window. "We'll figure something out, not to worry."

* * *

2012

Del wanted to hold the harvest festival at Coeur du Chêne rather than at the vineyard this year. The grounds were so lovely, and there was the magnificent estate kitchen where the food could be prepared and served. It would also be a more welcoming location to greet Michel Bast, as he would be flying into San Francisco on the afternoon of the festival, where he would be met by Francisco, and brought straight to the estate.

But first Del needed to confer with Clara to see if she was up to preparing the food, or whether it would be better to have it catered.

Clara was a still a striking woman at sixty-one. If one were to describe her it might be said that she came from pioneer stock. She was tall and strong. Her silver hair was pulled back from her face and tied in a tight bun at the back of her head. But she was not severe. Instead, she had a bright smile, sparkling dark eyes, and an easy laugh. Del had liked her immediately, and over the years they had shared many joys, sorrows, and secrets together. Del and Clara had become almost as close as sisters—Francisco and Lorne were as much a part of Del's tribe as Spritzer was a part of theirs.

"What do you think?" Del asked. "Is it too much to ask you to prepare the harvest festival food? You could certainly hire a staff to help if you felt the need."

Clara thought about the scope of Del's suggested project. "I think it might be fun. Have you planned a menu yet?"

"Oh yes, lots of champagne in honor of our new *Chef de Cave,* and I was thinking Mexican and Mediterranean dishes would be festive. But I don't have any specific recipes in mind. What do you think?"

"I think it sounds delightful. However, I'd reconsider the Mexican idea. Keep it simple and in keeping with the French theme. In fact, I would suggest a French Provençal menu to honor your new employee. That would be quite in the style of the Mediterranean food you suggested, and it would present a nicely unified theme."

"Yes, I like that a lot. Could you study some cookbooks and bring me a couple of sample menus?" Del asked. "Then we can proceed."

"And I *will* need to have a few sous chefs helping, if that's okay?"

"Absolutely, of course."

"And you can jump in and help too, if you feel up to it," Clara teased.

"You know, I might just do that. It does sound fun. After all my years in Paris, it might be fun to try my hand at cooking French food again."

* * *

It was a luscious, rich October day. The towering cottonwood trees were ablaze with shimmering yellow leaves. The Virginia creeper, covering Del's studio and the kitchen wing of the house, was a riot of reds and oranges.

Several open-sided pavilions had been set up on the flat land below the house. One of the pavilions contained the food and wine and the dining tables. Another pavilion covered a dance floor and a stage that hosted a dance band.

Del looked quite marvelous as she greeted her guests. She wore a deep-red and saffron sari. Her stunning auburn-gray hair was piled high on her head. She looked rested and vigorous. Spritzer, however, had been drinking steadily since late afternoon and was boisterously playful, almost prancing as he welcomed the guests alongside her.

After the first few guests arrived, Kan and her father, Dan, came forward.

"Hello, my dear," Del greeted Kan warmly.

"Hi, happy to see you," Spritzer said to Kan. "Glad you could come." He shook Dan's hand.

Kan took Spritzer's arm and leaned into him and whispered, "Easy on the booze, Spritz. It's still quite early yet."

Spritzer leaned back and laughed, speaking out a little too loudly. "Hey, this is our new beginning. It's a celebration. Don't you worry about me."

Kan looked around the gathered crowd. "Is Francisco back with the Frenchman yet? I'd really like to meet him."

"Nope." Spritzer took hold of Kan's hand. "Come on, let's dance." He dragged her to the center of the dance floor and grabbed her around the waist.

She freed herself from his grip. "Not yet, Spritz. I want to look around first. And I want to get Dad some food."

"Don't forget to try the champagne," he said, waving his glass in the air. "I'm gonna be pissing this stuff before you know it."

Kan came back to him and took his hand. "Hey, I think you need to take a breather. You're getting a little rowdy. Cool it, okay? Maybe get something to eat."

Del, seeing Spritzer's condition, came over. "My darling boy, come with me." She took Spritzer's arm and led him to one of the tables in the food pavilion. She sat him down, then sat beside him. She took his hand.

"I know this is probably a bit stressful for you, Stevie, but you've got to get hold of yourself. You're creating a spectacle. People are staring and starting to comment."

"Sorry," he said quietly.

"You are running the winery now, and have a lot of responsibility. Michel is going to be here any minute, and I want you to make a good impression. You two are going to be working together for four years, and I expect you to make me proud. You know how important this is for me— for both of us. We need this project to be successful."

"I know."

"So take it easy with the drinking, okay?"

"Okay."

* * *

Soon the sun set, and the groundsman began lighting the tiki torches placed around the perimeter of the party.

By now Spritzer and Kan were dancing, but Spritzer still had a drink in one hand and was obviously fully drunk. He was bumping into people and dancing crazily. Kan broke from him and pulled him to the edge of the dance floor. She was about to scold him again when they saw Francisco's car drive up.

Del was the first to go over to the car, along with a number of the guests.

"Hey, they're here," Spritzer said to Kan.

He dragged Kan after him as they headed toward the car, now surrounded by more guests anxiously waiting to meet the renowned Frenchman. Spritzer pushed his way through the crowd. "So where's our new *Chef de Cave?*" he bellowed.

"Right here," Del said, turning to Michel who was getting out of the car.

Michel stepped forward. Spritzer froze in place. He couldn't speak for a moment. The Frenchman was not what he expected at all. He wasn't some crusty wine gnome hobbling from the interior of some dusty champagne cave, but a very sophisticated and charming young man of about thirty. He was impeccably dressed in an elegant and stylish Saint Laurent beige suit. He was attractive, with recognizably French features—an aquiline nose, and dark hair that was loose but neatly framed his face. He had not shaved for several days and had a stubble beard. But he was not what one would call conventionally handsome. Rather it was the power of his character that one immediately noticed— especially his dark, penetrating eyes that seemed as though they could see through to the secrets of your soul. He emanated confidence, grace, and simplicity. Spritzer was caught completely off-balance.

Michel turned to Spritzer and extended his hand. "Hello, my name is Michel Bast. You must be Stevie."

Spritzer was, at first, too shocked to take his hand. "Spritzer. They call me Spritzer," he finally managed to sputter out.

Michel withdrew his hand. "Spritzer, then. That's charming. I'm pleased to meet you."

"My God, you're not much older than I am!" Spritzer bellowed.

"Why, yes. Do you see that as a problem?"

"And you're here to teach *me* how to make champagne?"

Michel answered very coolly, "No—sparkling wine. Champagne is only made in the Champagne region of France. Everywhere else it's called sparkling wine. Though I promise you I will do everything I can to make your sparkling wine as grand as *our* fine champagne."

Michel then turned to Del, smiled, and took both of her hands. "So you must be Del. I can't tell you how pleased I am to meet you."

"Me too, my dear. And what a pleasant surprise."

Kan eagerly stepped forward. "Hi, my name's Kan. I'm a buddy of Spritzer's."

Michel offered his hand. "*Enchanté.*"

They shook hands and smiled. But Kan seemed too nervous to respond.

Spritzer pushed between them and addressed Michel again. "Well, Del sure isn't going to be happy if she can't make her 'champagne.' Maybe we'll just have to pack you up and ship you back where you came from. 'Cause we sure intend to make 'champagne' here."

Furious, Del grabbed hold of Spritzer's arm. "You're drunk. Get a hold of yourself. Your behavior is totally unacceptable."

"Drunk? I most certainly am *not* drunk. In fact, I am not nearly drunk *enough!*"

Spritzer turned and grabbed a drink from a guest standing next to him. He chugged it down as fast as he could. When he'd finished, he dropped the plastic drink cup and went glassy-eyed. He wobbled. Kan tried taking his arm, but it was too late. Without warning, he lunged toward Michel, grabbed hold of him by both arms, fell to his knees, and threw up all over the front of his Saint Laurent suit. He looked up at Michel, closed his eyes, and fell over backward.

* * *

Spritzer was abruptly awakened when he fell out of bed. He was tangled in his sheets and had to free himself before he could sit up. *Oh my God—what a headache.* He sat on the floor and put his throbbing head between his hands. Had he ever had a hangover this bad? He searched for the bedside clock. Ten a.m. "Shit." But at least he was in his apartment and not passed out by some roadside. He tried to think back to last night but had no recollection except there were vague memories of dancing and puking. He could hear someone in the kitchen. "Kan? Is that you?" he croaked out.

Kan appeared at his bedroom door. "Well, well, well..."

"Was it *that* bad?

"On a scale of one to ten—twenty-eight."

"Do I want to know what happened?"

"I don't think you're going to have any choice. I think Del plans to disembowel you, disinherit you, and emasculate you—but not necessarily in that order."

"Thanks for being here."

"I stayed because you're going to need me to take you to Del's, where your car's still parked. No way could you drive last night."

"Hum. Got any coffee?"

"I do." She disappeared. A minute later, she came back with a mug and handed it to him.

"I'd better take a shower," Spritzer said as he realized he smelled of puke.

"Yes, you had...You stink."

Spritzer put aside the coffee and tried picking himself off the floor but couldn't seem to get a grip on the edge of the bed. Kan went over and held his arm as he found his footing, then she led him to the shower where he started showering with his boxers on.

"Ah, Spritz..." She pointed. "You might want to remove those."

Spritzer slipped off his boxers. He reached for the soap and dropped it, tried to pick it up, and slid to the floor of the shower. He realized it was pointless to fight the obvious, so he sat on the floor of the shower and soaped himself.

* * *

Del sat at her desk in the library. Her eyes were cast down as Michel paced before her.

"I can't. I simply cannot work with that man. It's impossible."

Del replied. "Last night was...was..."

"A disaster."

"A mistake, I was going to say. You must understand, Michel, that he was very nervous about meeting you. This is a very big change for him. He'd had a little too much to drink...He really can be very sweet, and he knows his job and the winery."

"Oh *là*...but you saw how he treated me, just because he thinks I'm too young to teach him. But I am the best at what I do. I could have any position I wanted. I do not have to put up with this. And I won't. I'm sorry, it is impossible. If you want me to stay you must find someone else for me to work with."

Del got up from her desk and walked over to him. She took Michel by the arm and led him to the two chairs by the fireplace. It was a chilly late-October morning, and Clara had laid and lit a small fire. "Please sit," she offered. Michel sat and stared into the fire. "Tell me, Michel, about your family."

Michel turned to her. "Of course, you know Domaine Bast Champagne?"

"Of course."

"That's my family's. We've been making champagne for over three hundred years. You could say it's in our blood."

"Yes, I know about your fine wine, but what I want to know about is your flesh and blood family. Your mother, your father, brothers, sisters..."

Michel nodded and smiled. "Well, actually it was my grandmother...and her mother...that were my greatest inspiration. After the war, the vineyard was a disaster. We'd not made any wine since the beginning of the war. When the Germans came through in 1940, they stripped the champagne cellars of every bottle and took them away for their high command. The men of the estate were off fighting, leaving those two women to run everything. After the Germans had moved on, after their first invasion, they were left with a vegetable garden, a few chickens, a hog, and a cow. Not as bad as many, but they refused to let their workers starve, and they fed every one of them and their families right through the war. It was brutal at times, but everyone pitched in and offered whatever they had for the communal pot, and they all pulled through."

Del spoke up. "Yes, I was in France not long after the war. I first came to Paris in the 1950s, and I remember, even when I first arrived, there were still shortages and some hardships—especially for folks in the country."

"Yes, just so. But it was my great-grandmother and my grandmother who started pulling the winery back together after the war before the men came straggling back. And, even then, there were many lean years. It takes three years to create a quality champagne, and it took even longer to get the vineyards back into shape and into full production again."

"You've got a fine lineage."

"I'm very proud of my family."

"As you rightly should be."

"Oh, there are many other stories I could tell, but let me leave that for now. I feel we still need to resolve the issue of Spritzer."

"Yes, I understand. And I promise to get to that in just a minute. But first I want you to also understand that while our family might not be as old or distinguished as yours, it is still a fine American immigrant family. We too are French, and we came to America in the early twentieth century, traveled west, and settled in California, buying this estate and establishing our winery. True, our current wine is not of the same quality as yours, but we have a vision for the future that I'm sure you can appreciate."

"Yes, I understand what you want to accomplish, but how is that relevant to my problem?"

"Because of family. You see, Stevie is more than just an employee. He's my family. I know you understand the importance of loyalty to family. You told me when we talked on the phone that it was your father who so carefully trained you. So, you see, I can't replace Stevie that easily. You must understand that one day he will own part of this business—he is one of my heirs...And so I'm afraid replacing him is just not an option for me."

Michel was thoughtful. "You make it very difficult. How can I possibly communicate with such a..."

"Michel, please I beg you, just give him a chance. I know your styles are very different. And I know it will be a challenge for both of you.

Believe me, last night was not Stevie at his best. But he is very knowledgeable about the business and very hardworking. And he is not a habitual drinker—I can assure you of that. It was just nerves on his part. Please give us a chance. We really need you."

"Hmm. Very well. I'll give it a try. But let me state, right up front, that if I feel it's not working out I will leave—agreement or no agreement."

There was a knock at the library door, and Spritzer came in. He was still hungover and looking very remorseful.

"So sorry I'm late," he said, as he came over to them.

Del stood. "I certainly hope you're sorry for more than that, young man," she said very sternly.

Spritzer cast a look at Michel, who remained seated and stone-faced. "Michel, yes, I am very sorry about last night, and I hope you can find it in your heart to forgive me."

There was an awkward pause as Michel simply glowered at Spritzer. He then turned to Del. "That's it? That's all the apology I get?"

Del could see Spritzer was not about to take cheek from this man, and he became fired up. "Okay, I gave you my sincere apology. So what else do you want? My head on a platter?"

"Well, it would probably be a whole lot more appetizing than the sight of you as a disgusting drunk."

Del spoke up. "Please, both of you..."

"And what about my suit?" Michel pushed.

Spritzer looked at Del. She nodded, suggesting he go further.

"Okay, I'll pay for the cleaning," he conceded.

Michel hardened. "It can't be cleaned. It's ruined."

"So why were you wearing such an expensive suit at a harvest festival? Certainly you should have known to wear something more practical."

"One does not wear farmwear flying first class."

"First class?" Spritzer sounded enraged. "I certainly hope we weren't paying for the ticket?"

"I upgraded at my own expense."

"Well, that's a relief."

"So what about my suit? Are you going to take care of it?"

Spritzer appeared to be doing everything he could to control himself. He looked over to Del. She nodded again.

"Okay, goddamn it. I'll buy you another. Men's Wearhouse is bound to have something..."

"I do not know this Men's Wearhouse. But that, my dear friend, was a three-thousand-dollar Saint Laurent classic.

"Oh shit," Spritzer moaned.

There was a long pause as each adversary evaluated their options.

"However, I am prepared to accept two thousand as it was not new," he added.

Del came over and took Spritzer by the arm. "I think you should know, Stevie, that Michel was ready to get back on the plane this morning after your behavior last night. However, he has graciously agreed to stay, on the condition that you behave yourself. If you want us to keep this winery, I suggest you do everything in your power to make this relationship work between the two of you."

Spritzer reached into his pocket and pulled out a wad of cash. He peeled off a couple of hundreds and threw them in Michel's lap.

"There. On account. I'll write you a check for the rest later."

Del carefully studied Michel. She knew Spritzer was definitely in the wrong last night, but she also felt the need to keep a wary eye on Michel. She could see how his arrogance might become a potential problem. She then addressed Michel. "Good. I hope that satisfies you." Michel nodded, as he picked up the money. Del continued, "Now, let's get down to making champagne."

Michel rose from his chair. "Please, madam, we will be making sparkling wine."

"Excuse me, sparking wine. Now then, Michel, I'll be putting you in charge of all the decisions regarding the making of the sparkling wine." She then turned to Spritzer. "And Stevie, you will manage the day-to-day financing of the operation, as well as coordinating and executing all of Michel's decisions." She turned again to Michel. "And, Michel, I promise you Spritzer will cooperate in every way to make this the best wine possible. I give you free hand to do whatever needs to be done to make this a success, but ultimately *both* of you are accountable to me. Is that clearly understood?"

They both nodded.

Michel took a list out of his messenger bag. He handed it to Spritzer. "Here. This is a list of the equipment we will need. Please go over it by this afternoon and let me know what you already have. Everything else will need to be ordered immediately. I will spend the morning with Francisco surveying the vineyards and examining locations where we might want to build the new winery. I will see you at three o'clock. Is that satisfactory?"

Spritzer was not used to being ordered about. He looked at Del, and she smiled at him and nodded her approval.

"I ah...yeah, sure. Three o'clock, my office," he said.

"Good."

Michel picked up his bag, turned to Del, and shook her hand quite formally. He turned to Spritzer and shook his hand, and then started to walk smartly out of the library.

"Excuse me..." Spritzer called after him.

He turned back. "Yes?"

"If you're going to go romping about the countryside, I suggest you wear something a little more practical. We don't want any more soiled haute couture."

Michel summoned all his patience and self-control. "Mr. Vallier..."

"You may call me Spritzer." He smiled.

"Spritzer, then...If it is humanly possible, do you think you could restrain your feeble attempts at sarcasm?"

"Sarcastic? *Moi?*"

Michel continued, "I am quite accustomed to taking care of myself, thank you. I am very comfortable with what I am wearing, and believe I know how to dress appropriately when carrying out my duties. Good day."

He turned and walked out of the library.

Del laughed. "Well, my dear, it sure looks to me like you've finally met your match."

* * *

Michel spent the rest of the morning and early afternoon driving around the vineyard with Francisco. He was taking an inventory of all the varieties of grapes they were growing and learning which were used for the commercial wine production and which could be used or adapted for the sparkling wine. He also took note of which land was lying fallow and could be planted with the types of grapes he would need for his wine.

Michel found it much easier to deal with Francisco than with Spritzer. But then, he was an employee and not in direct competition with him the way Spritzer was. Although he was finding this new adventure interesting and stimulating, he was still not certain he would be able to work with that annoying American. He was also embarrassed to find that Spritzer had been entirely right about his working attire. Driving around in an open Jeep, he found herself covered in mud and grime, and by the time he got to his office at three for their meeting, he looked like he'd been on a safari. Before going to Spritzer's office, he went to the men's room to wash his face and wipe down his mud-spattered slacks as best he could.

Spritzer was at his desk. His office had been rearranged and a second desk squeezed in for Michel's use. Michel came into the office and stood examining the room.

"That's your desk." Spritzer pointed. "We'll get you a phone and a computer, and set you up on the Internet, soon as we can."

"I don't get my own office?" he grumbled.

"Maybe when we get the new building...but for now, we've got to share."

"Huh..."

"Hey, I don't like it any better than you do. Sorry." Spritzer seemed to be making an effort to be civil with him, but he had a smug smile on his lips. He had obviously noticed Michel's disheveled state from his tour of the vineyard.

"You didn't tell me the vineyard roads weren't paved," Michel said as he went to his desk.

"I think you might find jeans to be a good idea."

Michel conceded the point. "Yes, thank you. I will try that next time."

As he sat in his chair, one of the wheels broke from the base, and he tipped over.

Spritzer laughed, but Michel could see he struggled to recover quickly.

"I'm so sorry about that. We'll get you a new chair. The office-supply catalog is on top of the file cabinet. Find what you like and I'll order you a new one right away." He got up and pulled a straight-backed chair over to Michel's desk before removing the damaged one. Michel sat down and tried to recover his composure.

"So...did you have an opportunity to go over the equipment list?" he asked as he settled himself.

"I did." Spritzer handed Michel the list. "I've marked in the right margin the equipment we have. And, as you can see, some of those are very similar to what you require."

Michel studied the list. "Well, with the exception of this these fermenting vats, all the rest are totally inadequate, inappropriate, or out-of-date. We must have the right equipment. Please order the rest as soon as possible."

He handed the list back to Spritzer with only one item marked as acceptable.

"Wait a minute. What's wrong with this bottler?"

"It doesn't include the bottle sterilizer, and has no mechanism for attaching the wire fastener and the foil caps—not to mention freezing the bottle necks and disgorging the sediment."

Spritzer studied the list further. "All this equipment comes from France. It's going to cost a fuckin' fortune."

"But it's the best. If you want the best wine, you must use the best equipment. Certainly even you can understand that."

"And why a shallow oak press? What's wrong with our crusher-stemmer? We could save a bundle right there."

"The oak press gently presses the fruit and does not damage the grape must the way a crusher does. It also allows the juice to flow more rapidly from the grape."

"Hey, come on, we have a great press right here. No one can ever tell the difference between grapes that are crushed or grapes that are pressed."

"The wine will know."

Spritzer threw his hands up.

Just then Francisco came in. He turned to Michel. "Ah, there you are. Ready to go back out?"

Michel got up from his desk. "Yes." He turned to Spritzer. "We're going back to the vineyard. We've planning which grapes to use for the first pressing. We'd like to show you what we're considering. Want to come along?"

"Yeah, sure." He looked at Michel. "Wait." He went to a locker and pulled out an old pair of overalls and a blue denim work shirt. "Here, you might want to try these."

Michel took them and smiled slightly. "Thanks."

* * *

After Michel changed into more appropriate clothing, the three left the office and went down to Francisco's truck. They got in and drove to the hill where Tom's memorial service had been held. It was the best location to get a panoramic look at the vineyard stretched out below. They got out of the truck, and Francisco spread a map of the vineyard over the top of the hood. Spritzer and Michel were on either side of him, studying the map.

Francisco pointed to sections on the map. "These areas definitely have the right soil and the best exposure for planting the new chardonnay. And over here we could put in the pinot noir and the pinot blanc."

Michel turned to Spritzer. "Do you have wine samples from the areas we're considering using for the first pressing?"

"I believe so. We can check in the lab."

"Good. But it's going to be tight." He studied the map again and pointed. "Can you commit these areas here, here, and here exclusively for the sparkling wine?" Spritzer nodded. "Excellent—but we're going to need at least that much more acreage to reach our eventual capacity." He turned to Francisco and pointed again to the map. "How old are the vines in these areas?"

Francisco thought a moment. "At least twenty to twenty-five years old."

"Good." Michel indicated several areas on the map. "We can T-bud all of this into chardonnay and pinot noir. It should be ready to harvest in two years."

"What do you suggest we do until then?" Spritzer asked.

"We'll use what we can from your vineyard and purchase the rest from local growers. I'm sure you must know some quality vineyards that would be happy to sell us their excess grapes."

"That's going to cost a lot more. Can't we make do with what we have here?"

"I'm afraid not."

Spritzer just shook his head.

* * *

Spritzer's apartment was what one might call pedestrian. He used it to sleep in and little else. He normally worked ten to twelve hours a day and came home after work, popped a frozen dinner into the microwave, watched an hour of TV, and went to bed. He was usually up at five and out of there with a mug of coffee and a slice of toast. He might clean the apartment once every two months, and make the bed and straighten up the living room if Kan was coming over for an evening of wings and beer.

It was Saturday night, and Spritzer had gone that afternoon to watch Kan at one of her rodeos. They'd come back to his apartment afterward, and he'd made spaghetti with a bottled Bolognese sauce and sprinkled it with nearly dried-up, Kraft parmesan cheese.

They were seated in their underwear, cross-legged on his bed, eating from large mixing bowls, as he'd had no pasta bowls. Kan was deeply engrossed in a slasher movie, and she was paying no attention, whatsoever, to Spritzer, who was obsessed with Michel and his arrogance.

"I'll bet you anything he's really into some kinky sex stuff too. Know what I mean?" Spritzer rattled on.

Kan answered automatically. "Uh-huh."

"That is, if he's into any sex at all. I can't imagine anyone being crazy enough to want to jump his bones. Can you?"

"Uh-huh."

"And let me tell you, he's just a bit too feminine for my taste."

"Uh-huh." Kan recoiled from a particularly gruesome hatchet scene and nearly tossed her spaghetti up in the air.

Spritzer glanced over at Kan. He could tell she was not listening to what he was saying.

"And he's got this thing for grapefruit. You can't imagine the erotic possibilities. He's a virtual encyclopedia on the use and abuse of citrus."

"Sounds great."

He stopped and stared at her. Then, in a single bound, he jumped over in front of her, shielding her from the TV. He'd clearly scared the shit out of her. She recoiled and then recovered—glaring at him with menacing eyes.

"Hey, I'm trying to watch the movie," she demanded.

"And I'm trying to talk to you."

She pushed him aside. "Later, okay?"

He slowly reached over to pick up a handful of spaghetti from his bowl. He pulled back the top of her tank top and flung the spaghetti down her front.

She sprang out of the bed, looking down at the mess he had created. He now had her full attention. She was furious but started laughing. Moving very slowly, they circled one another. She took a handful of spaghetti from her bowl with one hand, and, with a quick movement, opened the top of Spritzer's boxers and threw the pasta down his shorts.

He recoiled, hands up in the air, staring at her in wide-eyed disbelief, and declared, "Okay—holy war!"

He picked up his bowl of spaghetti and poured it over her head. She screamed. He was about to pounce on her and lay her flat with a kiss. But she managed to bring her bowl of spaghetti up, just in time, so instead of landing a kiss on her he ended up with his face in her bowl. They screamed and rolled all over the bed, both of them struggling for supremacy.

After they'd exhausted themselves, they cleaned up the bed. Fresh sheets (the first in weeks) and a long, rather sexy, dual shower calmed them down.

Spritzer was sprawled out on the bed, face down and half-asleep. Kan was beside him, reading a magazine featuring articles about France. She suddenly looked up.

"You know, I really rather like him," Kan said.

"Huh?"

"It must be hard, the first week or so in a new place, not to mention a new country." Spritzer mumbled something into the pillow. "He must be lonely too. No friends. Hum. Think I'll ask him over for dinner tomorrow night."

Spritzer sprang up. "No. No way! Not here."

Kan gave him a long, hard look. "Well, who invited you?"

* * *

Kan was not Spritzer's puppet. She'd called Michel the next morning and invited him for dinner at her modest little house at the edge of her father's olive grove. Michel had happily accepted.

He arrived with a bottle of his family's estate's nonsparkling red wine. Kan came out of her house as Michel walked toward her.

"What a beautiful location." Michel greeted Kan in the French style, with a kiss on each cheek.

"I like it."

"These olive trees are stunning. Are they yours?"

"My father's."

"So you make olive oil as well as wine?"

"We do. Actually, the olives are sort of my thing. Dad handles the vineyard, and I take care of these."

"Very impressive. I'd love to sample your oil. I have a special love of a good quality olive oil."

"Then be sure and try the salad. We'll be having some this evening."

"Good. But I'd like to try the oil plain and simple. Taste it as one would taste a good wine."

"Of course."

Michel stopped and stared at the olive grove. The sun had set, and the last fingers of sunset were splayed across the rapidly darkling sky—creating lacy, charcoal silhouettes of the trees.

He sighed.

"Are you homesick?" Kan asked, as she took Michel by the arm and led him to the house.

Michel thought about that. "Not so much. I'm excited by this opportunity to make my mark by creating my own wine. But...well, there are things about home I miss."

Kan opened Michel's wine. "Very nice," she said after tasting it.

Michel nodded. "Now, may I have a taste of your olive oil?"

Kan laughed. "I'm not used to having the oil tasted like a wine. But taste away."

Kan handed Michel a shot glass and a bottle of oil which he proceeded to taste. Michel smiled and inclined his head. "Totally different from the French, Italian, Spanish, or Greek oils, but very mellow and yet with a delightful peppery bite. I like it. Do you export any of this?"

Kan laughed. "Export? Oh no, we're lucky to make enough domestic sales to keep the doors open. We've never even thought about export. It seems all the good, high-priced oils come from Europe, not go to it."

"Let me look into that for you. Our marketing people in France are wizards at promotion on the continent, and I'm sure our distributors could handle what you might produce. If you're interested, that is."

"I'd be thrilled. We often leave more than half the trees unharvested because we don't have enough sales to warrant a full harvest."

"Oh my, what a shame. We'll have to do something about that."

* * *

After dinner Kan and Michel were mellow, continuing to drink wine, sprawled out in the living room. They were laughing, as Kan had just asked Michel about his romantic life.

Michel smiled and paused. "I guess it's going to come out eventually. My dear sister, you and I definitely have something in common. We both have a preference for gentlemen."

"You're gay?" Kan asked in astonishment. "But you don't look it."

"One can never tell by looks alone. Who knows, perhaps you are too," he said mischievously.

Kan gave a little scream of surprise and waved frantically. "Oh no, not me," she insisted.

"Very well, then, you ask about my romantic life. What could I possibly tell you that didn't sound ridiculous? I'm sure it's the same old story told over and over—everywhere. Meet the perfect guy. Discover he's a jerk. 'Jerk' is what you say in English, yes?"

Kan laughed. "We do."

"Then dump the jerk—or get dumped by him. It was disastrous. And the same story played out over and over again. I've seen it all. Each one seemed worse than the last. And you know what? I think I really don't like men very much. Attracted, yes—like, no. I was so glad when the opportunity came along to come here. I needed a fresh start."

"And has it helped?" Kan asked.

Michel laughed. "Well, the funny part is that Spritzer reminds me a lot of Jean-Claude—my last jerk. So it hasn't helped all that much. And I have to say, I have no idea what you see in him. Sorry, if I'm being rude."

Kan seemed a little uneasy with Michel's answer. "We get along. And remember, we grew up together, so we know each other pretty well. Sometimes I think we're lovers, and sometimes I think we're just good friends."

"Well, I really don't see how you can put up with him."

"He's good for a few laughs. You know...in moderation. But we've been playing around with the idea of marriage. I think I want it more than he does. I want kids. Not so sure about him."

Michel wanted to change the subject. "Do you like living here in northern California?"

"It's home. But sometimes, you know, I get real crazy and think I'd like to go off and do the rodeo circuit full-time."

"Rodeo?"

Kan laughed. "Yeah, I'm real good. You should see me on those wild horses. If you like, in August I'll be at the county fair."

"Yes. I'd like to see that."

Kan paused and was quiet for a moment. "Hey, I'd like to show you something." She got up from her armchair and went to the kitchen. She took a wine bottle out of the refrigerator, opened it, and brought it back. The bottle had no label.

"Here, try this."

Michel offered his glass, and Kan poured.

"This is the chardonnay my dad makes. Very light and dry. He won third prize at the state fair last year. These days we're contracted to sell most of the grapes we grow to commercial wineries, but he has one hillside he keeps just for himself, and he takes great care in making this. Here, try it."

Michel, like a true connoisseur, sniffed, swilled, and took a modest taste. He drew air into his mouth to aerate the wine, then swallowed and savored.

"Oh, very nice. Does he ever sell this?"

Kan waggled her hand. "Sometimes, but he really likes to keep it for the family. However, occasionally he gives it as presents to our suppliers. It's amazing how nicely he's treated when he walks into their businesses with a couple of these bottles. Who says oil is the only thing to grease a wheel?"

Michel laughed.

* * *

Spritzer wandered around his apartment. He had no interest in watching TV this evening—and he never read. He was a little angry at being excluded from Kan's evening with Michel, even though he had no desire to spend any more time around Michel than necessary. He had a fleeting moment where he wondered if Kan might be interested in Michel romantically. He paced the apartment, bored. He finally decided to go out. He got into his Jeep and drove off.

He found himself driving down Kan's street. He drove up to her house, parked, and then walked up to the front door. He could hear Michel and Kan inside, laughing and having a good time. He paced a bit more. He couldn't bring himself to go inside as he had not been invited.

He went to the side of the house and peeked in the window. He first heard Kan speaking.

"Your English is so good."

"Well, I was in London for almost two years. I represented our house for the English champagne market."

Kan sighed. "I'd love to go to Europe."

"Why don't you?"

"Oh, I don't know. No one to go with, I guess."

"Go alone."

"That'd be no fun."

"Wouldn't Spritzer go with you?"

"Oh, he'd complain all the time 'cause no one spoke English or served Coors."

"Yes, I've noticed his capacity for tolerance is maybe this big." Michel indicated about a foot between his outspread hands.

Kan answered. "Oh no, you must be mistaken. That's the size of his weenie. His capacity for tolerance is *much* smaller."

"Weenie? What is that?" Michel did not understand her reference.

Kan started laughing. "Oh, you know..."

Michel suddenly understood, and they both hooted with laughter, rolling around in their chairs. Spritzer, of course, overheard this. He was furious and stormed back to his Jeep, got in, and drove off.

CHAPTER FOUR

1988

"Let's take a look at those." Francisco reached out for Brian to hand him the shears. He took them and examined them closely. "Yep, for sure need sharpening. Leave them with me and I'll check out the others too. Might as well get them all taken care of at one time."

"Sounds good." Brian picked up his jacket to head home.

Francisco reached for his. "Stevie got a birthday comin' up soon, no?"

"One year. Can you believe it?"

Francisco shook his head. "Doesn't seem possible. Gonna have a party?"

"Just the family. He's too young to know what it's all about yet."

Francisco had been looking for an opportunity to talk to Brian privately. "Got time to catch a beer?"

Brian threw his jacket over his shoulder. "Sure. Why not? Fran's not fixin' dinner tonight anyway—got some girly function. I'd just have to rummage in the fridge for leftovers. Maybe we can grab a meatball sub as well? Wanna hit Tony's?"

"Sure. Sounds good."

* * *

"Bacon cheeseburger. And make that with blue cheese," Francisco ordered, as the two sat at Tony's counter.

"Fries with that?" the waitress asked.

"Naw, side salad. Ranch dressing."

"And what for you, Brian?"

"Meatball sub—coleslaw." Brian turned to Francisco and asked, "Pitcher?" He nodded. "And a pitcher of the Pilsner."

"You got it."

Brian was the son of Tom's and Del's sister, Lara. She'd passed away when Brian was in high school. His dad passed away soon after.

Brian had married his high school sweetheart. He had been considered quite a catch at the time. A linebacker on the football team, he had a tough working man's body, but with a handsome face, green eyes, and the same wild, curly hair that Spritzer had inherited.

He had apprenticed well under his Uncle Tom, and it was assumed he would work as manager at Vallier, and that is exactly what he did.

The waitress brought over the pitcher of beer and two glasses. The two sat drinking in silence as they waited for their food order. Francisco kept shooting furtive glances at Brian. Finally, Brian turned to his friend and asked, "You got sumpin' on your mind? You're makin' me nervous."

"Sorry." He turned back to his beer and stared forward. He suddenly turned back. "Yes. Yes, I do. I need to talk about something personal. You okay with that?"

Brian nodded. "Long as it's not about sticking your tongue down my throat."

Francisco laughed. "No. No. Nothin' like that, I assure you."

"Okay then, shoot. Let's hear it."

Francisco bowed his head for a moment, staring at the counter. "It's about me and Clara," he finally offered.

"Trouble in paradise?"

"Not like you think. Things are fine between us, but we got another kind of problem."

"Money?"

Francisco shook his head. "No. Not that either."

"Okay, buddy, you gonna tell me or are we going to play twenty questions all evening?"

"Sorry. No. But it's really difficult to say it out loud."

Brian appeared to become a little annoyed. "Okay, just tell me. I'm not gonna bite. What?"

Francisco said very quietly. "We can't have kids."

"Oh, man..."

And just at that most inopportune moment, the waitress brought their food.

"Gentlemen, enjoy." The waitress smiled, as she put down their plates. "Let me know if you need anything else, okay?"

"Sure." Francisco stared down at his food, suddenly without much appetite.

The two began eating and didn't say any more for a few moments.

Then Francisco continued, "We've been to several doctors, and Clara's just fine." He paused. "It's me." He couldn't look Brian in the eyes.

"Is it functional? I mean—can't you get it up?"

Francisco shook his head. "No, that's fine. But I'm infertile."

Brian put his hand on Francisco's shoulder. "Oh, man, I'm so sorry. That's gotta be hard."

Francisco chuckled at seeing a joke. "Yeah it's hard, but it don't shoot bullets."

That set the two of them laughing, and it helped break Francisco's nervousness.

"So no kids? That's gotta be tough for Clara."

"Devastating. You can't imagine. It's eating her up."

"Gonna adopt?"

Francisco looked at Brian directly, as he was gaining more confidence. "No, she wants her own."

"So—sperm bank, then?"

"No, not that either."

Brian looked puzzled. "What's left?"

"A substitute." Francisco let that suggestion linger.

Brian seemed to be thinking about that. "You mean...another guy?"

Francisco nodded.

"And you're okay with that?

"I am."

"Who have you got in mind?"

"We want to know if you'd consider...?"

"Me and Clara?" Brian waggled his finger back and forth, indicating the two of them together. "Wow."

"We've discussed it, and we both agree. It should be you. It would mean so much to us, Brian."

"I don't know, buddy. That's a lot to ask." Suddenly Brian seemed very nervous. "But Fran—I'd have to discuss it with her. I'd have to see how she'd feel about that. I have my doubts about her. We've been having a rough patch..."

"But if she agreed, would you do it?" Francisco asked eagerly.

Brian was thinking through this proposal. "I'd like to talk to Clara first. Would that be possible?"

"Absolutely. We thought you might want that. The three of us could get together and talk it over. You could ask questions and see if you and she would be okay."

"I'd want to make sure she's comfortable with this."

"I understand." Francisco was conflicted but he felt he had to ask. "And what if you didn't tell Fran? Just bypass the issue. It could be just between the three of us. And it's only a one-time event."

"But what if Clara doesn't get pregnant the first time?"

Francisco hadn't thought about that. "Oh...Yeah, that could be an issue."

"I'm gonna have to think about this."

"That's fine. Just let us know. But we want to start a family as soon as possible. Clara's thirty-six, and it's getting a little late for us to be having kids."

Brian took a big bite of his meatball sub. "Man, this is some supper."

* * *

2013

Spritzer was raking in the vineyard when his cell rang. It was Del.

"Hi, doll, could you stop by when you have some free time?" she asked. "I've got a few things that need fixing on the house. And you know me. I'm about as useful as a kite in a hurricane when it comes to working on the house."

"How urgent is it?" he asked.

"Oh, not at all. Just come when you can."

"Whatcha needing?"

"There's a small leak in the library roof. I've got a dimmer switch in the studio that's kaput, and the cord on the vacuum needs patching or replacing. And maybe a few other little things."

"Michel and I are going into Santa Rosa later this morning to meet with the architect to review the final drawings for the champagne winery."

"Sparkling wine," Del corrected.

"Yeah, yeah, yeah...sparkling wine. Jeesh. Who gives a f— Sorry, Del."

"Not to worry. You should hear me when I'm in the studio alone and a pot goes all wobbly on me."

Spritzer laughed. "Okay, I could come by later this afternoon if that would work for you?"

"That'd be just fine, Stevie. And pick up a dimmer switch for the studio while you're in Santa Rosa."

"Okay. See you later."

"Oh, and Stevie, any idea when we'll be able to break ground for the new building?"

"If Michel deigns to let us finalize the drawings this morning, then we can go ahead with the permit process, and we could expect to break ground in about two months after that."

"Excellent."

* * *

"Would you mind if I just stop in here for a moment?" Michel asked Spritzer as they were passing a pharmacy after visiting with the architect in Santa Rosa.

"Not at all." He looked around the area. "I was thinkin' of havin' a coffee anyway. Why don't we meet over there?" Spritzer said, pointing to a coffee shop across the street. "What can I get you?"

"Yeah, sounds good. Order me a medium nonfat latte, please. Meet you there."

"Okay."

While Michel went into the pharmacy, Spritzer strolled over to the coffee shop and went inside. He placed his order, and while he was waiting to pick it up, he looked around for a table.

He was surprised to see Lorne sitting at a table with another young man in a far off corner. Wasn't he supposed to be at work? Then Spritzer remembered that Wednesdays were one of Lorne's days off. He was about to go over and say hi when he saw the other young man reach over and take Lorne's hand. It was clear from Lorne's reaction that he welcomed the young man's touch. And it was also clear they only had eyes for each other.

Not that Spritzer was shocked, but he was surprised. All indications pointed to Lorne being gay. He'd never suspected that before, but it made sense.

"Stevie," the barista called out, with Spritzer's order ready.

Spritzer turned back to the counter to collect the coffees.

"Thanks." He picked up the drinks and was surprised to find himself nervous and flustered. He didn't know how to react to this new discovery. At first, he thought he should find a table as far away from Lorne as possible. But then he realized Lorne might see him and be embarrassed. But, if he was honest with himself, he found that it was *he* who was embarrassed. He needed time to assimilate this new discovery, and decided to wait outside for Michel—hoping that Lorne would not catch sight of him on his way out.

Spritzer stood nervously outside the shop, expecting that Michel would come before Lorne came out. He did.

"Aren't we going to have our coffee in the shop?" Michel asked.

"I forgot I've got to make a stop at Lowe's. I've got to get some things for Del," he said, still a bit flustered.

"Okay. But can't we have our coffee first? I feel like relaxing a bit before we go back."

"No. No. I promised Del I'd do some work on her house this afternoon. We gotta go now. You can drink your coffee in the car."

"Well, okay." He took the coffee from Spritzer, and they started walking to the car.

Spritzer cast a last quick look at Lorne and his companion before they left.

* * *

It was an easy patch on the library roof. It took Spritzer only fifteen minutes to complete the task. While he was up there, he walked around, looking for other potential problems, but the flat roof had been replaced just five years ago, and it all looked pretty sound.

When he was done with that, he went to visit Del to replace her dimmer switch.

"I could use a progress report," Del announced, as Spritzer was installing the switch.

"On what? We approved the drawings this morning. Is that what you mean?"

"Well, I'm glad to hear that, but I was really thinking about you and Michel. How are you two getting along? It's hard for me to keep an eye on the both of you. Give me a report card."

Spritzer laughed. "Hmm. Well…let me see. I'd give me an A plus and Michel a D minus."

"And what would he say if I asked *him*?" Del smiled.

"Probably just the reverse."

"You two! Really...What am I going to do with you guys?"

"Well, I certainly know what you can do with him..."

Del became stern. "Just know that whatever I do to one of you, I will also do to the other. So please keep that in mind."

"Aww, Del...I'm your sweet little Spritzer—kith and kin."

"Makes no never mind. If *either* of you screw up, you *both* go. So I would advise you to help him out as much as possible, and make sure you behave yourselves. I'm putting every cent I have into this venture, and if it fails we all fail. Just remember that."

"Are you going to have this talk with him too?"

"Already have. So just watch it, buster."

Spritzer was finished with the dimmer. He tested it, and it worked just fine. "See, you couldn't do without me, now, could you?" He smiled.

"Don't test me." She scowled.

He wasn't going to. He knew the cat could scratch. "All done. And I've repaired the vacuum cord. Is there anything else?"

Del mellowed a little. "Sit down. Want some tea?"

"No thanks." He sat.

Del proceeded to make some tea for herself. "Stevie, how old are you now? Twenty-eight?"

"Almost twenty-seven."

"So what are you doin' with your life?"

"Workin' for you."

"No. I mean *your* life. You and Kan planning anything serious?"

Spritzer thought about that. "We've talked...around...but I'm not ready for that kind of thing just yet."

"You're not getting any younger, my lad. Before you blink an eye you'll be thirty. If you want a family, don't leave it too late."

"You never had a family," Spritzer pointed out.

"Well...*I'm* the nutcase, remember."

Spritzer laughed. "I guess it runs in the family, then."

"I led a different kind of life. I found my creativity in my work, not in a family. Sometimes I regret it, but mostly I don't. But you've always been a homebody kind of boy. Never had a hankering to kick up your heels and wander the world?"

"I've thought about it once or twice."

"But you haven't done it."

"I still could."

Del shook her head. "Don't know 'bout that. You know, Stevie, you're really good at what you do. You are going to make a world-class wine one day. And it seems to me you're gonna need someone alongside you on that journey. Do you think Kan is that person?"

"Maybe. Just not sure yet."

"Kan is a fine person. Don't make her wait too long."

"I understand." Spritzer was thoughtful for a moment, then asked, "Del?"

"Yes?"

Spritzer couldn't look Del in the eye. "Something happened in town today."

"Oh? Care to share?"

"I know you and Clara are real close."

"Yes, we are. Like sisters."

Spritzer looked up at her. "Has she ever said anything about Lorne?"

"All the time. She just adores him. But what are you getting at?"

"I saw him in town today...with a guy."

"And..."

"They were real close." Spritzer looked at her, hoping she would get what he was saying.

Del nodded.

"So you know?"

She nodded again.

"Why didn't you tell me?"

"I thought it was his place to tell you if he wanted to."

Spritzer was sad. "But he never has."

"Does he have any reason not to? Have you said things that might make him hesitate to be open with you?"

Spritzer thought about that. "I may have called a couple of guys fags when we were out together sometimes. But you know I didn't mean anything by it..."

"Uh-huh."

"Ever since I got back from Davis, he's been really cool to me. We talk, but not about anything important. I thought maybe it was because I was his boss now. It never occurred to me that he might be...you know."

"Go ahead, Stevie, you can say it. It's not going to make you gay by saying the word." She laughed.

He laughed too. "I know. But it's just not something I'm familiar or comfortable with."

"Then talk to him, Stevie. You were such close friends. It's a shame to let your friendship languish just because you feel uncomfortable."

He nodded.

Del hesitated. "And Stevie, you may have more in common with him than you know."

"What does that mean?"

"Just talk to him."

Spritzer turned to leave, but Del stopped him. "Stevie, I don't think I'm breaking any confidences here, but Michel told me right up front, before he signed the agreement, that he was gay. He didn't want it to be a problem because he wanted to be totally open about his sexuality. I thought you ought to know."

"Michel's a fuckin' fag too? Oh shit."

* * *

Spritzer was *so* nervous. His mind kept churning as he drove over to Michel's house. First, there was the shock about Lorne and now Michel. He parked in front, but it took him a moment to pull himself together, get out of the Jeep, walk up to Michel's front door, and knock.

"Spritzer..." Michel said with some surprise after answering the door. "Did we have a meeting?"

"No. Sorry. This is personal. I need to ask you something."

Michel seemed a little hesitant. "I was just making dinner, but come on in. Would you like some supper?"

"No. No thanks. I'm sorry to show up like this, but I've just come from Del."

"Okay. Is everything all right?"

Spritzer stood rigidly. "She told me you were gay."

"Uh-huh. And?" He was obviously waiting for Spritzer to elaborate, but Spritzer wasn't sure what to do or say next. "Would you like to sit down? Do you have any questions for me?"

"I don't know. This has been a weird day. I just learned that my friend Lorne is also gay. What is this, gay awareness day, or something?" He started to laugh.

Michel took Spritzer by the elbow and led him to the sofa. "I like to think that every day is that." Spritzer could see Michel was being open with him and in no way embarrassed. "Sit with me for a moment. Ask me anything you want."

They sat down.

"Okay. Have you always known you were gay?" Spritzer asked.

"Pretty much."

"But how did you really *know?*"

"When I used to play around with my buddy, Philippe, and found I *really* liked it."

"How old were you?"

"Eight."

"That young?"

"Yes."

"Did you ever play around with girls?"

"I brushed their hair, and did the most charming flower weaving."

Spritzer laughed. "And that's all?" Michel nodded. "Have you ever had sex with a girl?"

"Might have...I had a mad crush on the brother of a girl from my school. She invited me to her birthday party, and he was there. There was a lot of drinking. Somehow, the three of us drifted into her bedroom. She went into the bathroom and, while she was gone, the brother and I started kissing like crazy. She came in, discovered us, and somewhere in all of that sex might have been involved. I was never completely clear on who did what to whom, but I later had vague feelings that vaginal intercourse was a part of it."

"And you've had a lot of lovers?"

"No, not a lot. A few. I'm more interested in relationships than random sex. And, of course, these days I am totally dedicated to my work and don't have a lot of time, in any case, to pursue the sort of relationship I want."

"I see." Spritzer sat with his hands in his lap—his head down, thinking. He suddenly looked up and stared directly at Michel. "Do you find me attractive?"

Michel considered that carefully before he spoke. But he finally answered. "Yes, as a matter of fact, I do." He paused. "Does that make you uncomfortable?"

"Don't know...maybe a little." Spritzer said quietly.

Michel continued, "But I would certainly never act upon it. As far as I can ascertain you are completely heterosexual. And I have no interest in changing that. I can assure you, you will be completely safe with me—if that is your concern."

Spritzer sat silently.

"Anything else I can help you with? Short of quantum physics, medieval Catholic doctrine, or international economic theory, I can expound competently on most subjects."

Spritzer looked up at Michel and laughed. "If I think of anything else, I'll let you know."

* * *

The new Maison Vallier Winery building was to be situated near the main entrance to Vallier Winery, across from a park used by visitors, and separate from the commercial winery. The land had been cleared, and construction was ready to start. Del wanted to have an official groundbreaking ceremony with the press and a champagne toast with wine from Michel's estate in France.

Del arrived at the site a little before ten, when the ceremony was to start. She was dressed in a flowing autumn-colored dress with a long Isadora scarf, her auburn hair beautifully dressed by Clara with a crown of autumn leaves.

"Del, you look charming," Kan greeted her, giving her a hug.

"Thank you, dear, and thanks for coming. I know it's taking up part of your workday."

"Any excuse..." She laughed.

Spritzer came over and put his arm around Kan. "Hi, glad you could make it." He turned to Del. "Well, old girl, the day has arrived. We can finally get this show on the road now. I talked to the construction manager, and he thinks it's going to take about four months from breaking ground to handing us the keys. Not bad."

"In plenty of time for the harvest," Del added.

Spritzer nodded. Just then, a limo drove in and parked near to where the ceremony was going to be held, but it was blocking the entrance to the construction site. Spritzer was about to go over and ask the driver to move the limo when Michel and Nelson stepped out of the car. Spritzer was completely taken by surprise. What was Nelson up to? And, for that matter, what was Michel doing with Nelson? The last thing Spritzer needed was for Michel and Nelson to become allied against him. He knew how Nelson worked, and wouldn't be at all surprised to find Nelson ingratiating himself with Michel so he could manipulate Michel in his favor.

Michel looked over their way and waved, and then he and Nelson began a leisurely stroll toward them. They looked very chummy, laughing and leaning in toward one another to speak. Spritzer was definitely uneasy.

"Well, well, well..." Del commented as the two walked up to the assembled group.

Nelson came forward. "Darling Aunt Del, how divine you look. Like an autumn forest."

"Better than a swamp," she replied. "And you're still wearing your white suit after Labor Day? Shame on you."

Nelson laughed. "It's a personal style choice. White flatters me, don't you think?"

"You look like an iceberg." Spritzer smiled.

Nelson turned to him, ignoring his comment. "Coz, splendid day for new beginnings. Michel was telling me all about the new winery. You must be very excited. And I just *had* to be here for the launch of the new building."

Spritzer cast a glance at Michel. But Michel was not making eye contact with him.

"Shall we begin?" Michel asked, as he came over to Spritzer and Del.

Francisco stood by with a shovel spray-painted gold.

"You ready?" Spritzer asked Michel. He nodded. "You want to say anything? After all, you're the *Chef de Cave*."

"Just a few words. Really just want to get the construction started."

Michel gathered the press around him. He spoke about the plans for the new winery and then took the shovel from Francisco and offered it to Del. "Please will you do us the honors?"

Del took the shovel and turned the first earth, followed by Michel, and lastly Spritzer. Francisco and Lorne popped the corks on several bottles of champagne and poured. The six of them toasted. The press took photos, recorded segments for TV, asked a few stock questions, and then disappeared.

Spritzer looked over to Lorne, hoping to finally have that catch-up chat with him. He tried to catch his eye, but Lorne didn't look over. He would have to corral him another time. Spritzer then turned to Nelson. "The construction crews are ready to work but your car is blocking the entrance."

"I'll be leaving shortly," he said. "But first, a quick word with Del."

Spritzer was not going to put up with Nelson's nonsense. "No, Nelson, I need the car moved now. The crews need to start work immediately. Every minute wasted, is money wasted."

Nelson waved his hand, dismissing Spritzer, and turned to Del.

Spritzer was furious and strode over to the limo. The driver was not to be found, so Spritzer got in the car and moved it himself, and then waved for the construction crews to begin work. He went back to Del. She was in an intense conversation with Nelson. It was clear she was scolding Nelson for his rude behavior toward him, and he backed away. He was sure Del could handle Nelson more effectively and with a far greater impact than he could.

* * *

Kan came over to Spritzer. "I'm gonna head out."

"Oh, okay," he said distractedly.

"Oh, don't go yet," Michel said, reaching over and taking Kan by the arm. "I've got some great news for you about your olive oil."

"Really?" Kan turned to him with shining eyes.

"I got a very positive e-mail from our marketing people back home. They said they could certainly take a look at your oil with the idea of distributing it in Europe. They said it's an untapped and potentially lucrative market for US olive oil. So far, there's little competition from other California growers."

Kan became very excited, "Oh, that's wonderful. What do I need to do now?"

"Let's get together later in the week to discuss it. But, in the meantime, get a selection of your entire line together and we'll ship it over to France so they can look at it and develop a plan."

Kan gave Michel a hug. "Michel, that's so exciting." She turned to Spritzer and took his arm. "Dinner sometime soon?"

"Yeah, sure," he said.

Seeing he was still focused on Del and Nelson, Kan backed off. She left without either noticing.

* * *

Michel stood looking at the commencement of the construction.

Spritzer came over to him. "How did you happen to come with Nelson? You two have a hot date?"

Michel turned to him and laughed. "Nelson? Really? You've got to be kidding..."

"Nelson was the first gay person I ever knew. I just figured he'd be interested in someone...like you."

"I'd walked over to get a soil sample from the new field, and he offered me a lift on my way back."

"Un-huh."

He reached into his coat pocket and pulled out a baggie with soil. "There. Done being an asshole?"

* * *

Michel stood before the massive, ancient oak doors at the Cain Winery. *What a magnificent stone building,* he thought, *worthy of any European winery.* He had an appointment to meet Kan. He looked around but didn't see any workers, and the double doors were closed. He went up to the doors and knocked. An echo reverberated through the quiet building. "Hello," he called out as he opened the right door and peered inside into the darkness.

"Hello," he heard from the back of the building. "Is that you, Michel?"

"Yes, shall I come on in?"

"Yes, sorry. I should have been outside to meet you," Kan said as she came forward to greet Michel.

Kan pushed the heavy doors the rest of the way open to allow light to flood inside, casting a mellow glow over the myriad of stacked oak barrels.

"Come in, come in. So glad you could make it," Kan enthused. "The olive-oil warehouse is at the back. I was just organizing for your visit. Come on back."

Michel looked around the cool interior of the winery as they walked toward the back.

"What a splendid operation," he said, as he studied the impressive collection of oak barrels. "These look to be very old."

"Yes, they are. But, unfortunately, we're not the operation we once were. We're only making the family wine here these days. All the rest of the grapes are contracted out. Dad's not as young as he once was, and he's let go of most of the staff."

"That's a shame," Michel stated. "This must have been a magnificent operation in its time."

"After Mother passed, he seemed to lose heart and interest."

"Yes, I can understand."

They had reached the back warehouse, and Kan welcomed Michel inside.

"This is it. Not all that impressive, but you can see we do have a wonderful old olive press. Makes a really high-quality product."

"Yes, I was impressed when you let me sample the oil."

"So what do you think? Where should I start?"

Michel gazed over the warehouse. It was stacked with a modest amount of olive oil cartons.

"What's your current inventory?" Michel asked.

"I've got about fifteen hundred boxes."

Michel guessed each carton held twelve bottles. "Is all of this from your last harvest?"

"No, it's from several years. We still make more than we sell, unfortunately."

"And you say this reflects only a small portion of what you could harvest at full capacity?"

"Oh, yes. Exactly." Kan handed Michel a bottle of the oil. "What do you think about the bottle and the label?"

Michel studied it. "The bottle has a nice shape. Do you have different sizes?"

"Yes, we have three." She placed the other two sizes on the bench.

"The label is okay, but not great. I'm sure our marketing people could come up with some killer designs. Would you be averse to changing the label if we found the right one?"

"Not at all—if it will help sales."

"What I'm concerned about is the amount of oil you have. It's not nearly enough to satisfy the needs of our distributors for the European market."

"But that's good, isn't it? If you could let me know what you'll need, then we could certainly ramp up production for the next harvest, no?"

"We're going to need, at the very least, three to four thousand cartons a year to create a sufficient supply. Do you think you could do that?"

Kan was thoughtful. "We'd have to hire more staff. And I might have to curtail some of my rodeo activities."

"Are you willing to do that?"

"I'd better be." She laughed.

"Do we need to talk to your father about this?"

"No, this is entirely my operation. But it sure would be great for the family to have this expansion. I'm totally ready to go for it."

Michel thought about what else might help with sales. "And what about awards or citations? Has the oil ever been adjudicated?"

"Just locally—county, and the state fairs. But we did well." She pointed to the wall where a series of framed awards were hanging.

"Excellent. Make up a list of those for me and I'll send them along to the team."

"Happy to. Michel, I'm really excited, and I want you to know how much I appreciate your interest and help."

"Okay then, let's ship these sample bottles to my team, and see what they suggest."

Kan hesitated a moment. "But it doesn't seem fair. What are you going to get out of this? Do we need some kind of agreement between us where you get a share of the profits?

"That's very kind of you to think of me, but I'll be getting a share through the distribution end. My family has a piece of that business."

Kan came over and gave Michel a hug. "You're the best."

Michel laughed. "Well, not always, as I'm sure Spritzer could attest."

* * *

Most of the framing was completed on the new building, and already the siding was going up. Spritzer was in his office with a stack of bills and invoices, writing and printing out checks. As he studied the Maison Vallier account balance, he kept shaking his head. He just couldn't believe the stuff that Michel insisted they *must* have for the new building. He saw Del's precious funds just melting away. He didn't know if he should consult with Del or not. She had put him in charge of the finances, but he couldn't seem to get through to Michel that their funds were limited. And he had to keep reminding himself Del had expressly insisted that Michel should get everything he needed to produce the best sparkling wine. He held the strings of the purse, but Michel held the reins of the winery.

There was a knock at Spritzer's door.

"Yes?" he called.

Jack, the construction foreman, came in. "I need you to authorize an upgrade."

"What do you need?"

Jack spread out a blueprint on Spritzer's desk. "Michel said the capacity of the warehouse air conditioner in the specs is too low. He wants to go ahead with the top-of-the-line unit, but said I'd need to clear it with you first."

Spritzer shook his head. "How much more are we talking about?"

"About twenty-five hundred. But it *is* the best unit."

Spritzer was furious. "Absolutely not. What we have in the specs should be just fine."

"Okay."

Jack picked up the blueprint and left.

For Spritzer this was the last straw. He swept up his papers and marched out of the office, mumbling to himself. He got into his truck and headed over to Coeur du Chêne.

* * *

Spritzer stormed out of the truck and into Del's studio. She was in the process of glazing a platter.

He could hardly contain himself. "That Frenchman is ruining us! Look, Del. Look. This is our intended budget and here's what he's already spent. I've tried to reason with him, but he is *so* stubborn and insists that everything be his way." He spread the papers out on her table. "We have some perfectly good equipment that we could use, but no, it's got to be new...and French...and cost about four times as much."

Del washed her hands and calmly walked over to study the papers. She looked them over, considered for a moment, and said, "Yes, well...we've come this far. I don't see how we can turn back now. Quality costs. But as one of my teachers used to say, 'The cost of quality only hurts once.'"

"Del, he's going to bankrupt us...you."

Del was thoughtful, then reached over and took Spritzer's arm. "Honey, I'm willing to take the risk. After all, it is my money."

"But Del, you have no reserves. What we've budgeted is *all* you have. Where is this additional money going to come from?"

"Maybe Nelson will want to invest some more."

"That would make me very nervous. If he were to invest *more*, I'm sure he'd want *more* control as well, and I'm not willing to accept that."

"But if we're running out of capital we might have to ask for his help—eventually."

"Then let me put a cap on that French bastard's spending."

"No, Stevie. He's doing what he thinks is best for the wine. We'll do what we have to do when the time comes. I'm sure we'll find a way."

* * *

When Spritzer got back to the office, Michel was sitting at his desk, a row of sample sparkling wine bottles in front of him. Each one was numbered. Spritzer strode in, threw his papers down on his desk, and turned to Michel.

"What's all this shit about an upgrade of the AC?" he asked.

Michel calmly turned to him. "We have to keep the fermenting bottles at an even cool temperature or there is a chance they'll overheat and be damaged. The spec unit is not sufficient in this climate to maintain an even temperature for the square footage of our building. I've done some research, and I see that the summers here can get a great deal hotter than in the Champagne district of France. I should have caught that when we approved the plans, but I see now the need for the upgrade."

"Well, Jack came by to get my approval, and I denied it."

"What?" Michel stood.

"I'm sure the architect knew what he was doing when he the approved the spec unit, and I just cannot approve such an expensive upgrade. I have to think of Del and our budget. I understand there is some equipment you just must have to make the wine, but this is one item I must insist on."

Michel was obviously weighing his options. Finally, he said, "Very well. I'll not argue that with you right now. But we have to choose a bottle in order to get delivery in time for the bottling process. These are the samples I've selected. What do you think?"

Spritzer went over to Michel's desk. He studied them. "What are the differences? They all look about the same to me."

"There are differences in shape, coloration, and tensile strength."

"And the costs?" he asked.

Michel scooted a paper over to him. He picked it up and studied it. The manufacturers were listed and the bottles numbered and priced— each number corresponding to a number on the bottle.

"Which one do you prefer?"

Michel pointed to one. "This one."

Spritzer referred to the list. He threw his hand down. "The fuckin' most expensive, of course."

Michel defended his choice. "It's strong, has good protective coloration, and a pleasing shape. It's reminiscent of the Dom Pérignon bottle, which will have a good psychological effect when we start marketing."

"Damn it, you drive me crazy. When are you going to hear me? We can't afford it. Every single item on the budget is overrun. We've got to cut some corners, Michel. We'll take this one." He pointed to a bottle.

"The cheapest? But that hasn't even been tested for strength."

"What do we need strength for? It's just got to hold wine."

"Yes, but under five atmospheres of pressure, remember. This is not your jug wine."

"Then tell me...will the bottle affect the quality of the wine?"

"Well, no, but..."

"If the wine doesn't know, then we won't tell it. Order the cheapest."

* * *

A few days later, Del invited Spritzer, Michel, and Nelson to attend a business meeting at Coeur du Chêne. Clara was in the kitchen, preparing lunch for the group. Del came in to see how the meal was coming along prior to the meeting.

"My darling Clara, something sure smells good in here," Del said, coming up behind where Clara was chopping onions.

"Cinnamon cookies in the oven for dessert," she answered.

"Do you need any help?" Del offered.

Clara turned to her, tears in her eyes. Del put her hand out and touched Clara's arm. "Are you all right, my dear?"

Clara laughed. "Oh, yes, it's just the onions." She wiped away the tears. "But if you want to help could you take out the silverware, placemats, and napkins, please?"

"Of course." As Del took the napkins out of the sideboard drawer, she said, "Stevie saw Lorne in town with Robert the other day, and it seems he's figured out about Lorne being gay."

"Oh...he told you that?" Del nodded. "And how does he feel about it?"

"Ambiguous at best." Del began taking out the place settings.

"I'd hoped they would get close again after Stevie's father died and he came back from university, but it still hasn't happened," Clara said sorrowfully.

"I know. Me too. I tried talking to Stevie about it—tried to encourage him to reach out and talk to Lorne. I hope he will."

Clara turned to Del. "You know, we can't keep it from them forever. They need to be told."

Del nodded and took Clara's hands. "I've wanted to tell Stevie, but I didn't think it was proper for me to do that until Lorne knew the truth."

Clara nodded. "I know. But I've been afraid to tell him myself."

"And Francisco hasn't told him either?"

"No. He's as big a baby about it as I am. We've talked about telling him together but we always lose the nerve and chicken out."

Del thought about that. "Well, I've been thinking that if Stevie and Lorne warm up their friendship again, then you and me—maybe we could tell them together."

"Oh, I'd like that. I think that would be better for them—and for you and me." She laughed.

"Let's give them a little more time. I know Stevie wants to reach out to Lorne," Del suggested.

"And if he doesn't?" Clara asked.

"Then we'll have to decide what to do."

* * *

Del and her guests gathered in the library after Clara brought out the light buffet lunch.

They were seated at the big table and had just finished eating. Del had been evasive when asked what she wanted to meet about, and had skirted any questions that dealt with today's agenda during lunch. Nelson was engaged in conversation with Michel, and Spritzer with Del.

Nelson was shamelessly flirting. "So, no romantic attachments back in the old country?"

"I've had my adventures," Michel replied, enigmatically.

"But nothing current?" Nelson was insistent.

"I have a four-year contract here. Not conducive to maintaining a long-distance relationship, wouldn't you say?"

"Well, I'm delighted to hear that."

"But don't get ahead of yourself. I'm totally dedicated to my work and have little time to socialize."

Nelson saw an opening. "But you have *some* free time. After all, one must sup. No?"

Michel nodded but didn't comment.

Del tapped a knife against her wine glass. "May I have your attention, please? They turned to her. "I've asked you here this afternoon to discuss the progress on our mutual project. Michel, would you like to start? Just a few words about where we are in the timeline."

"Of course. I'm very happy to report that we are slightly ahead of schedule on the building. It's coming along nicely. And we are progressing exceptionally well with the vineyard. I've organized all the plots and allocated the grapes that are available to the sparkling wine production. We will need to purchase additional grapes from outside for a few years, but I'm planning to plant new vines and adapt some older ones to our production. All in all, it's going very well."

Del turned to Spritzer. "And your report?"

Spritzer was cautious. "I have concerns about the budget."

Nelson leaned forward. "And how is that?"

Del took the answer. "We underestimated the cost of some of the equipment we would need. Michel has very demanding standards..."

Spritzer squirmed in his seat. He wanted to say more but was holding his tongue.

Michel stood and turned to Nelson. "Monsieur Wayland, I can see that you are a gentleman of true discrimination." Nelson nodded. "I would say you are a connoisseur, is that not so?"

"That is correct," he replied, beaming.

"As with all fine things of quality, there can be no short cuts in its manufacture." Nelson nodded again. "And nowhere is this truer than with fine wine."

Spritzer observed Michel's masterful buttering-up of Nelson, and he couldn't believe Michel was getting away with it. Spritzer just had to smile. Michel was leading Nelson along a very definite path.

Nelson nodded. "I quite agree."

Michel continued, "Then I know you would not want your name associated with any wine that was less than absolute perfection. It would not do you or your family justice."

Nelson seemed to be enjoying this immensely. Del smiled with a twinkle in her eye as she watched Michel at work. Spritzer also enjoyed watching Michel, and he was very impressed.

"And such a wine is not possible without the most select grapes, the loving care and knowledge of dedicated professionals, and the right equipment."

"Yes, but Del spoke of underestimated costs. What exactly are we talking about here?" Nelson sounded suspicious.

Del handed Nelson a paper with the revised budget. "This is more in line with our current reality."

Nelson studied the paper. "I see." He looked up at Del. "And why, exactly, were you not able to estimate these additional costs in the original budget?"

Del answered. "When we made our previous estimates, we didn't have Michel's expertise and input yet. We couldn't foresee his requirements."

Nelson turned to Spritzer. "And why couldn't *you* foresee these costs? After all, you know about making wine."

Spritzer made an effort to control himself. "Champagne was not my thing."

Nelson glared at him. "Well, is it your 'thing' now?"

"I'm learning."

Del spoke up. "It's a matter of doing this right—and covering our investment. I know we can produce a quality product with time and patience..."

"And more money, it would seem," Nelson added.

"Yes."

"My money." He tapped the paper. "And this is the additional amount you require?"

"It is."

"Hm. I don't know about that."

Del asked, "Would you prefer we look elsewhere?"

Nelson was thinking about that when Michel stepped in.

"I have a splendid idea. I would suggest that if Monsieur Wayland has the vision to support our efforts with an additional investment we should name our special reserve label after him. *The Grand Reserve Wayland Demi-sec.* Don't you think that has a nice ring to it?" Michel turned to Nelson. "How do you like that?"

Nelson registered a slow smile. He looked at Michel.

"Do you have papers to sign?"

Spritzer beamed in delight. This was a side of Michel he'd not seen before, and he totally got it.

* * *

Spritzer had finally agreed to have dinner with Kan. She'd been bugging him for a few days now, but he never felt up to it. He was not feeling very social. There was so much going on at the winery.

This evening he'd agreed, and they were shopping for dinner fixings at the market. But Spritzer was in a foul mood, and he leaned with his arms crossed on the handle of the market basket, as they reluctantly browsed the aisles.

Kan was consulting her list. "One can of kidney beans."

Spritzer found a can and tossed it in the basket.

"Large can of chopped tomatoes."

He found that and tossed it in too, making no effort to place it gently in the basket.

Finally, Kan barked, "What *is* the matter with you tonight? Huh?"

"Nothing."

She studied him. "When are you gonna grow up and stop behaving like a spoiled brat?"

"What does that mean, for Christ's sake?"

Kan reached for a package of ground beef. "Ever since Michel arrived and you're no longer the top honcho, you've been acting like a class-A prick."

"Oh, great, now you're siding with him too."

"I don't see what the problem is. He's just doing his job, and from what I hear he's doing it very well."

"He's impossible. He's got an ego the size of a barn."

"Oh, come on, it's not that big."

"Well, is it as big as my weenie?"

Kan stopped dead in her tracks. She glared at him, but he knew he'd caught her out.

"How did you hear about that?"

"I have my ways."

Kan studied him. "Were you spying on us?"

"I came over to say hi, but you two were having such a good laugh at my expense I didn't want to spoil your fun."

"Why, you stinker. You scummy, low-life slug." She grabbed a bag of potato chips and hit him over the head with it.

* * *

Spritzer and Michel were squeezed into their office, each concentrating on paperwork at their desks. There was a knock at the door. They looked up. A delivery man was standing in the doorway.

"Mr. Bast?" he asked.

"Yes," Michel answered.

"I have a delivery for you."

Spritzer spoke up. "Oh, deliveries should go to the receiving dock round back."

"It's not that kind of delivery. One moment, please."

He disappeared. Spritzer and Michel looked at each other. In a few moments, the delivery man returned with several helpers. Between them, they were carrying dozens of flower arrangements which they brought into the office.

"Wait, wait, there's not room for all of those in here," Michel insisted, rising from his desk.

The men brought in what they could and the rest they left in the hallway. Spritzer was disgusted by the blatant excess.

When they were finished, the man handed Michel an envelope. "Here's a card for you, sir."

"Thank you." Michel reached into his wallet for a tip. "Here."

"Thanks, a lot." The man nodded, and the delivery men left.

Michel sat down at his desk and smiled. He opened the card slowly and read. Spritzer was dying to know who the flowers were from. Michel read what appeared to be a rather lengthy message. He smiled and chuckled. "Well, well..."

Spritzer couldn't stand it. "Who's it from?"

Michel answered coyly. "An admirer."

Spritzer laughed as though he didn't care. "Someone from France, no doubt."

"Not at all."

"Is it your birthday?"

"No, it's a token of esteem."

"My, my, my. Now can we get on with our work? If you don't mind, that is."

Michel maintained his sly smile. "Yes, certainly." He put the card face down on the desk. Spritzer was going crazy with curiosity. He couldn't stand it any longer, and he jumped up, reached over, grabbed the card, and read it.

Spritzer shouted, "Nelson?"

Michel got up and grabbed the card from him.

"How dare you! That is private. Get out. And don't come back till you can behave yourself like a gentleman."

Spritzer was shocked at Michel's fury and stormed out, muttering, "Nelson? Nelson? Scumbag Nelson?"

* * *

Spritzer practically ran to his Jeep, seething. He couldn't believe how Michel had treated him. He considered going to Del to complain, once again, about the insufferable Frenchman. But he knew exactly what she was going to say. *Trust my judgment. Cool your head. Look at everything that is at stake.* Yeah, yeah, yeah. He knew all of that. But there were times when his anger just couldn't be contained. What was the fun of being a bad boy if he couldn't express himself?

But then he stopped and asked himself why he was so angry. What the fuck did he care what Nelson was up to? Unless he was trying to manipulate Michel in some way for his own ends concerning the winery. And then he had a vague feeling of unease as an unwelcome thought crossed his mind—could he be jealous of Nelson's attention to Michel? Ridiculous. He dismissed the thought immediately.

He sat at the wheel of his Jeep and considered where to go. Away. Certainly that, but where? He didn't want to go home to pace the apartment and stew. He'd not reconciled with Kan since their brawl in the supermarket. They'd never made it back home together that evening for supper. Maybe this would be the time to make up with her. And, if she was forgiving, they might launch some great makeup sex, and he could release some of his pent-up energy, frustration, and confusion. He turned the ignition and spun out a spray of dirt and gravel as he charged out of the vineyard.

* * *

Spritzer went to Kan's house, but she wasn't in, so he drove over to see if she might be at Dan's.

"How's it goin'?" Spritzer shouted out to Dan above the chug of the tractor he was parking next to the stone winery building. The Cain Vineyard was as neat and orderly as a chess board, in a truly lovely but unpretentious setting. Towering elms and eucalyptus trees shaded the area around the sturdy building where the fermentation tanks and oak barrels rested.

"Pretty good," Dan drawled, as he climbed down from the tractor. He wiped his hands on a rag snatched from his back pocket and shook hands with Spritzer. He was a man of few words.

Spritzer looked around for Kan's car, but didn't see it. "Is Kan here?"

Dan adjusted his overalls and smiled. "Hear you two had quite a squabble."

Spritzer shook it off. "Yeah, well, a little difference of opinion, one might say." He shuffled and didn't look Dan directly in the eye.

Dan went back to the tractor. "She's at the rodeo in Santa Rosa."

"Oh, was that today?"

"Yep."

"Will she be back later?"

Dan dug into the bowels of the tractor with a wrench. "Nope. Said she's staying the weekend. Won't be back till Monday."

Spritzer pushed on. "So who's she staying with? I didn't know she had any friends in Santa Rosa."

"Didn't say. And I didn't ask." Dan gave Spritzer a look that suggested he might want to back off now.

"Oh. Okay."

Spritzer had no choice but to leave. He got into the Jeep and drove over to Tony's for a beer, a slice, and a couple rounds of pool with a few old high-school buddies. Anything to avoid going home.

But when he got there he was still restless. The beer and pizza didn't help get Michel out of his mind, and he had no taste for a round of pool. What he needed was a friend he could talk to. His pool buddies were only that—pool buddies. Not true friends. And then his thoughts turned to Lorne. He pulled out his phone and dialed. "Lorne, it's Spritz," he said, not without some hesitation.

"Spritz?" Lorne reacted with surprise. "Is there a problem at the vineyard?"

"Not at all."

"Then what do you want?" he asked curtly, but not unkindly.

"You." There was silence at Lorne's end of the line. "Can I come over?"

"If you like."

Spritzer laughed. "Where are you now? You're not still living at home, are you?"

"No. Hold on." Lorne texted Spritzer his address.

"I'll see you in twenty."

* * *

Spritzer pulled his car up in front of Lorne's apartment. He was a little nervous as he knocked on Lorne's door. It took a minute for him to answer.

"Sorry, wasn't expecting company tonight. I was just straightening up a little. I'm still as messy as ever."

They stood looking at one another.

Spritzer was the first to speak. "I've missed my old buddy."

Lorne had a faint smile. "Yeah, me too." He reached out and pulled Spritzer into his arms for a deep hug.

Spritzer was the first to disengage. He pulled back and looked at Lorne. "What happened? How did we become such strangers?"

"Not an easy answer. You'd better come in," Lorne suggested. "Take a seat. Beer?"

"Sure." He sat on the sofa while Lorne went to the kitchen to fetch a couple of beers.

When Lorne came back, he gave Spritzer his bottle and sat down opposite. "It's been a long time." He offered up his own bottle for a toast.

"It has. To best friends," Spritzer toasted.

"To friends."

Spritzer noted he had not said "best friends," but let it pass.

They both sat back and looked at each other, sipping their beers to keep from speaking. It seemed to be difficult for either of them to proceed. So much time had passed. So much buried feeling. So many casual slights.

Finally, Spritzer leaned forward to speak, but he couldn't look directly at Lorne. "I was in Santa Rosa not long ago, and I saw you…"

"Yeah?"

"With a guy. You looked very chummy together."

Lorne was briefly silent, and then said, "Robert, probably."

"Are you…?" Spritzer said, not able to actually ask the question.

But Lorne understood and nodded.

There was a long pause, then Spritzer asked, "Why didn't you tell me?"

Lorne looked intently at Spritzer. "I didn't know how you'd take it."

"Lorne…" he said with disappointment.

"You were away at university…It was all new and scary for me when I first came out. I was confused and bewildered. You'd never been gay friendly, and then you came back to Vallier and became my boss…" He paused to gather his thoughts. "By then, I had a new set of friends, and you really didn't seem all that interested in picking up our friendship or getting to know me again. I guess I just let it drift."

Spritzer looked at Lorne. "You could have told me. It would have been okay."

"Maybe."

"So is this Robert…is he your boyfriend?"

Lorne nodded. "For now. Don't know how serious it is yet. It takes time to get to know someone, build trust, and develop a relationship."

Spritzer nodded.

"And what about you and Kan?" Lorne asked. "One time I see you and you're all lovey-dovey, and the next time you're screaming at each other like banshees."

Spritzer laughed. "Yeah, that's about it."

"So where's *that* headed?"

Spritzer just shook his head. "Not a clue."

"Another beer?"

"Sure."

Lorne went to the kitchen and returned with two more beers.

"Have you told your parents?" Spritzer asked.

"Mom knows and is great about it. Dad suspects—but we've never discussed it. I'll get around to it eventually. Doesn't seem to bother him, though."

"And what about the rest of your life? Are you happy just being a worker at the vineyard? You've always been a pretty bright guy. Isn't there something else you want to do?"

Lorne smiled. "I guess what you don't know is that I'm really into renewable energy. I've been taking advanced courses from Santa Clara online, and should be getting a certification in renewable energy technology by the end of the year."

Spritzer was stunned. "Lorne, that's fantastic. What do you plan to do then?"

"I don't know. There's a lot of need out there. Guess I'll see what comes along."

"You know, I've been thinking about how we might apply new energy technologies to our operations. With the new winery and the massive energy use we have with Vallier, it's costing us a fortune in electric bills."

"Funny you should mention that." Lorne went over to his desk and pulled a folder out of a drawer. He came back and handed it to Spritzer. "My thesis. *Renewable Energy for Use in Commercial Wineries.* And guess who I had in mind when I wrote it?"

Spritzer looked at the folder then up at Lorne. "Wow. Can I have a copy?"

"You bet. Take that one."

"Don't think we could change over all the way until we get the new winery producing a profit but it's something I want to do—and I think Del and Michel would go for it too."

"Well, keep me posted. I'd like to be your go-to guy on this."

Spritzer leaped up and went over to Lorne. He gave him a hug, and whispered in Lorne's ear. "I am so glad to have you back in my life again."

"Me too."

* * *

Walking through the construction site of the new winery, Spritzer was greatly impressed. The building was taking its final shape. The large fermentation tanks had been installed. The walls and ceiling structures were already in place and crews were at work framing the interior spaces. The contractor was at a worktable in the center of the building going over blueprints with several crew bosses. It was the start of the workday.

"Lookin' good," Spritzer greeted him.

The weathered, saggy-eyed boss looked up. "Movin' right along."

"Got a completion date in mind?"

"Not a fixed date yet. But I promise we'll at least make our scheduled completion."

"Glad to hear it." Spritzer nodded and stood by the boss, expecting further attention, but the contractor turned back to his crew. He had work to do, and Spritzer was just a distraction.

Spritzer got the message and headed back out and over to his office. He was *not* looking forward to facing that cramped room filled with cloyingly scented flower arrangements. But he was pleasantly surprised to find that the office had been emptied out, except for one modest arrangement sitting on Michel's desk and, to his surprise, one on his. He had to give Michel a point for that. But he was not in the office.

Spritzer really didn't want to be stuck at his desk this morning, and started to look for Francisco, hoping there was some outdoor work he could put his mind to today. Benny, the maintenance man, was mopping in the ladies' room. "You seen Michel or Francisco this morning?"

"I heard them say they were heading up to R-6 to do some T-budding."

"Thanks."

Spritzer got back in his Jeep and drove to the new pinot noir vineyard. He parked and looked over the field. He didn't see Francisco, but Michel was hunkered down with a flat of pinot noir cuttings. He was working intently on T-budding the cuttings to the old chardonnay root stock. The process involved slicing a slit in the root base and inserting the pinot noir cutting, then closing the opening using grafting tape to wrap, and seal the new bud.

Spritzer went over to Michel. He was on his knees. A large straw hat shielded his face, and his stubble beard was accented by the shade of the brim. Spritzer was taken by Michel's intense concentration and the firmness of his gaze as he worked. He was wearing gloves, but they were dirty, and his strong arms were covered in sap from the root stock. He looked up. "Hey there."

"It's going to get very hot later. You ready for a break?" Spritzer suggested.

Michel leaned back on his haunches. "Are you kidding?" He waved his hand toward the field stretching out forever before them. "With all of this work to do?"

"Where's Francisco? I thought this was his job?"

"He turned his ankle this morning. I sent him home to a tub of Epsom salts and a couple of aspirins. But this has got to be done, so here I am."

"You've done a lot already, and it looks great."

"Thanks."

"Why don't you have some of the other fellas helping out?"

"Everyone else is tied up right now on other necessary projects."

He went back to work—focused and intent on getting the job done. Spritzer started walking back to the Jeep but stopped, turned, and went back. He stared at Michel, but finally made up his mind.

"Want some help?"

Michel stopped his work and looked up at him.

"That would be most welcome. But do you know how do to this? Have you ever done it before?"

"At Davis. But it's not something I routinely do."

Michel sized him up and narrowed his eyes. "Hmm. You got any tools in that Jeep?"

"Got a box cutter. Will that work?"

"If it's good and sharp." He rummaged in his box and tossed Spritzer a roll of grafting tape. "And you'll need this. There's another box of cuttings covered with a wet cloth under that tree." He pointed.

Spritzer went to his Jeep, got out his blade, retrieved the box of cuttings, and came back.

"Ready and willing," he announced.

Michel took a deep breath and got up. "We'd better start on the next two rows. You take one, I'll take the other. That way you can see what I do, and I'll be able to answer any questions you might have as we go along."

Both were ready to start. Each had their tools and cuttings. Michel launched right in. His cutting was quick and efficient. He inserted the bud stock and wrapped the tape around the insertion with just a couple of movements, and then scooted over to the next vine.

Spritzer, on the other hand, seemed to be all thumbs. He was slow, plodding, and inefficient. Michel had already completed three vines by the time Spritzer had completed his first one. He looked up and sat back. Already his back was hurting from bending over. He watched Michel whizz through another vine. Boy, he was good. Spritzer took a deep breath and began work on his second vine.

After several hours of unrelenting work, Michel was way ahead of him. He had completed two-thirds more vines than Spritzer had. Spritzer looked up at the cloudless sky. The sun was unrelentingly bearing down on them now. Spritzer's shirt was soaked through. He called over to Michel.

"I've got a jug of water in the back of the Jeep. Wanna take a break?"

Michel held up his water bottle. "I'm good. You go ahead, though."

Spritzer pried himself up from the ground. He didn't remember ever being so stiff—except after riding that horse. He hobbled over to the Jeep, sat down on the passenger seat, picked up the jug of water, and held it up over his head, releasing the spigot so the water could pour over the top of his head. *Oh Lord, what have I got myself into?* He shook and let the cooling water spray off his head and run down his neck, and then he took a long, refreshing drink. He stared out across the field and watched Michel. *How the fuck can he keep going on like that? That is one tough dude.* But Spritzer was not about to let Michel see him yield the field to him. So he pried himself up from the Jeep and stiffly went back to work, covering his head and neck with a handkerchief he kept in his back pocket.

Michel finally suggested they a break for lunch. Spritzer looked dirty and exhausted.

"I've got to run up to the office. My lunch is up there, but I'll be right back," Spritzer said rather lamely.

"You take your time." Michel looked at him and smiled with a naughty, teasing grin. "And if this is too much for you, or you have other more pressing things you need to do, don't hesitate to quit. I'm quite capable of carrying on by myself."

*Oh no...*Spritzer was having none of that. "I'll be back. Don't you worry. There's more than enough work for the two of us. And I'll schedule some more workers for out here tomorrow."

"As you wish," was all Michel would say, as he sat down under the tree and opened his Greek salad lunch.

* * *

Spritzer did, indeed, return after lunch, and the two of them worked the rest of the afternoon as Spritzer continued to labor away purposefully and with rugged determination.

Spritzer glanced up at the sky and could see the sun had passed below the western ridge. It would soon begin to fade to twilight.

Michel stood from where he knelt, shielded his eyes, and looked over to where Spritzer was working. "Enough, yes?" he called out to him.

Spritzer sighed with relief. He was not about to be the one to call it quits first. "Yeah, sure. You must be tired," he said, mischievously.

Michel came along his row toward Spritzer. Spritzer couldn't believe how good he looked after such a grueling day. He looked down at himself. His jeans were coated in dirt. And even though he had changed shirts at lunchtime, the one he wore was soaked through again.

"That was great work. We got a lot done. I really appreciate your help. Thanks," Michel said.

Spritzer got up from the row and smiled at him. "You are sure some fine worker. God, you're fast."

He nodded, and they both walked back—Spritzer to his Jeep and Michel to his truck. They put away their tools and stowed what was left of the cuttings. Michel looked up at the evening sky.

"It gets dark quickly here, doesn't it?" he said.

"Yeah, once the sun sets, the light just goes."

The two stared at each other. And Spritzer noticed with some discomfort how attractive Michel looked in the fading light. Even though he was thin, he was lithe, and tight. And Spritzer couldn't get Michel's sly smile out of his head.

"How about I invite you to dinner?" Michel asked. "I've got some cassoulet I could heat up. With a salad from my new garden."

Spritzer was not sure whether to accept or not. He hesitated briefly but said, "Okay, why not?" After all, it was just one coworker offering dinner to another.

* * *

As part of Michel's work contract he had requested a one-bedroom furnished house, with room for a garden, in a rural area not too far from the vineyard. Michel led the way into the cozy house, followed by Spritzer. He turned on some lights and headed for the open kitchen.

Spritzer looked around the house.

"Please, make yourself comfortable," Michel said. "It won't take long to heat up the cassoulet and throw a salad together."

"You have a nice place. It's so orderly and—*clean*. You should see my hovel."

"What would you like to drink?"

Spritzer laughed. "A spritzer, of course."

"Oh..."

Spritzer went over to the kitchen counter. "What? Is that a problem?"

Michel was looking in the refrigerator. "Well, all I have is really good wine. It would be such a shame..."

"Okay, I'll try it your way. Hell, with the kind of jug junk we make, a spritzer is the only way to drink it without gagging. Just got used to it, I guess."

Michel laughed, and poured two glasses of a nice cold and refreshing Pouilly-Fuissé. He looked at Spritzer, his face streaked and his hands grubby. "Would you like a shower?" Michel asked as he handed Spritzer his wine. "There are towels in the cupboard."

"Oh yeah, I would love that. Feel like a musk buck during rutting season."

"Glad I'm not a doe, then."

Spritzer seemed a little taken aback by the remark but didn't respond. "Okay, shower it is." He started for the master bath.

Michel called out to him. "Sorry, I didn't make the bed this morning."

Spritzer called back, "No problem. This is a palace, what's an unmade bed?"

After a few moments, Michel heard the shower running. He popped the cassoulet into the oven and began washing greens for the salad.

There was a knock at the front door.

"Yes?" he called out.

Kan burst in through the door and headed toward the kitchen.

"Hi. Hope this is okay—me stopping by? I saw your light. I hope you don't mind."

"No, of course not. The door's always open to you."

Kan plopped down on a kitchen counter stool and began snacking on the red pepper slices Michel was cutting into the salad bowl.

"I've just been dying to talk to you." Kan bubbled with enthusiasm. "I had such a great weekend. I didn't get back till just now. I haven't even been home yet."

Michel heard that the shower had stopped. He was about to inform Kan that Spritzer was here for dinner, but was interrupted.

"Hot! Hot! I mean do you know what I mean by *hot*? I mean, this guy had asbestos sheets."

Michel, sensing where this might be going, tried to break in. "Spritzer…"

But Kan was on a roll. "And cute! His lower lip has this little quiver thing going on…" She demonstrated by shaking her whole body.

By now Michel was pointing toward the bedroom where Spritzer stood naked, listening in evident horror to Kan's narrative. "Kan…Kan, you should know…" But his words were to no avail.

"Well, let me tell you, we saw daylight once for about five minutes when he got up to pee, but aside from that, it was Saturday night for a day and a half. And talk about the fish that *didn't* get away…" She spread her hands about two feet apart.

Michel spoke forcefully and pointed to her bedroom door. "Kan…"

Kan turned to look and saw Spritzer standing in Michel's bedroom doorway, without a stitch on. Kan froze. Spritzer looked furious. Kan stared at him, dumbfounded, then turned back to Michel.

"You…you seduced my Spritzer?"

Kan got up from the stool and strode over to Spritzer. She pushed at his chest. "What are you doing here? What have you two been doing?"

"Nothing. What the fuck…!" He couldn't find his words.

Michel tried to break in. "Please calm down. Let me explain."

Kan pushed Spritzer into the bedroom. Michel followed after. Spritzer's clothes were thrown on the floor by Michel's unmade bed.

Kan turned fiercely to Spritzer. "So…this is the passion pit. You scum. Get dressed, you degenerate."

"What are you talking about? I just had a shower, is all. We've been working all day in the vineyard, for Christ's sake."

He struggled to get dressed, clearly repulsed at having to put on his still dirty, stinky clothes.

Kan turned and snarled at Michel. "And I thought you were my friend."

Michel replied indignantly. "Now wait…just one minute…"

Kan pushed Michel away and turned back to Spritzer. "Good. Pretty good. Make up some classic story about some epic battle between you two to cover up your sludgy goings-on. But you're not even gay. How did he seduce you? Were you drunk?"

"Me? Me? What about you?" Spritzer turned the assault back on Kan. "I heard everything. Screwing some Santa Rosa bar cowboy. No doubt some dumb grease monkey with tats."

Kan was suddenly surprised. "How did you know?"

Spritzer seemed equally surprised. "Good guess, I guess."

Michel took advantage of the lull. "Shut up, you two!"

Kan and Spritzer turned to look at Michel, suddenly united by a new common enemy.

"Keep out of this. It's none of your damn business," Spritzer shouted to Michel.

"Yeah, who asked you, froggy?" Kan belted out.

By now Spritzer was mostly dressed. But Kan started pushing him around the room, as he hopped, trying to get his last sock on, with his shoes under his arms. He collapsed onto the bed and pulled the last sock up, then rose and stormed out of the bedroom, Kan following.

"Well, I guess that pretty well shows me to what level our relationship has plummeted," Kan shouted.

Spritzer stopped and turned. "Relationship? Wait a minute, what relationship? I thought we were just buddies?"

"Buddies? Buddies are what you are with your dog when you're six. What about our understanding—that night at Tony's? Three children, two dogs, and a cat, with a white picket fence—or was that some more of your endless bullshit?"

By now, Kan was forcing Spritzer out the front door. Michel just stood and shook his head. He could still hear them squabbling outside as they headed toward their cars. He sighed, chuckled, sat down with relief, and began dressing the salad, after starting up a CD of soothing Mozart piano sonatas.

CHAPTER FIVE

1988

Brian found he was unexpectedly nervous as he followed Francisco's car home. They pulled into the drive and parked in front of the rural house. A flurry of chickens came scooting over. Had Clara missed feeding time, he wondered.

Clara came out onto the porch and shaded her eyes from the setting sun. She waved to Brian, then took a scoop out of a box on the porch and proceeded to throw feed to the chickens.

Brian and Francisco came up onto the porch. Francisco gave Clara a kiss on the cheek.

"Hope you're hungry." Clara greeted Brian with a smile. "Got one of these critters in the pot."

Brian laughed. "Hope you don't name them. I'd hate to be eating Martha or Geraldine."

The three laughed and went inside. Brian always marveled at what a wonderful housekeeper Clara was. Fran was a slouch at housework. But he wasn't surprised by Clara, as he knew how well Clara managed the family home as Del's housekeeper.

Brian noticed that Clara kept giving him furtive glances. He surmised that she was probably just as nervous as he was about this meeting, even if it was over a casual dinner.

Dinner went well enough, even though the small talk was strained and awkward at times, as all three knew what was on the others' minds.

Finally, after food could no longer be a distraction, they sat at the dinner table in momentary silence.

Francisco finally took charge of the situation by asking, "Have you thought about our proposal?"

Brian nodded and then turned to Clara. "I know this must be very awkward and difficult for you, Clara."

"Not that much," she said softly. "It's a necessity. And I'd be so grateful if you would consent to our plan."

"You don't have any reservations?"

She laughed lightly. "Well, of course, but we want a child so badly. And we don't have any other viable options."

"Yes, Francisco told me you'd rejected adoption and artificial insemination."

She nodded. "They just don't seem right to me."

Francisco turned to Brian. "Have you talked to Fran about this?"

Brian bit his lip before answering. "I haven't."

"Are you going to?" Clara asked.

"I haven't decided whether I can do this or not yet."

Clara seemed deflated. "Oh, Brian..."

"But I haven't rejected it either," he added, seeing her disappointment.

"Is it a moral issue?" she asked.

"Hmm. No, not exactly. It's not like I'm having a wild affair. I understand. And I sure do want to help you folks out. But...well, it's just strange. If we were complete strangers I think it might be easier. But I'm going to keep seeing you guys forever after. And every time I'd see the child I'd know it was mine."

"Maybe it would it be easier if you just donated sperm and let us do the rest?" Francisco suggested.

Clara shook her head. "No, honey, we've already discussed that."

"And what about parental rights?" Brian asked. "You see, I would be one of the legal parents."

Francisco nodded. "We'd have to ask you to give up those rights, Brian. The whole point is we want it to be our child. I mean, you've got a son now, and I assume you could have others, but for us, this is our one chance. We'd have to ask you to sign papers."

"But why me? Couldn't you find someone who's a complete stranger? Wouldn't that be easier?"

"You're family," Clara said softly. "We know you. We trust you. We know where you come from."

Brian was thoughtful. "How would we go about this, then?"

Clara took charge. "I'd let you know the best time in my cycle, and we'd set a date." She laughed. "Francisco could go bowling or something, then you'd come over."

"And you'd let nature take its course," Francisco added, smiling gently.

"And if it didn't work the first time?"

"We'll look at that later, if that's the case," Clara answered.

Brian considered. "Okay. I'll do it. But only because it's you guys."

"And what about Fran?" Clara wanted to know.

"I think it's best if we don't involve her. I can't see her being able to handle knowing your child came from me. I don't think she could separate herself from the situation. She has a tendency to brood."

"Whatever you think's best," Francisco said. "And I hope this won't create a strangeness between us three."

"Not from me," Brian said.

"Nor me," Clara added. "I will have nothing but gratitude." She stood. "Then you will hear directly from me when the time is right." She offered her hand.

Brian shook.

Clara went to the kitchen as Brian prepared to leave. Francisco put his hand on Brian's shoulder and whispered, "Thank you. You have no idea how much this means to us—and especially her."

Clara came back with a carton of eggs. "Tell Fran they're fresh from the chickens today."

Brian just had to smile at the irony of Clara giving Fran eggs.

* * *

2013

"That's not what I heard," Del chuckled, as she reached for a package of broccolini from Trader Joe's produce display, traveling down the aisle in her electric grocery cart.

"And what, exactly, *did* you hear and from *who?*" Spritzer was more amused than angry to learn Del had challenged his assertion that he and Kan had *not* had an epic battle of nuclear-war proportions.

Del reached for a package of spring onions. "Well...Michel and I were having our weekly chitchat and he happened to mention..."

"Ah...I see..." Spritzer said noncommittally, as he threw a package of hickory smoked almonds into the basket. "And don't you think his perspective might be a little nonobjective? After all, he sees me as some sort of a Neanderthal throwback."

"Oh...I wouldn't go that far. In fact, he said some very nice things about you."

"Really?" He was genuinely surprised and intrigued.

"Yes. He said you'd manned up real nice and were a great help with some operation or other out in the vineyard somewhere."

"Well, that's nice."

"Except you were a bit bumbly at it," she also teased.

"Great...now I'm a *bumbling* Neanderthal."

Del reached out and patted his arm. "Not at all." She smiled, with the slightest of twinkles in her eyes, delighted to be teasing Stevie. "In fact, he also said he thought you were rather cute." Spritzer was shocked. "But he didn't indicate whether you were cute as in hot. Or cute as in like a puppy."

"Thanks for that little bit of information."

Del laughed. "Oh, Stevie, don't take it too seriously. Nothing's that serious."

Just then, Kan came around the corner of the aisle, pushing her cart. She appeared to be completely engrossed in her shopping list. Spritzer saw her and abruptly directed Del into the next aisle. He did not want another confrontation with her in front of Del—or anyone else, for that matter. Best to avoid her altogether.

"Kan's here," Spritzer whispered to Del. "And I really *do not* want to deal with her right now. So if you don't mind, I'd like to finish the shopping and get out of here."

"Oh my...Can't tell you how glad I am at my age not to have to deal with these romantic dramas."

"Come on, Del..."

"Okay, here's the list. You run around and get what I need, and I'll run interference for you if I see Kan."

"You're a doll."

Spritzer scampered off to finish the shopping. When he returned, he saw Kan chatting with Del at the end of the aisle. Kan was actually laughing. Dare he approach? No—absolutely not. He retreated behind the coffee and peered over the frozen food to wait until Kan left. *What a wuss I am,* he thought. Michel was right; he was a Neanderthal.

* * *

Spritzer was pacing his bedroom. He had the TV on and was channel surfing but not finding anything he wanted to watch. Actually, he was really not paying much attention to the TV at all. He couldn't get what

Del had told him out of his mind. Did Michel really think he was cute? How cute? He thought back to the day they'd worked in the vineyard together. He couldn't get the image of Michel striding elegantly from the field at the end of the day out of his mind. He shook his head. And if he was really honest, he had to admit he *did* find Michel sorta cute as well. Well, not cute—handsome, perhaps. Manly.

No. No. This was ridiculous. He couldn't possibly have any feelings for Michel or he for him. And yet...*He did invite me back to his place for dinner. You don't suppose...No. He was just being friendly after we'd done a hard day's work together. Still...*

He picked up his phone and sat down on the edge of the bed. For a moment, he hesitated. But he finally dialed Michel's number.

"Hello?"

*Oh, shit. He's answering...*Spritzer couldn't speak.

"Hello. Hello. Spritzer, is that you?"

Of course—caller ID. Michel could see it was him calling. *Dumb fuck. Why didn't you remember that*? He panicked and hung up.

His phone rang. It was Michel. *Think. Think.* He answered. "Hello?"

"Spritzer?"

"Yeah, who's this?"

"Michel. You just called me." He sounded a little annoyed.

"I did? No. Not me."

"You did. I could clearly see the call was from you."

Spritzer forced a laugh. "Oh you know what? I bet it was a butt call."

"A butt call? What's that?"

"You know, you have your phone in your back pocket and sit down, and the phone dials some random number..."

"Butt call...huh. Never heard of that. Okay. You have a nice night. Bye." He hung up.

Spritzer stood frozen in place. *He said to have a nice night. He likes me. He does.* He paced the room some more. *No. No. This is all just a fantasy. I'm not gay. I must be under some kind of crazy French spell.*

The phone rang again. He whipped the phone up to his ear as he answered. "Michel?" he asked brightly.

It was Kan. "Michel. Michel, huh? Just as I thought. Pig!"

* * *

"It's just beautiful." Del had her arm through Spritzer's, as they gazed up at the newly completed winery, the entrance covered in festive flags for the day's celebration.

"Yeah, it is, isn't it?" He leaned down toward her and gave her a kiss on the cheek. "What's it like seeing your dream becoming a reality?"

Del turned to him and squeezed his arm. With her other hand, she gave Spritzer a pat on his cheek. "Well, we still need to see how the wine comes out, don't we?"

"We'll do our very best."

"Have you seen Michel?"

"Don't think he's come yet."

Del waved to Kan and her dad, who had just arrived and were headed over toward them. Kan was dressed in her rodeo cowgirl outfit—bloodred boots, fringed blouse and skirt, and a yellow kerchief around her neck, topped off with a black Stetson.

As they approached, Kan didn't even look at Spritzer. She went right up to Del and gave her a hug. "It's great. What a joint. Great day for the grand opening. Looks like there'll be a lot of folks showin' up."

There was already quite a crowd. Aside from the industry invites, a lot of locals had shown up and were taking tours of the new building. A refreshment tent was set up and a quartet was already playing smooth jazz.

Dan shook hands with Spritzer. "How's it goin'?" he asked. "Looks like a winner."

"Sure hope so," Spritzer replied.

Kan turned awkwardly to Spritzer. "Hello."

"Hello," he answered as neutrally as he could.

Clara came up and whispered in Del's ear. Del turned to Spritzer and Kan. "If you'll just excuse me for a moment—got a catering issue." Del left with Clara.

Spritzer and Kan just stared at each other.

"How ya been?" Spritzer finally asked.

"Hangin' in. You?"

"Oh, you know...busy."

"Yeah, me too." Kan looked over at the food tent. "Food looks great."

"Yeah, the chef is from Territorial in San Francisco. Nelson arranged it. Said he wanted class."

"And he got it."

"Yep."

Nelson's limo cruised down the driveway and drew to a halt in front of the food tent. Nelson got out, followed by Michel, as he climbed out of the backseat and stood tall like a lord surveying his domain. Spritzer caught his breath. Michel looked magnificent—like always, simple, masculine, and elegant.

Michel glided up to them. "Sorry, I'm late. Is everything all right?" he addressed Spritzer, putting his hand on his shoulder and squeezing slightly.

Spritzer flashed a big grin. "Everything's just fine—now."

Michel took hold of Spritzer by both arms and kissed him on each cheek in turn—French style. He then turned to Kan and did the same with her.

Michel smiled genuinely at her. "Good to see you. Are you still angry with me? I hope I was able to clear everything up for you about that awkward evening."

Kan took Michel's hand. "Yes. I'm sorry I flared up at you before you could explain."

"Just to let you know, your olive oil arrived at the marketing people. They'll be getting back to you as soon as they've settled on a promotional plan."

"Excellent. I look forward to it."

Michel turned back to Spritzer. "Is Del here?"

"In the catering tent with Clara." He pointed.

Michel thought for a moment. "I wonder if we shouldn't have the ceremony soon so people can get on with enjoying themselves."

"Sure. Whenever you want."

"Let me go confer with Del. Be right back." He headed over to find her.

Kan reached out and took Spritzer's arm. "Can we talk later?"

Spritzer was distracted as he watched Michel amble over toward the tent. He turned back to Kan. "Yeah, sure. We can do that."

* * *

A short while later, the winery tours were completed, and the guests were assembled in the tent and already snacking at the buffet. Del, Michel, Nelson, and Spritzer were at the edge of the dance floor. Michel held a microphone. He turned to Del.

"Do you want to say anything? After all, it is your baby."

"Oh no, dear. I'm fine."

"You?" he asked Spritzer.

"You'd be much better than I would. You go ahead."

Michel turned to the guests. "Welcome. Welcome, everyone. May I have your attention, please?" They quieted down and turned toward Michel. "I would like to extend a great big Maison Vallier welcome to you all." The crowd applauded. "It is such a pleasure to have you with us to help celebrate this very special occasion, as we officially launch our new winery." He turned to Del and then to Spritzer. "It is a great honor and privilege for me to be here to help make this really delightful dream of Del's come true. And as a small token of my appreciation and esteem for these three new friends—" He indicated Del, Nelson, and Spritzer. "I have shipped over a number of cases, not of sparkling wine, but true vintage champagne from my family's estate where I grew up. We'll leave it up to you to compare the two wines when our first bottling comes out in its proper time. Thank you all, so much. Enjoy your afternoon."

Waiters immediately spread out amongst the guests with flutes of champagne. One waiter came over to Michel, who handed a glass to each of the principal group. He raised his glass and toasted, "To the beautiful dream. Thank you all for your part in making Del's dream come true."

The others also toasted. Then Spritzer grabbed a bottle from a passing waiter and filled up their glasses again. "Here, enjoy. Let's all have a great day."

Del leaned in to Spritzer and whispered. "Easy on the champagne today, okay, Stevie? We don't want a repeat of last time."

Spritzer smiled. "I promise. No embarrassment from me."

The guests flowed over to, and around, the group. They offered congratulations and well wishes. It was quite a crush. But, finally, the band started up again, and the crowd dispersed, and people begin to dance.

Spritzer poured another round of champagne. Del told him she was tired and sought out a chair with some of her friends to chat. Nelson removed his coat and carried it to the car. Kan stood across the floor by the food table with her father.

Spritzer suddenly wanted Michel all to himself. He looked at Michel—who smiled back. Not some *hail fellow well met* smile, but a real smile. A sexy smile. A *come to me* smile.

Spritzer reached out to him, and as he did, he saw Kan starting to walk over toward them. He also noticed that Nelson was coming back from the car with Michel as his intended target. He leaned in to Michel and whispered, "Would you care to dance?"

"*Bien sur.* Very brave of you," he said, and took Spritzer's hand.

They went to the center of the floor and began to dance. And suddenly it was like they were in a movie. The camera pulled back, revealing the rich, lush colors of the flowers draped around the tent, entwined with twinkle lights. It caught the sparkle of the champagne in the glasses, held in each of the couple's hands, arms wrapped around each other. On the soundtrack, a lush and sexy saxophone moaned. And they danced. Eyes locked. Entranced. What was happening? Was it the champagne? The magic of the day?

And Spritzer realized that Nelson and Kan both saw what was happening. Anyone watching could see. The two were close and closer. Their lips almost touched, brushed, turning away and brushed again—tantalizing but not connecting.

Kan saw, and seemed to understand. She'd had enough of the Spritzer/Michel show and left the party.

Then the music stopped. The dance floor began to clear as people went back for more food or wine. Michel and Spritzer continued just looking at each other.

But Spritzer broke from the spell and became frightened. He withdrew into himself and abruptly backed away. Michel nodded to Spritzer, let go of him, and walked over to sit with Del. Spritzer just stood looking after him.

Nelson came over. "Now, coz, what was that all about? Eh?"

Spritzer was still in a daze. "I have no idea."

Nelson took a firm grip on Spritzer's shoulder. "Well, what have we here? Is this a new dimension to our rather staid and narrow cousin?"

"Don't know what you're talking about," Spritzer stated defensively.

"Beware, coz. From what I saw, it looked like you were prospecting in territory where I have already staked my claim."

"What?" Spritzer, still in his daze, turned to look at Nelson.

"A friendly warning. Keep your relations with Michel strictly professional, or else..."

Spritzer shook his head and challenged. "Are you threatening me, Nelson?"

"Telling you."

"Michel's his own man. I doubt you could have any hold on Michel that he doesn't want."

"Maybe. But I control the financing on practically everything around here. Cross me and I could call in all my chips. Just you remember."

Nelson turned away and casually sauntered over toward Michel.

* * *

It was a sure sign that autumn was approaching as a V formation of Canadian geese honked overhead heading south. Spritzer looked up and thought about his father, remembering the early morning when he was six—staked out in the blind waiting for geese or ducks to land on the upper pond during his first hunt. It was one of the few activities that the two of them shared together. He remembered sipping hot chocolate from a thermos and munching on a frosted ginger cookie with sprinkles that his mother had packed for them early that morning.

Little did he know that within two months his mother would run away—never to return. It was difficult for his father to explain, and even more difficult for a six-year-old to understand why his mother had abandoned them. It was only years later that he learned she had run away with another man to Alaska to start a new life. But all contact was lost, and she was never heard from again. Spritzer had tried talking many times to his father about why she left, but he never got a straight answer. His father was always evasive and, even up to his death, always skirted the issue, leaving Spritzer with no answer and a gaping hole in his family history. But the one thing Spritzer knew was that his father blamed himself, though he would never disclose the reason why.

Now both of his parents were gone. It was just him alone—except for Del, of course. And he certainly was *not* going to count Nelson as part of his immediate family.

* * *

"I think we should wait," Michel said, as he studied the crushed grape between his fingers.

This brought Spritzer back into the moment—standing at the edge of one of the established chardonnay vineyards with Michel and Francisco. "Why?" he asked. "We've already harvested our regular crop."

"If we can get the sugar content up just a bit more, it will be just perfect. I'd say one or two more days with these on-and-off cloudy days we've been having."

Spritzer looked over at Francisco who waggled his hand, indicating he was uncertain.

"I think we should go now." Spritzer was adamant.

"Why? This is California—the weather is stable. It's not like France, where a frost could come overnight and wipe out the crop."

Spritzer was nervous. "We've never waited this late before. I don't think we should risk it."

"And you've never made sparkling wine before."

Spritzer was trying to be fair. He turned again to Francisco. "What do you think?"

Francisco squinted and looked up to study the sky. "I don't know. Michel's right about the sugar. But the weather's strange. There've been reports of hail a little north. If that came our way, it could land us a sucker punch."

Spritzer turned back to Michel. "There, what do ya say now?"

Michel considered. "I still think we should wait, and remember, it's my call." He glared at Spritzer and was not about to budge. Spritzer just stared him down without answering.

Finally, Michel pulled out his truck keys and said, "Francisco, we'll check the sugar content again tomorrow morning. For now, I'll be in my new office unpacking if you need me."

* * *

Michel opened one of his viticulture books. It was nice to be reading in French again. His books had been packed away until the new winery was completed, but now he had his own office and was finally able to unpack. He closed the book and put it on a shelf behind his desk.

His walkie-talkie buzzed. It was Spritzer. "Yes?"

"Have you been outside?" he asked in an urgent voice.

"Not since this morning. I'm in my office."

"You've got to get back to the chardonnay field right now," Spritzer commanded him. "We've got a situation."

"I'll be right there." What could be happening that demanded his immediate attention?

He dashed out of the office, down the stairs, and out to his truck. He drove over to the vineyard. As he approached, he could see what the problem was. Dark, threatening clouds towered over the field. Already there was thunder, but no rain as of yet.

He parked and ran over to where Spritzer, Francisco, and a group of other workers were picking grapes as fast as they could—snapping bunches of grapes with their shears and dumping them in baskets. Michel had demanded they harvest the champagne grapes the traditional way. He insisted they not use the mechanical harvester, as it would bruise the grapes and not produce the best sparkling wine.

"Can we get any more workers over here?" Michel shouted to Spritzer across the row, as he began picking too.

"These are all we have right now."

There was a loud clap of thunder down the valley, followed by several strikes of lightning. It suddenly began to rain. Michel was fairly flying down the row now, his shears snapping and flashing.

And then, without warning, it began to hail in white waves of ice. It splattered hard against the delicate ripe grapes, bursting the skins and ruining the grapes left on the vines. But the shower passed quickly—the dark clouds moving farther down the valley. A blanket of white covered the ground, soon to melt. But the damage was done.

Michel reached out and took a bunch of damaged grapes in his hand. He was trembling in the cold and wet. He nodded as tears rolled down his cheeks.

Spritzer stormed around the row and strode up to him.

"Well, are you satisfied now?" he bellowed.

"I'm sorry," Michel said.

Spritzer looked around the vineyard. "We'll be lucky if we can save half of this mess." He turned his fury back to Michel. "Always so goddamn sure of yourself. Think nobody else knows shit."

Spritzer stopped his rant and just stood before him. Michel looked so totally vulnerable, and he raised no defense. Spritzer was conflicted about what to do next. Mind made up, he turned and charged toward his Jeep. But he stopped, turned, came back, and took Michel in his arms. He leaned farther in to whisper, "I don't know whether to kill you or comfort you."

"How about neither? I think we need to focus on rescuing what grapes we can for now." He smiled wearily.

* * *

Fortunately, only a small portion of the field had been damaged by the hail. Quite a large amount of the grapes were salvageable, and Spritzer and the crew harvested them during the next two days. And, mercifully, the good weather held.

Michel was in the new winery, overseeing the use of the new coquard press. The last of the final truckload of grapes was being pressed. The first pressing had gone into one tank, and the second pressing, which produced a smaller amount of lower-quality juice, went into a second tank, to be proportionately blended later with the first pressing to achieve just the right cuvée.

"Is that it?" Michel asked, using his walkie-talkie to communicate with Spritzer out at the vineyard.

"Yep. We're done here. Be back in ten."

Michel was cleaning out the press with the help of a few workers when Spritzer arrived.

"How'd we do?" Spritzer asked.

"Not too bad." Michel showed him the totals in the fermentation tanks from his clipboard. "Numbers one and two have the first press. Number three has the second press." Then Michel shook his head slowly. "But it's just not going to be enough."

"Really? I thought we saved enough of the grapes from the hail."

"Almost."

"So what do you suggest we do now?"

"We'll have to buy more grapes from some of the locals."

Spritzer turned and slapped the top of the press. He hung his head. "Oh, great. More expense. How much are we gonna need?" he asked, turning back to Michel.

"At least a thousand gallons more."

"Come on...I know for a fact we can do the first bottling with less than that. The totals indicate quite enough."

Michel folded his arms. "For the first bottling—yes. But we need a reserve to mix with the following harvest."

"Can't we do without a reserve for this one year? What the fuck difference is that going to make?"

Michel did not admire Spritzer's short temper or petulance. "It makes a lot of difference. With a reserve, we can blend the cuvée to have continuity. We can establish a house character and maintain it. Without the reserve, we're completely at the mercy of a single season's harvest."

Spritzer turned and leaned back against the press. "I see. You've got to have it," he said in a softer tone.

Michel smiled. "I've got to have it."

They both laughed.

"Okay, who do we know that was spared the hail? Let's call around," Spritzer said.

They went up to Spritzer's office where he had a list of all the growers in the area. He took the directory and tore it in half. "Here, you take M through Z, and I'll take the rest. Is that okay?"

Michel was surprised Spritzer had torn the list in half, but took his share and began to call on his cell.

* * *

Spritzer was finishing up his seventh call. "You too? I'm sorry. You know anybody else who might have some quality chardonnay or pinot noir who'd be willing to sell? Okay, thanks."

Michel had been working his phone, as well, and was coming up completely blank.

Spritzer kept calling. "George, I need six to eight tons of chardonnay or pinot noir. What can you do for me? Sorry. Okay, next year, perhaps." He turned off his phone and turned to Michel. "Any luck?"

"Not yet, but I just remembered something important." He pushed the list aside.

"What's that?"

"Kan's father makes his own wine. She gave me some, and it's pretty good. I'm sure you must have had it."

"Yeah, sure."

"I know their area wasn't hit by the hail, and he normally doesn't contract out his personal grapes to anyone. Maybe we could persuade him to sell to us this one time. What do you think?"

Spritzer thought about that. He couldn't see any options left to them. "Hell, let's give it a shot."

* * *

Michel was pensive as they drove over to visit with Dan Cain. He was feeling a little homesick. He rested his head against the headrest and stared out the window at the passing scenery. There were many similarities between the Champagne region of France and Sonoma but, also, a number of differences. Around his home, almost all available land was laid out in neat, tidy vineyards on the flat lands and rising up the sides of every available hillside. Here in Sonoma, besides the vineyards, there were areas of woods, open fields, barren hills, and small towns, giving this area a looser, wilder feel.

Spritzer parked in front of Dan's house, and they got out.

The house, with its large front porch, was built of stone, just like his winery. It was shaded by live oaks and pines. Besides loving his vineyard, Dan loved gardening and the house was surrounded by lovely shrubs, bushes, and a border of annuals along the walkway leading up to the house.

Spritzer knocked on the door.

Kan opened the door abruptly, glared at them, and said, "Well, if it isn't the two dancing lovebirds." She stood, barring the entrance.

"You're here?" Spritzer said with some surprise.

"Dad wanted me to sit in. But don't think I want to be here."

"Okay."

Dan came from behind Kan and put his hand on her shoulder. "Come on in," he said to Spritzer and Michel. Dan ushered them inside. He turned to Kan. "Now, you behave yourself. We got guests. I didn't ask you over here to bully them."

Dan and Kan sat on the sofa, and Michel and Spritzer sat in chairs opposite.

"Have you harvested your personal grapes yet?" Michel asked.

"Was going to do it today until I got your call. They are ready, and need to be harvested as soon as possible."

"Then we have a proposition for you." Spritzer wanted to get right to the point and made his offer to buy Dan's personal supply of grapes.

"Over my dead body," Kan burst out.

Dan turned and looked at her with surprise. "What's going on here?" he asked Kan.

Kan pointed and waggled her finger. "These two have been trying to pretend that nothing's goin' on between them."

Michel was surprised. "Kan. I've explained to you. You know that's not true."

Spritzer cast a look at Michel, and then at Kan, and actually blushed.

"I saw you two dancing at the grand opening. Everybody could see what was going on between you two," Kan insisted.

"That's between you three," Dan said sternly. "But we got other business here today."

Spritzer leaned in to make his point. "That's right, and I'm appealing to you, Dan, to please consider our business proposal. We really need your grapes for our sparkling wine. We're tried getting them everywhere—but no luck. Either the other wineries were hit by the hail or they've already contracted out their crop. You're our last and best hope."

Dan sat back in the sofa and stared at the ceiling, considering the offer. He turned back to Spritzer. "Hey, I'd like to help you out but these grapes are what I use to make my own wine. It's a family tradition that goes way back. And I use the wine to give to family, friends, and business associates. They would all be very disappointed if I didn't make my wine this year. So, sorry, I can't help you out."

Spritzer seemed resigned to Dan's answer and nodded in acceptance. "Yeah, I'm sorry too."

Michel, clearly not willing to give up so easily, stood and went over to the sofa. He sat between Kan and her father. He put an arm around each of them. He turned first to Kan.

"Look, I don't know how you got it into your head that there's something going on between Spritzer and me, but I can assure you there is absolutely nothing other than an improved working relationship." Spritzer definitely looked upset by that remark. Michel went on. "And if you'd talked to me I could have made that abundantly clear. So, please, put your mind at ease."

"But I saw you two at the party, and I was pretty certain that *something* was going on," Kan said, a little pouty.

"Yes. And it's called champagne. There was the music, the occasion, and the wine—a sometimes lethal combination. What you saw was a momentary lapse—an emotional interlude brought on by the sentiment of the festivities. That's all it was. I can absolutely assure you of that."

Michel turned to Dan. "Dan, I truly understand your feelings about your wine. My father had a couple of acres of his own grapes, and each year he would put aside a special wine for the family. Not a champagne, but a very lovely still wine. Delicate and rare. And I've been thinking, and I believe, there may be a way we can both benefit from this."

Dan looked suddenly interested, "Oh, and how's that?"

"Well, if you'll let us buy your grapes I'll make a very generous deal with you."

"Yeah?"

"We'll start by paying you 20 percent over market for the whole lot." Spritzer groaned at that. Michel ignored him. "Then we'll press the grapes in our press. And after pressing, we'll take only the amount of juice we need for our reserves. The balance we'll give back to you for your wine—for free. It won't be as much as you're used to, but it will be at least something for your friends and family. What do you say to that?"

Spritzer just had to speak up. "Wait a minute..."

Michel raised his finger in warning for Spritzer to shut up.

Dan looked over at Kan. She seemed to have gotten over her anger and nodded.

"Sounds like a deal to me." Dan took Michel's hand and shook it in agreement.

"Excellent." Michel looked over to Spritzer with his "you'd better accept this" face.

Spritzer nodded.

"I'll harvest the grapes first thing tomorrow and bring them directly to you," Dan said, finalizing the deal.

* * *

Outside in the Jeep, after their business was concluded, Spritzer sat at the steering wheel, brooding. Michel turned to him. "What are you waiting for? Let's go."

Spritzer turned to look at him with a pained expression. "Then what was that between us that day at the party?"

Michel turned and looked straight ahead. "Like I said to Kan, it was the champagne—for you and for me."

"I don't believe it."

Michel paused, looked down, and said softly, "Then it was a mistake on my part. I am so sorry. Spritz, I can't get involved with you. You're not even gay. What do you think is going to happen?"

Spritzer didn't want to voice this, but he did ask, "Is it, Nelson?"

Michel flashed a moment of anger. "Don't be ridiculous."

"Then why did you go to the opening with him?"

Michel turned to him to make his point. "Because he respects me. He listens to me. He doesn't push me. And he asked me."

"But it was real what we felt there on the dance floor. I know it, and you can't deny it."

Michel wouldn't respond and just stared ahead, so Spritzer put the Jeep in gear and shot off too fast.

* * *

Dan and Kan had brought the grapes as promised, and Michel had pressed them in their fine new coquard press with two pressings.

"Your wine is here." Michel indicated a small fermentation vat. "You are perfectly welcome to leave it for the full fermentation if that suits you. We have plenty of space. You can even bottle it here, if you like. And you can pick it up anytime you want."

"That's great. Think I'll wait till it's finished." Dan looked around the new winery. "This is quite an operation. You must be very pleased."

"We are, and the next big test is coming up in a few weeks when we prepare the cuvée and bottle for the second fermentation."

Dan nodded and smiled at Michel. "I guess that's where you come in—with your expertise."

"And a challenge I feel up to," Michel said confidently.

Spritzer came over and put his hand on Dan's shoulder. "If you'd like to come to my office, I'll write you a check for the grapes."

Spritzer led the two Cains to his new office. He sat at his desk, took out a checkbook, and wrote Dan's check.

"Here you are." He handed Dan the check.

Dan looked at it. "Very nice. Thanks." He turned to Kan. "I'm going home. You coming or staying?"

Kan looked at Spritzer. "You'll give me a lift, won't you?"

Spritzer got up from the desk and went over and put his arm around her waist. "You bet."

"Yeah, I'll stay then," she said to her father.

Spritzer glanced at Michel to see how he was taking his new friendliness with Kan. Michel showed no reaction.

Dan waved the check at Spritzer. "Well, thanks again, Spritz. I'll be off then." He left.

Kan reached up and began to massage Spritzer's shoulders.

"Oh that's nice," he groaned. "It's been a rough few days. You sure know how to make a guy feel good."

Kan smiled at that, and checked out Michel to see how he might be reacting, but he was engrossed on his computer.

Spritzer sighed. "Well, we did it. I can't believe the first harvest and the pressing are all over.

"Well, we need to wait a few weeks for the first fermentation to complete, and then the *real* work begins," Michel insisted.

"Let's party to celebrate," Kan suggested enthusiastically.

Spritzer replied. "Sounds good to me."

Kan turned to Michel. "You coming?"

Michel hesitated and answered coolly, "No thanks. I've got to pack."

"Pack?" Kan asked, surprised.

"He's going back to France for a few weeks," Spritzer answered.

Kan smiled. "You're kidding?"

"Everything's in hand here until we bottle," Michel said. "Spritzer can oversee the first fermentation by himself. And I've got some family business to attend to back home."

"You sure you can trust this yahoo to take care of things all by his little ol' self?"

Michel hesitated and then smiled very slightly. "I've got him well trained."

Spritzer glared at Michel.

"Well, we'll miss you." Then she said to Spritzer, as she gave him a kiss on the cheek, "Won't we, dear?"

"Uh-huh," he grumbled, but showed no emotion.

Kan smiled. "But we'll be fine. Just fine—just the two of us."

CHAPTER SIX

1988

Francisco was shaving in the bathroom after his morning shower. The bathroom was steamed up, and he had to keep clearing the mirror with the back of his hand. The door opened, and Clara came in and put her hands around Francisco's waist and leaned her head against his left shoulder.

"It's time," she said softly. She didn't need to explain; Francisco understood. "I was thinking this afternoon after work."

He took a deep breath and stared into the sink. "Do you want me to call him?" he asked.

"No, I'd better do it. I think the less you know about the details the better, don't you agree?"

He had to laugh. "Yeah, probably. But you'll let me know for sure when he's coming over, so I can give you your privacy?"

"Of course." She paused and looked at him in the mirror. "You going to be okay?" she asked, patting his still wet cheek.

He nodded. "You bet. It's our goal that matters. Remember, I've always got my eye on the prize."

"Where will you go?"

"Think I'll catch the early showing of *The Presidio* after work." He laughed out of nervousness.

"But I thought we were going to see that together. You know I have a big thing for Sean Connery." She bit his shoulder.

"Ouch." He turned and took her in his arms. "Okay. Then I'll go see the Michelle Pfeiffer movie instead."

"And you be good." She turned and grinned at him as she left the bathroom.

* * *

2013

Being one of the oldest of the premiere estates in the Champagne region, the Domaine Bast Champagne house and vineyard was anchored by a beautifully symmetrical, modest-sized, seventeenth-century chateau. A central circular tower with a conical slate roof was flanked on either side by the main body of the house. At either end were two squared-off towers with high, pitched roofs in the same slate. The chateau was constructed of white sandstone with just the faintest yellow tinge. The windows were tall, with white shutters folded back against the outside walls. Stately trees surrounded the sides and back of the house, but not so close as to restrict sunlight from flooding the interior of the house during the day.

The view from the front of the house was unobstructed, and it looked over a formal garden laid out with an *allée* of arching plane trees, extending down a stone path that connected different smaller formal gardens, matrixed in a green lawn and adorned with fountains and neatly clipped boxwood hedges.

Not far from the main house was the working winery. Nestled into the side of a hill, chalk caves extended deep into the hillside, providing the estate with its champagne cellars. And a magnificent stone building housed the pressing, fermentation, and bottling equipment.

At the east end this building, on the third floor, was Michel's office. It was surrounded by lacy, light-filtering trees.

Michel had been back home from the United States for a week now. And surprisingly, even though he had been homesick for France in California, now that he was back in France he found himself already homesick for California. He had not expected that. He had been happy to see his family, and they him, but now he was bogged down in endless winery paperwork that required his personal attention. He picked up a stack of contracts that needed vetting from the desk, and a photograph dropped to the floor when he moved the papers.

He reached down and picked it up. It was of him and Spritzer at the dedication of the new winery. He smiled. Michel had been wearing one of his stunningly fitted suits, and he had to admit he did look pretty damn good. And then there was Spritzer. With his quirky grin and wild hair, he looked more like an overgrown boy than a man. But there were also Spritzer's knowledgeable, piercing eyes. They seemed to look right into Michel's soul. But he shook free of this reverie, reminding himself that while Spritzer might be having a brief infatuation, ultimately, he was straight.

Michel leaned back in his chair, closed his eyes, and reflected on his time in California up until now. He was surprised, but had to admit he couldn't wait to get back.

* * *

Spritzer had a little breathing space now that Michel was in France. He hadn't had the opportunity to look at Lorne's thesis before with all the drama at the winery, but now he had time. He threw the thesis on the passenger seat of his Jeep and headed out to his favorite spot in a small state park not far from the family home. There was an outcropping of rocks where he liked to nestle down, hidden amongst the boulders, sheltered from the wind, and where he could lean back and read undisturbed.

He quickly became engrossed in the thesis and, after reading one particularly compelling section, he pulled out his phone and called Lorne.

"Hey, Lorne."

"Hi, Spritz, what's up?"

"Sorry, but I'm only just now reading your thesis."

"That's okay. No rush."

"But I've been studying your implementation timeline, and I really got excited."

"Yeah?"

"I really like the way you've set up incremental implementation so that there's not a huge cost up front."

"I figured most businesses would need to do it that way."

"What ya doin' now?"

"Studying," Lorne said.

"Could you spare a little time to meet me at my office? I'd really like to have you take a look at our operation with me and see where we could start small. I'm sure I could get Del and Michel behind a startup plan for energy conservation. Could you do that?"

"When?"

"Half an hour?" Spritzer said, as he got up to leave.

"Okay, see ya then."

* * *

Lorne was leaning up against his car waiting for Spritzer as he drove up and parked.

"What the fuck?" Spritzer exclaimed as he got out of the Jeep and saw Lorne up close. "What happened?"

"It's nothing..." Lorne insisted, waving away Spritzer's concern.

Spritzer went over and looked closely, putting his hand on Lorne's shoulder. He leaned in to examine his face. "No, it's not nothing. You've got stitches on your forehead and cheek, and a hell of a black eye."

Lorne nodded. "Robert and I were in Guerneville last night. We'd just come from the movies and were going for a frozen yogurt. Some thugs were following us and began making rude remarks."

"Fag stuff?"

"Yeah. We hurried on, but they caught up with us and shoved us in an alley and began hitting and kicking us."

"Oh, Lorne..."

"Fortunately, a cop car was cruisin' nearby, saw what was goin' on, and squawked their sirens and flashed their lights. The thugs lit off faster than a prince from a whorehouse."

"Did they catch them?"

"Don't know. We didn't stay around to find out."

"Was Robert hurt?"

"A little, but not as much as me. He fell among some cardboard boxes, and they couldn't get to him."

Spritzer was riled up. "Do you know the attackers?"

"I've seen 'em 'round. But don't know any names."

"Man, if you ever see them when I'm around let me know, and I'll bust their asses wide open."

Lorne shook his head. "No. That wouldn't help anything."

"It might make them think twice..."

"I think education's better."

"Yeah, well, I'll educate their boney asses."

Lorne laughed and put his hand on Spritzer's arm. "Thanks for the offer, but I think I need to handle this myself."

"And how are you gonna do that?"

"Learn to run faster."

Spritzer laughed. "That might do it." He studied Lorne. "You up for this? We don't have to do this today if you don't want to."

"That's okay. I need a study break, and I'd like to help. And maybe I'll be able to test my thesis if you decide to go forward."

"Okay, then...let's go to my office."

* * *

Spritzer was in his office at the end of the workday, an array of champagne labels spread out on the desk. Kan was leaning over him, her arm resting on his shoulder.

"What'd ya think?" Spritzer asked, as he studied the labels.

"Um..." She studied them and pointed to a brightly colored one in a very contemporary design with sparkling champagne bubbles. "I like that one."

"Yeah, that's nice." He pointed to another. "But I think this one is the best, and perhaps more appropriate for what Michel is trying to do." It was dark green, with gold lettering edged in black—very plain and simple.

"Hmm. It's okay, but a bit dull, don't you think?"

"It's called classy," Spritzer informed her. He studied the label, then took his pen and scratched out the word "champagne" and wrote in "sparkling wine."

"He got to ya, huh?" Kan said snidely.

"Calling it sparkling wine."

"Oh...yeah."

Kan leaned over and put her arms around him from behind. "Spritz...hon..." she cooed as she nuzzled his ear with her nose.

"Yeah?" He turned his head away.

"You've been so busy this past week with Michel gone and all, and I was wondering if there might be some way I could help you more?"

Spritzer was a little cautious. "Oh? And how's that?"

Kan rolled Spritzer's chair away from the desk, swung him around, and sat on his lap with her arms draped around his neck. "Well, if we were in a more permanent situation, I'm sure I could help in all sorts of ways.

"Permanent?"

"Yeah, you know, knot tying...and things like that."

Spritzer removed her arms from around his neck. "I don't think we should rush into anything right now. I told you we've got to get the sparkling wine launched first."

"The harvest party's coming up real soon, and I thought that might be a time to, ah...jump right into a little connubial bliss."

He didn't answer and turned away.

Kan got up from his lap and turned to confront him. "And I thought you weren't all that interested in making that old champagne anyway?"

"Sparkling wine," he reminded her.

"Well, it seems to me that a lot of the time we used to spend together is now being taken up with all this crap." He didn't answer. "Or is it just an excuse not to spend time with me at all?" He still didn't answer.

* * *

It had been just over a year since Michel first arrived, and Spritzer was taking stock and contemplating his return from France in a few days. He realized how much they had accomplished together. Besides the fine new winery, they had put in several new fields of pinot noir and chardonnay vines that would be producing all the grapes they would need for the sparkling wine in just a few years. And now they had completed their first harvest, and the first fermentation was ready to be bottled as soon as Michel returned.

Today, Spritzer was doing his morning rounds, checking on the fermentation tanks. Each tank had a chalkboard where the type of grape, which field, the date pressed, the vat number, and the state of fermentation were recorded. It was his job to check the temperature, acidity, and alcohol content of the wine every few days. He used a cart to carry his test materials and recorded the results on a chart on his tablet.

"Hello, stranger," a voice rang out behind him.

He turned and saw Michel striding toward him.

"Michel," he said in great surprise, "you aren't due back till Thursday."

Michel came up to him and put his arm around Spritzer's shoulders. "I know, but I became homesick."

Spritzer laughed. "But you *were* home."

"I know. But it seems my heart is in California these days."

"Really?" Spritzer smiled broadly, not exactly sure what he meant by that remark. "Hi, I'm really glad you're back." He took Michel's left forearm and held on.

Michel just stood and smiled. "Me too."

They looked at each other, not sure what to say next. Finally, Michel released himself from Spritzer's hand and looked up at the vats. He went over and put his hand on a vat, caressing it lovingly. "Are my babies okay?"

"They sure are. And just waiting for your return."

"Well then, what do you say we get down to work?"

* * *

Spritzer—encouraged by Michel's warm response to his welcome back to California—appeared at Michel's door, on the first Saturday morning after his return, with several brace of frozen ducks from his last hunting season. He knocked, but didn't wait for Michel to answer and barged into his living room. Before the scene fully presented itself to him, Spritzer said, "I was just driving by..."

He was surprised to recognize Nelson sitting on the sofa with Michel. It was clear they had been having an intimate chat. Michel stood.

"Spritzer...I wasn't expecting you."

Spritzer was stunned. "No, I can see that. But...I brought you these."

He held out a plastic grocery bag toward Michel, who crossed over to him and took the bag.

"What's this?" Michel asked.

Spritzer stammered. "Ducks...I know how you like to cook fancy...thought maybe..."

"How very nice, thank you." Michel turned to Nelson. "Very sporty, eh?"

Nelson was his usual smooth and snarly self. "Oh yes, so charming. Hi, coz. Quite jolly to have Michel back, isn't it?"

Michel leaned in toward Spritzer and spoke softly. "I was going to call you later this morning."

Spritzer turned to Michel and also spoke softly. "I didn't know you were busy."

"I think you and I need to talk," Michel said earnestly.

Spritzer was really pissed off now. "Yeah, well, let's do that. But it's obvious you are otherwise engaged right now."

They stood looking at one another, but at an impasse as to what to say next.

"I'd better go," Spritzer finally said.

"I'm sorry..."

Nelson stood. "Are you leaving...so soon?"

"Yeah, was just driving by." He turned to Michel. "I'll see you at the lab Monday morning."

He left quickly—hurt, confused, and completely lost.

* * *

The new laboratory at the winery was state of the art. It was equipped with every imaginable instrument needed in modern sparkling wine production. This was where the magic would take place. The nature and signature of the new sparkling wine would be constructed right here. Michel was at a workstation with a series of glass beakers filled with the various types of wine they'd pressed a few weeks ago—both first and second pressings. Each beaker was labeled.

It was early morning when Spritzer came in.

Michel looked up, knowing what would be on Spritzer's mind. "I'm sorry about Saturday. I had no idea Nelson would drop by," he said apologetically.

Spritzer answered briskly. "Forget it."

"I want to explain..." Michel tried to say, turning his attention to Spritzer.

"Want some coffee?" Spritzer busied himself at the coffee maker.

"I already had some. Can we talk, please?" Michel insisted.

Spritzer turned to him, abruptly. "Why? What's there to say? You are obviously in some sort of relationship with Nelson. It was quite clear when I came into your house Saturday. I have nothing more to say on the subject. So can we just get to work? The sparkling wine is not going to make itself. And, after all, that's what you're here for, isn't it?"

Now Michel was pissed. He just stared at Spritzer. *If that's the way he wants to play it, okay.* He turned back to his work without answering him.

Spritzer came over with his coffee. He studied what Michel was doing.

"What's this?" Spritzer asked, pointing to the beakers.

Michel answered coolly. "I'm working on creating the cuvée. Different blends of this harvest and some of the Vallier reserve from last year; and different percentages of different grapes. I'm trying to create the unique identity for our wine."

Spritzer picked up a beaker and sniffed. Then he tried to take a sip, but Michel slapped his hand and took the beaker from him.

"Hands off."

Spritzer was not to be deterred. He picked up another beaker and sipped, making a horrible face.

"Ugh. That's terrible. That's our cham...sparkling wine?"

"It's not finished. It needs to be blended, have the *liqueur de tirage* added, go through the effervescent fermentation, and then rest for eighteen months."

"What's that *liqueur de tirage*, anyway?"

"It's a mixture of sugar and yeast. We introduce it when we bottle the wine, and it causes the second fermentation. And that's how we get sparkling wine."

"How in the world can you tell what it will be like from tasting this piss?"

"Well, that comes with about three hundred years of experience. This is an art as well as a science."

"And these are all the different wines you work with?" Spritzer asked, pointing to the various beakers.

"Yes. I've been working to blend these to create exactly the base I'm looking for."

"Have you blended any yet?"

"Yes. These." Michel indicated four beakers.

"Let me." Spritzer picked up each beaker in turn, smelled it, and took a small taste. He pointed to the second one. "I like that one."

He handed it to Michel who took a taste. "Oh, no. That would come out far too sweet and harsh. I've pretty well decided on the fourth one."

Spritzer tasted it, but spit it out. "You're crazy. It tastes like turpentine."

"Maybe now, but not when we're through."

Spritzer shook his head. "No, no. This one is definitely better," he said, going back to his original choice.

Michel stepped back and confronted him. "I can't believe this. You know nothing about preparing the cuvée and you're telling *me* which one is best?"

Spritzer's anger flared. "Hey, I'm not some dumb-ass, you know."

"No, I don't know. You're certainly behaving like one." Michel covered the beakers and began putting them in into the refrigeration unit.

"We'll let Del decide, then."

Shaking his head, Michel began wiping down the workstation. "Ah...you are so stubborn."

"*I'm* stubborn? Ha!"

Michel looked up at him. "You still haven't learned to trust my knowledge and expertise yet, have you?"

"God, you are *so* arrogant and full of yourself!" Spritzer blurted.

"And just when I thought you might be a human being after all, you behave like a spoiled brat." Michel returned fire with fire.

"And you drive me crazy." Spritzer's phone rang. He checked the ID. "Clara." He answered abruptly with his phone on speaker, "Yes?"

"Del's just had a terrible fall in the studio. You'd better come." Clara said.

"Be right there." He turned to Michel. "I've got to go."

"Me too," Michel said.

They ran toward the door.

* * *

Spritzer and Michel hopped into Spritzer's Jeep. They raced toward the house, an uneasy truce between them.

As they were driving, Michel looked over and could see that Spritzer was concerned about Del. He put his hand on Spritzer's shoulder. Spritzer nodded to Michel, adding a very slight smile.

They pulled up to the house, got out, and dashed toward the studio. Spritzer flung the door open and went inside. Del lay on the floor by her potter's wheel. Her head was resting on a pillow. She had her hand on her right hip. Clara was kneeling beside her, holding her other hand and stroking it.

"Stevie," Del said weakly, looking up at him. "I think I've broken my hip." She looked ashen.

"I called 911," Clara said.

"How did this happen, Del?" Spritzer asked.

"Oh, darling, it was so silly. I was trying to stand on a chair to get a ceramic from the top shelf, and it wobbled, and I fell."

"Oh, Del, you should know better than to do that," Spritzer said.

"I do. I was being lazy. Didn't want to go get the steps from the closet."

"Next time, you'll know better." Spritzer wiped her brow where beads of sweat were starting to run down the side of her face.

"If there is a next time," Del said sadly.

"Of course, there will be." He turned to Michel. "Can you get me a wet cloth, please?"

"Certainly." He went to the sink, picked up a clean towel, wet it, and wrung it out. He folded it as he brought it over to Spritzer, who placed it on Del's forehead.

"That's nice," Del said weakly. "No one heard me calling for help for the longest time, and I was afraid to move. Then Clara brought me some coffee and found me."

"Well, you'll be all better now." He turned the wet cloth over and reapplied it to her forehead. "How's that feel—better?"

"Oh, yes, thank you, dear."

A siren blared in the near distance. "I hear the EMTs," Spritzer said. "They'll take good care of you."

Clara got up. "I'll go greet them. Be right back." She left.

"Are you in any pain, dear?" Michel asked.

Del nodded. "Some. But I'm more embarrassed than anything. I feel so stupid."

"Well, you don't have a monopoly on stupidity," Michel joked and smiled at Spritzer.

The EMTs came in with a gurney and a backboard.

"Hey there, young lady...this nice lady tells me you fell and broke your hip," the first EMT said, kneeling down. The second EMT brought over the backboard and put it down next to Del. "We're going to take good care of you. Don't you worry. We're going to need to transfer you to this board, then we'll lift you onto the gurney. Okay?"

Del nodded.

"I'll go pack a bag for the hospital," Clara said, then disappeared.

Spritzer and Michel stood back as the EMTs prepared Del for transport. When they wheeled her out to the ambulance, Spritzer and Michel followed.

"You going with her?" Michel asked Spritzer.

He turned to the EMTs. "Can I come too? I'd like to be with her."

"Are you family?"

"Her nephew."

The first EMT nodded. "Yes, if you like."

"How about me?" Michel asked.

"Can you drive the Jeep?" Spritzer asked Michel.

"Absolutely."

"Then why don't you bring my Jeep to the hospital in an hour or so, then I can drive you back later after Del settles in. And bring Del's bag with you when Clara has it ready."

"Sounds good."

"You gonna work on the cuvée some more?" Spritzer asked.

Michel nodded. "I may, but I think I'm about there. I still need to calculate the amounts I'll need for the mixing vat. Then we'll be ready to bottle."

Spritzer reached out and put his hand on Michel's shoulder. "Thanks for your help."

"Sure."

"We're ready," the first EMT announced.

Spritzer got into the rig. He sat down next to Del and took her hand. "See you shortly," he called out to Michel and waved as the EMTs shut the ambulance doors.

* * *

Del was being expertly cared for at the hospital. She was on the mend, and on the way to a long but, hopefully, full recovery. At her age, as the medical staff had explained to Spritzer, these things were uncertain and mending could take longer. He told Del that he was needed at the winery for the crucial bottling stage, so he wouldn't be able to spend a lot of time with her over the next few days. But Clara was at her side daily, so she was well looked after, and had company and assistance if she needed anything the nurses couldn't provide.

Spritzer was intrigued by Michel's new bottling machine. It was much more sophisticated than the one used for the jug wine, as he had expected, but it was intriguing to watch it in operation. Michel had made an exact blend of the select premier fermented wines from the various vats, combining them together in the mixing vat. From that vat, the bottles were filled with the mixed wine. The *liqueur de tirage* was then added to each bottle. Farther down the line, each bottle had a crown cap attached. It was the same kind of cap used on a beer bottle. But this was only temporary, while the second fermentation took place—a process that lasted up to eight weeks. During this time the carbonation of the sparkling wine was created, forming the bubbles. This would produce the same pressure in the bottle as a bus tire.

Michel was overseeing the operation, and Spritzer was driving the forklift, moving the bottles from the bottling machine to the storage area in the new warehouse that still smelled of new wood, fresh paint, and newly set concrete. As the warehouse was receiving its first consignment of bottles, it reverberated and echoed with the sound of Spritzer's forklift as it zoomed into the empty space.

Michel had accompanied Spritzer to the warehouse with his first batch of bottles. He instructed the workers how to lay the first, and subsequent, rows. Spritzer stood with him to see how it was done.

The workers laid the bottles horizontally along a straight line, neck of one bottle to base of another. Slats were placed between each stacked row, creating space for the air to flow through. And here they would rest as the second fermentation took place. When the bottling had been completed, and all the bottles had been stacked in their separate rows, Michel stood and admired his accomplishment.

"Good. Good." Michel nodded, then turned to Spritzer. "We'll need to restack these inside out later. That's why I've left enough space between each group so we can create the inside-out stack next to it."

"Why do that?"

"As the bottles ferment they heat up, and restacking helps cool them down."

Spritzer said, slyly mocking, "Okay, you're the boss."

Michel answered playfully, "And don't you forget it."

Once the bottling was completed, they were done except for monitoring the stacked bottles over the next two months. They would spend their time cleaning the vats and preparing for the spring vineyard cultivation. But there was still one decision that needed to be made—the labels.

Spritzer laid out the label selection on Michel's desk.

"Kan favored this one," Spritzer said, pointing to the label with the bubbles.

Michel laughed. "Yes, I bet she did."

"And I sort of favored this one," he said, pointing to the dark green one.

Michel looked up at him. "You do, really?" He nodded. "You're sure?"

What's he getting at? "Why, is something wrong with it? It seemed to fit exactly with your idea of a sophisticated look."

After studying all the labels carefully, Michel nodded. "And you are exactly right," he said, smiling.

Spritzer felt much relieved and pleased with himself.

"I'll put in the order," he said.

* * *

Del was finally back from the hospital and propped up in her bed in the master bedroom. Clara, ever attendant, was cleaning her bathroom, after dusting and vacuuming. When she'd finished, she came over and sat down next to Del on the edge of her bed. She took Del's hand.

"What do you want for lunch?" she asked.

Del sighed. "I still don't have much of an appetite."

"I know, but you've got to eat to get stronger. Think of all you've got going on in your studio. I know you want to get back to that."

Del leaned her head back against the pillow. "Oh yes...but..."

"But what?" Clara asked. "I'm not going to allow you to wallow in self-pity, my dear friend. We're going to fight this together, and you're going to win. No doubt about it."

Del laughed. "Well, I'm glad at least one of us is resolute."

"I've got some nice potato-and-leek soup. Or there's still some quiche left over from the other day. Or a salad? I picked some fresh greens from the garden. What's your fancy?"

Del reached out and patted Clara's hand. "What would I do without you?"

"Well, you don't have to."

"The salad sounds nice. With some of your famous avocado dressing...and maybe just a small slice of quiche heated up."

"Sounds perfect."

Just then Spritzer and Michel appeared at Del's bedroom door.

"Knock, knock." Spritzer came into the room, bearing a bunch of tulips. Michel was carrying one of his homemade clementine glazed tarts.

Del immediately lit up. She sat up straighter and smoothed her bedding. She was wearing a light blue, knitted bed jacket. "Oh, how nice to see you both. Please come in."

They walked over to her.

"Oh, how lovely the flowers are. You know how much I like tulips."

"I certainly do," Spritzer said, presenting them to her.

"And look at that lovely tart. How delicious looking. Did you make it?" Del asked.

"I did. One of my family favorites from home."

"Clara," Del said, "would you put these flowers in water for me please? And take this lovely tart and put it in the refrigerator. We'll have some later."

"Of course," Clara said, "I'll be right back."

It was clear that Del had lost weight and she didn't seem to have a lot of strength, Spritzer thought. An array of papers was spread around her on the bed. Del lay back against her pillows and shut her eyes. Spritzer and Michel pulled up chairs next to the bed. They waited for her.

Del opened her eyes. "Sorry, just needed to rest my eyes a minute. I've been studying these reports from Vallier Winery you gave me the other day, Spritzer."

"Not great, huh?" he said. "The whole state has had such a bumper crop of grapes this fall, the prices are greatly depressed. Don't know if we'll be able to maintain our prices on the jug wine."

"Any idea what the competition is doing?" Del asked.

"Their costs are lower, so they're trying to be competitive by lowering their prices."

"So we'll need to do that too?"

"I don't see how we can avoid it—we've always been the low-price selection." Spritzer scratched his forehead, trying to figure out an alternative. "But I don't think it will be more than ten to fifteen cents a unit."

Del put on her glasses. She picked up a paper from the bed and studied it. "But Stevie, you know how close our margin is. Even that seemingly small amount adds up and becomes a huge figure spread out over an entire year."

"I understand."

"I don't know what we're going to do. Nelson has been breathing down my neck about the costs on the new venture, plus he is pushing for a higher and faster repayment figure on the mortgages. I don't see how we can handle all of this and keep going."

Michel spoke up. "I can handle Nelson. Give me the figure you need for this to work and I'll speak with him."

Spritzer looked over at Michel at his mention of handling Nelson, but he avoided Spritzer's eyes.

"How bad do you think it will be?" Spritzer asked.

"We'll eat, but it's really going to bite into our profits." Del thought for a moment, then turned to Michel. "How long before the first bottling of the sparkling wine is ready?"

"Eighteen months," he replied.

"Could you go with nine months or ten?"

"Not if you want the quality you insist on."

Del nodded. "If we could release the sparkling wine sooner, say before the end of next year, I think we could be okay."

Spritzer supported Michel. "You said you wanted the best, Del. Eighteen months is the minimum. I think we should wait, like Michel says."

Del and Michel both looked at him with some surprise as he was, for once, siding with Michel.

Del appeared to be contemplating the consequences of less revenue and waiting the full term for the sparkling wine. "Okay, we'll wait, but I think we'll need to cancel the harvest festival this year. Don't see how we can afford it."

Spritzer was shocked. "Give up the party? Del, we've had that for fifty years, without a break."

"I know, but I think we've got to cut costs everywhere we can. I'm going to use my income from the winery to pay Nelson."

"Del..." Spritzer protested.

"No, I've got enough other income from my ceramics to keep me going. Not to worry. And remember, if we can't get through this season, the winery becomes Nelson's."

Spritzer and Michel looked at each other.

"We'll make it work, I promise," Spritzer said. "I'll cut my salary in half this year. I've got some savings."

Del reached over and patted his hand. "You don't have to do that."

"I want to."

"And I'll pay for the harvest festival," Michel said.

Spritzer looked over to her and smiled. "No. We both will."

"No, I'll pay for the whole thing. You've already done your part by cutting your salary. I'm not willing to do that, but I will stake the party."

Del nodded. "Then I think we just might just make it work."

* * *

It was an unusually warm day for mid-October. The projected high was to be in the low nineties. Spritzer was in the Maison vat room looking for workers. With the projected heat, Spritzer was afraid the unpruned vines might start budding, and it was way too early for that. He needed to get as many workers as possible out into the vineyard to complete the pruning for the year. He saw a worker atop one of the vats, filling it with water, preparing to clean it.

"Hey, Leo, I really need your help over at the vineyard today. Could you finish that up later?"

"Don't you need this done now?"

"Let it soak. I need you to help me and Francisco today. We've got to get the rest of the vines pruned. Take your shears and go on over."

"Okay, boss."

"Anybody else about?"

"Haven't seen anyone around except Michel. He's in the warehouse."

"Great."

Spritzer went into the warehouse. Michel was inspecting the stacks of bottles.

"Hey." Michel greeted him with a tense expression. "It's time to restack now. The bottle temperature has risen significantly."

"Can it wait? We've got to get the rest of the pruning done today. Everyone's over at the vineyard now. I'm afraid the unpruned vines are gonna start budding."

"Then help me get this done right now. This is equally important."

Spritzer shook his head. "Sorry, Michel, I've got to be over there today. And you should come too."

"Spritzer, this is just as, if not more, important."

Spritzer thought for a moment. "Well then, turn up the air conditioner. We'll get to the bottles later this afternoon—I promise." He turned to leave. "Come on, we need you in the field."

Michel shook his head. He went to the thermostat and turned the dial way down in an effort to keep the bottles at an acceptable temperature. "Okay, let's go."

* * *

The warehouse was now completely empty, with all the doors shut in an effort to keep the building cool. A hot wind was blowing steadily west from the Sacramento Valley, but with occasional strong gusts. An outside thermometer registered eighty-four degrees. And the warehouse thermostat was showing a decent sixty-eight. An hour later the external temperature had risen to eighty-nine, and the internal temperature was now seventy-four.

As the heat intensified, waves of heat began radiating off the metal roof of the warehouse. And there was a separation of inside and outside temperatures of many fewer degrees. The rooftop AC was cranking at full blast as the inside temperature struggled to reach its set point.

Finally, the outside temperature reached ninety-four and the inside temperature eighty-two. The AC struggled, but became overloaded, and tripped the switch in the circuit breaker.

A half hour went by. The inside temperature continued to rise, reaching eighty-six. An hour later, with the metal roof getting even hotter, the inside temperature hit eighty-nine.

Suddenly, a bottle in one of the fermenting stacks exploded. This sent other bottles exploding, setting off a chain reaction from one stack to the next. Shattered bottles were strewn across the floor, and sparkling wine spread in flowering circles across the warehouse floor.

Francisco had come back to the warehouse to get the necessary paperwork to make an important call. As he was nearing the offices he heard one explosion and then another from the warehouse. He ran over and threw open the sliding door. The devastation before him looked monumental. He pulled out his phone and called Michel.

* * *

"What happened?" Michel asked, in utter shock, as he surveyed the devastation spread out before them.

"I have no idea," Spritzer said flatly. He went to the thermostat. The interior temperature was registering ninety-two degrees. He checked the thermostat switch and saw that it was turned on, but the AC was not operating. "Christ, the AC's out. It must have overloaded in the heat and shut off. Francisco, check the circuit breakers."

"Sure." He went over to the breaker box and could immediately identify the tripped AC switch. He flipped it back on, and the AC started up again. "Yeah, that was it," he called over.

Michel charged at Spritzer. "That does it! I'm finished. I'm through! This is all your damn fault."

"My fault?"

"Who refused to upgrade the AC when it was being installed? Who wanted to save money on these cheap fucking bottles? Who wouldn't shift the bottles when I said they *must* be? Huh? Huh?"

He reached out to Spritzer and pushed him at both shoulders, sending him staggering off balance.

The problem was, Spritzer *was* in the wrong. This disaster was all down to him, and he knew it. But he went crazy too. "Don't push me, you French bastard. Who the fuck do you think you are, anyway?" Spritzer pushed right back after regaining his balance.

Michel stumbled backward and fell against a stack of undamaged bottles. The sides of the stack gave way, and the bottles slipped and began rolling across the floor. He was not hurt, but now he was absolutely furious. He got up and ran right up to Spritzer. Grabbing him by the shirt, Michel swung him in half a circle till he slammed into a stack of folded packing cartons. These came tumbling down. Spritzer picked himself up, and now was really ready for a fight. He lurched toward Michel, growling.

"Don't you dare!" Michel shouted, backing away and beginning to laugh at the absurdity of the situation.

Spritzer looked around for a weapon and pulled loose a board from a broken pallet. He waved it over his head like a broadsword and charged at Michel, shouting like a Celtic warrior.

Michel had nothing to protect himself with and was not going to wait around. He started running. Spritzer chased after. Michel ran into the vat room and climbed the ladder that led to the catwalk along the top of the vats. He reached the end of the walk which overlooked the vat that had been soaking. Spritzer was running at full speed, waving his pathetic piece of wood. Michel had nowhere to go. He put his hands out to protect himself. But, just before Spritzer reached Michel, he slipped, the sword flying into the air. He landed with his full body weight against Michel, and they both toppled over the railing and into the vat of water, letting out identical surprised screams.

Together they surfaced, sputtering and gasping for breath. They grabbed onto the side of the vat.

"I'm sorry. I'm sorry," Spritzer spit out. "You were right. It *is* all my fault. I'm such a stubborn ass."

Michel was gasping, and shook his head as he ran a hand through his hair. "It's done. It's done. Let's just forget about it and get the mess cleaned up so we can see what we've got to work with."

Spritzer suddenly grabbed Michel's shoulder as he continued holding onto the side of the vat with his other hand. He sputtered out, "I didn't know how much I cared. Seeing all our work...damaged...it's made me realize..." He stopped and stared at Michel, who was regarding him with surprise. "Made me realize...how much I care about...you."

"Stevie...?" Michel said. "Don't...You don't know what you're saying."

Spritzer reached out to throw his arms around Michel's neck, but Michel backed away out of reach, let go of the vat, and began to sink.

"I can't swim!" he called out, panic in his voice.

Spritzer swam over to him. He put his arm across Michel's chest from behind, and began pulling him back to the edge of the vat. After reaching safety, they hung on to the side and began to laugh.

Francisco had climbed to the catwalk and was leaning over the railing. He shouted, "Here, take my hands. I'll pull you out." And he began laughing too.

First, he pulled Michel out, dripping and frazzled as a baby chick in a birdbath. Spritzer was able to lift himself out, looking like an abandoned puppy.

At first, they just stood there, looking intently at each other. Then Spritzer gently put his arms around Michel and asked, "Can you forgive me?"

Michel pulled back and glared at Spritzer, then gave him a whopping slap. He started laughing. "Now I can."

* * *

Michel and Spritzer both kept a spare set of work clothes in their offices. They retired to the restroom, dried off, changed, and met back at the warehouse to assess the damage.

Francisco and two other workers were already cleaning up the mess. "It's not all that bad," Francisco announced, as he and one other worker began restacking the unbroken bottles. "I'd say we didn't lose more than about ten percent. Fifteen at the most."

"That's not impossible to live with," Michel said, as he picked up a bottle and examined it. "Be sure and check for cracks before you restack the bottles."

Spritzer was on his phone with the AC service people to see what could be done about upgrading the system. As he was speaking, he watched Michel with a big smile, despite the recent catastrophe.

After everything had been cleaned up, Spritzer and Michel stood looking out over the warehouse, which was once again restored to order.

Spritzer turned to Michel and put his arm around his shoulder. "Well, at least you got the bottles restacked."

They laughed.

* * *

It had definitely been a stressful day. Spritzer stood outside the winery in the twilight watching the birds circle and settle in the trees for the night. It had cooled down significantly from the heat of that disastrous afternoon. He had checked the weather on his computer and had seen a cold front was headed their way and would be in place by the morning.

Michel came outside to stand beside him. "Are you okay?" he asked, putting his hand on Spritzer's shoulder.

Spritzer nodded. "I feel like one of those cartoon characters that gets rolled over by a steamroller and then peels himself off the pavement and jumps back to life."

Michel laughed, then was quiet and thoughtful. He reached up, put his hand on the back of Spritzer's head, and ruffled his hair. "Don't you think we need to talk?"

Spritzer thought about that. "Yeah, some things happened today, didn't they?"

"I think you could say that."

Spritzer turned to Michel and looked at him openly and without defenses. "What's happening?"

Michel moved in closer and put his arms around Spritzer from behind. "Want to come to my place for some dinner and we can talk about it?"

"Not sure I could eat right now."

"Whatever you want. But come over and let's figure out what's going on here. Then if you're hungry at any point I can fix us something."

"Okay. You lead."

They went to their vehicles. Michel drove away, and Spritzer followed.

* * *

"I bet you'll have some wine," Michel offered as they went inside his house.

"You'd win."

"Red or white?"

"Whatever."

"I've got a nice Beaujolais."

"Okay."

Michel poured them a glass each and came over and sat down on the sofa, after turning on some lamps.

Spritzer continued standing. He was pacing, unable to settle.

"Okay, let's take a look at what happened right up front," Michel stated. "Do you think you might be gay?"

Spritzer stared at him like a dog caught chewing on the sofa cushions. "I don't know. How could I be?"

"Well, Spritz, you know human sexuality can be fluid. We pin names on things that sometimes don't fit, or they can change. You have thought of yourself as straight all these years, but our meeting may have triggered a dormant aspect in you, and you might, in fact, be bi. That is what you will need to decide for yourself. But I can tell you with absolute certainty that I am pretty much, sometimes, occasionally, but at least today—totally gay."

That got Spritzer laughing, and he felt comfortable enough to sit down in an armchair across from Michel.

"Now what I want to make very clear to you is that I will do nothing that you are not comfortable with. If you think you might have feelings for me, and you decide you'd like to explore that part of your sexuality, then I support that. I want you to know that I find you very attractive and I also have feelings for you. For both of us, these feelings are just tender shoots right now that need to grow, but if we decide to move forward, I want you to know I will do nothing to harm you in any way. If at any point you feel threatened, then just step back and tell me. I promise I will not take advantage of you."

Spritzer nodded. "I appreciate that. But that doesn't really answer my question."

"Okay, then let's look at what it is you feel. Can you tell me?"

Spritzer thought about that before answering. "You know I really hated your guts when you first came here."

Michel laughed. "Yeah, I got that."

"And then...over time...working with you...seeing how dedicated you were—and fair. Yes, fair. We often disagreed but you always kept to the integrity of our purpose. Well...I just began to admire you more and more.

"I guess it really started for me that day we worked in the vineyard T-budding together. I so admired your strength and dedication...And when we were done, I looked at you...and I saw...you. You were just so beautiful. And I didn't know what to make of that."

Michel nodded.

"And then Del, of all people, mentioned quite casually that you thought I was cute."

Michel laughed. "Yes, I did."

"And I couldn't get that out of my mind. Remember that night I called you and hung up, and then I told you it was a butt call?"

"Yeah."

"Well, it wasn't. I wanted to call you to talk, but I got scared."

"Kind of thought that..."

"And then it all just kept growing until today. I was so angry at you, and you were so stunning in *your* anger. It just...Something happened...and I wanted to break you and mend you, and to kiss you and hold you all at once. You tell me. What does it mean?"

"Hmm. And what about Kan?"

"What about her?"

"She must mean something to you. You've been together forever."

"Yes. That's both the reality and the problem. Cozy and unthreatening. We are never going to marry. We are both lazy and have been unwilling till now to face up to the truth of us. There is no passion there—just habit."

Michel got up and went to the kitchen. He came back with the wine bottle and filled up their glasses. He leaned over Spritzer and kissed the top of his head very gently.

"I think it's best if we both just *be* with this new situation for a while," he said as he walked back to the kitchen and deposited the bottle. "I don't think either of us is ready to move ahead just yet. You need time to sort out your feelings, and I need time to think through what I want. Remember, I am only here for a short time. I will be going back to France and resuming my life there. We both need to be sure what we really want before entering into any sort of...relationship. You understand?"

Spritzer nodded.

"That being said, I would really like a hug." Michel opened his arms, and Spritzer stood. He went over to him, laid his head against Michel's shoulder, and they hugged.

After the hug, Michel pulled away and, holding Spritzer at arm's length, said, "Don't know about you, but I'm starved. I have some fresh clams and could pull together a really great clam pasta dish. You up for that?"

"Why not?"

CHAPTER SEVEN

1989

Brian stood on the ridge behind the winery where he liked to go to watch the sun set before going home to dinner, when he could afford the time. It was his moment to unwind from the usually hectic day, and he could reflect on things other than work, which he rarely got to do.

The slivered new moon hung in the western sky. He felt a presence and turned to see Francisco approaching. They nodded to each other. Francisco came over and stood next to Brian, and they watched the evening spectacle unfold before them without speaking. After a few moments, Francisco reached into his jacket pocket. He pulled out a cigar. He turned and offered it to Brian.

"It's a boy. Seven pounds, three ounces. Lorne Brian Delgado."

"Lorne?" Brian asked.

"Clara's grandfather."

"And Brian? Really? Isn't that a bit close to home?"

Francisco put his hand on Brian's shoulder. "Couldn't have done it without you, old buddy. Clara insisted. And why wouldn't I name my only child after my very best friend?"

"I'm honored. And very happy for you."

* * *

2013

Spritzer and Michel were in Del's studio.

"Damn this hip. It's so slow mending. Can't wait till I can use the wheel again." Del was sitting at her workstation, but was unable to operate the potter's wheel with her foot.

"Maybe you should join the twenty-first century and get yourself an electric wheel," Spritzer suggested, a little snidely.

"What—and ruin my reputation as the last of the crazy old broads?"

"At least you still have your sense of humor," Spritzer observed.

"So how bad was it?" Del wanted to know, referring to their news about the exploding bottles.

"About ten to twelve percent of the bottles were lost through breakage. And maybe another one to two percent had cracks and needed to be destroyed," Michel said.

"I see. What do you think? Do I need to call Nelson, to bail us out once again?"

Michel turned toward Spritzer and smiled. "No way."

Spritzer smiled back. "You're learning."

Del noticed this new and warmer familiarity between Michel and Spritzer, but was still focused on the bottle disaster. "But we were hoping for ten to twelve dollars a bottle, wholesale, from the first bottling just to cover our expenses. Now we'll have a modest percentage less. And what we have is what we have. We've got no means to increase the inventory this year. I'm concerned."

"We'll find a way," Spritzer announced confidently.

Del momentarily closed her eyes and just sat at her workstation. "I feel old, Stevie. Never did before...And tired. I just don't have the sass I used to."

"You don't have to, but I do," Spritzer reminded her.

"And me too," Michel added.

"Honey, I don't see any way out," she said, opening her eyes.

"I do," Michel said.

"What you thinkin'?" Spritzer asked.

"Well, about the time our first bottling is released, the biannual Grand Prix d'Or will be held in San Francisco. It's only *the* most prestigious wine competition in the world, and that year it's going to be held just next door. Fantastic press coverage for winners. If we were to enter, and did well, we might be able to get a better price for our first release. It might not cover all the expenses, but it might bring us up to fourteen or fifteen dollars a bottle wholesale."

Spritzer turned to Del. "It's a chance." He sounded enthusiastic. "We've a really good reserve this year, and with the new grapes coming on we'll have a much larger release in the next year or two. If we were able to set our price at that higher level the first year, we could really do well with the second release and make up most of the loss. What d'ya say? We really don't want to give up this early. And I certainly don't want Nelson taking over the winery. There might be bloodshed."

Del laughed a little. "Okay. If you really think you can make it work. Go for it. And let's hope I can sell a few more of my high-end ceramics to keep us going."

* * *

"Have you spoken to Kan?" Michel asked. "Regardless of what we decide to do about us, you might want to free yourselves up, so you can both get on with your lives."

Michel had his arm linked through Spritzer's as they strolled across the ridge up behind the family home at sunset. They had just finished their visit with Del and decided to take a walk to watch the sunset from the best vantage point. It was such a fair evening for late October.

"I haven't. I'm afraid I'm a terrible coward when it comes to Kan."

Michel turned to him. "It's not fair. You've got to talk to her. She's going to find out sooner or later that there is something developing between us—you know that. Don't you think it would be better if it came from you directly rather than from some third party—or me?"

"You're absolutely right." He took a deep breath. "I'll do it tomorrow, I promise."

They stopped at the crest of the ridge and looked out across the valley to the opposite ridge. The sun had just set, casting a magnificent display of color as the light caught an array of low, scattered clouds, creating a tapestry of intense red, orange, yellow, and violet.

Spritzer put his arm around Michel's shoulders. He leaned in and gave him a tender kiss on the left side of his neck.

"Are you sure you're ready for this?" Michel asked, turning to look at Spritzer.

"I want to try," Spritzer replied. "And how about you?"

Michel was thoughtful. "I want to remind you, once again, that I am only going to be here for a short time. You do realize nothing permanent can come from this?"

"I understand. But you have to realize too, that I am not completely sure this is going to work for me either. This is all new to me, and at this stage, I am just exploring. But it's something I want to do. Are you willing to explore with me?" Spritzer looked at Michel, scared but also excited.

Michel smiled slightly and slowly enfolded Spritzer into his arms, then whispered, "I can't promise you the world. I can't promise you the moon. But I will promise to be true to who you are, coming from who I am."

"Be patient with me, okay?" Spritzer whispered back.

"Whatever you need."

As they separated, Spritzer looked at him and asked, with an implication he knew Michel would understand, "Maybe tonight?"

"Maybe," he said. "But first we eat. Okay? I'm starving."

Spritzer laughed. "I have a hankering for fish and chips."

"Sounds good. Is there a decent place to get it around here? After my years in London I miss the good stuff."

"The cook's from Manchester. I think you'll like it. The fish is dripping with grease and crispy as toast. And the chips are golden with a creamy-soft center."

"Fantastic…" Michel laughed.

* * *

"What were you like as a child?" Michel asked, with a mouth full of vinegary, crispy fish.

Spritzer thought about that. "A brat, I guess. Loved playing space cowboys and aliens in the vineyard, but was always reluctant to come inside when called. And a vineyard is a great place to hide out if you don't want to be found, except in winter when the vines are pruned."

"Who did you play with? Did you have any special friends?"

"As you know, we live pretty far out from Santa Rosa. I had to take the bus to school. And as the vineyard is so large, there aren't a lot of houses close by. My best friend was Francisco's kid, Lorne."

"Our Lorne—who works for us now?"

"One and the same."

"How come you two don't hang out anymore now? You hardly speak to him."

Spritzer's gaze clouded over. "I'll tell you sometime—but not now."

"Oh shit." Michel became distracted as he dropped a sloppy piece of fish on his lap. "Shit, shit, *merde*. That spot is *not* going to come out."

"I'll buy you a new pair of pants from Sears."

They had a good laugh after that, remembering the first item of clothing Spritzer had to buy him.

"And what about you?" Spritzer asked. "What were you like as a child?" He wiped his greasy hands on another flimsy napkin from the dispenser on the table.

"Oh, just the perfect little boy," Michel said with a wicked smile.

"Yeah, sure."

Michel became sober and gathered his thoughts. "No, I was okay. I was basically raised in a household of women. My father was away, traveling for business a great deal of the time. It was mostly my mother and my grandmother who raised me—and a bossy housekeeper-nanny named Colette. I didn't have any siblings. My mother had an ectopic pregnancy after I was born and couldn't have any more children, so, like you; I grew up on the vineyard with few other children to play with. When my father *was* around he was teaching me the business, because it was eventually all going to fall on my shoulders and he was determined I would be successful."

"Then why aren't you at home taking care of your vineyard now? Why are you here?"

"Spirit of adventure, you might say. When you grow up in an isolated place, you either become a part of it, like a stitch in an old sweater, or you break away and unravel to experience the rest of the world. And that's what I needed to do. Not forever, but for now. My ties are too strong and too deep for me to abandon France and our vineyard altogether. Besides, it's a very successful brand, and we make a lot of money."

"Like you're going to do for us." He smiled.

"But of course."

Spritzer picked up and studied the menu, with dessert on his mind. "Want anything else?" Michel appeared to be thinking about it as he wiped down his fingers. "There's a real nice yogurt place down the block. Sound interesting?" Spritzer added.

Michel had a slight grin. "Actually, I was thinking of something a little more adventurous."

"Oh, and what might that be?"

"I make a dynamite dessert crepe. Want to come back to my place for coffee and crepes?"

Spritzer suspected where this might be heading. "I think that's a splendid idea. Shall we go?"

* * *

It was just past the October full moon as they drove back toward Michel's house. The burnt-orange moon was low on the horizon and looked unnaturally large—like a Spanish war galleon at full sail, cresting the horizon. It lit up the pale, ghostly mists settling into low places in the landscape. Spritzer turned to Michel. "What do you know about our Halloween? It's just around the corner."

"You have something called treats and tricks, I believe."

Spritzer laughed. He reached over and patted Michel's hand. "No. Trick or treat. It's for the kids."

"You Americans...always with your little take on our European traditions. Something to do with witches, no?"

"Close enough." He shook his head, but didn't feel like giving him the Wikipedia treatise on Halloween this evening. But he kept casting appreciative glances at Michel.

What a marvel these last few days had been, he thought. Bitter enemies when they met, and now...what? Playmates? Lovers? Rivals? Equals? So many possibilities and permutations. And the anticipation and mystery of it all was sweet to savor. And then there was Kan. Oh dear...Kan. What to do about her? Yes, tomorrow he must have *the* talk. Because, regardless of what ultimately happened between him and Michel, he still needed to break up with Kan. He was very clear about that.

Spritzer drove into Michel's driveway and parked.

"Such a lovely evening," Michel said, as he hopped out of the Jeep. "Look at that moon. A hunter's moon, we call it. My mother has a saying, 'safe as a rabbit on a hunter's moon'—meaning not so safe."

Michel led Spritzer inside and turned on the lights. He patted his back before heading for the kitchen. "Make yourself comfortable. I won't be long."

"Can I help?"

"Sure, if you like. You can make the coffee."

"Do you like your house?" Spritzer asked, as he rummaged through the cupboards searching for the coffee.

"I do. And here's the coffee." He handed Spritzer a bag of beans from the refrigerator. Michel continued with the crepe batter by also taking out the milk.

"Where's the coffee maker?" Spritzer asked as he surveyed the counter tops.

"Bottom shelf on your left."

He opened the cupboard. "I don't see it."

Michel sighed and went over and pulled out a French press.

"You make coffee with that?" Spritzer asked, with some astonishment. "How do you plug it in?"

Michel smiled. "I think you'd better let me take care of that. Why don't you go sit in the living room? I won't be long."

"What—and miss out on your sympathetic company and rapier wit?"

"How about you take out the coffee mugs, then? Think you can do that?"

"You bet."

"And the napkins are in the sideboard," he added.

Michel had his batter whipped together in no time, and was deftly making paper-thin crepes, stacking them on a plate between sheets of wax paper when they were done.

"Now, if you can find a nice selection of jams in the refrigerator and the powder-sugar shaker on the shelf behind you, then we will be all set to go." Michel had already made the coffee, and it was waiting to be pressed.

Together, they moved everything for the dessert feast to the dining table. Michel lit a few candles, put on some smooth jazz, and they sat down to eat.

"I guess you're not much of a cook," Michel said, as he rolled up several crepes, each filled with a different jam, for Spritzer.

"Can't fuss with it. That's what takeout's for."

"But it's such a pleasure to shop for wonderful ingredients, then prepare, and finally serve and eat a scrumptious meal for yourself and friends."

"Eh…" Spritzer tucked into a crepe with an apricot-jam filling. "Um, tasty."

"Tell me, what do you like to eat, the very best in all the world?" Michel asked.

Spritzer thought about that. "A nice, smothered batch of baby back ribs, slow cooked all day in a smoke cooker and just dripping in smoky-sweet sauce."

Michel nodded. "Um yes, that's nice. And it takes a master to make good ribs like that, I imagine."

"Just like making good champagne, I bet you're gonna say?"

Michel laughed. "I wasn't—but you're right. No, what I wanted to say was that my favorite meal is a gathered meal."

"What's that?"

"It's something I'd do regularly on our estate in France. My father would go hunting—usually for quail or pheasant—and I would go foraging for the rest of the meal. Then we'd go home and prepare the most splendid feast for the family."

"Foraging? What do you mean? Never heard of that."

"You don't know the word?" he asked incredulously.

"Well, it means to look for food in the wild, doesn't it?"

"Yes. Exactly. And that is what I would do. I'd find wild potatoes, asparagus, salad greens, herbs, garlic, and onions, and have enough for a whole meal."

"In France?"

"Certainly, why not? You just have to know where to look and what to look for."

"I thought that's what savages and nomads did. Do real people still do that?"

Michel laughed. "Of course. I'll tell you what. Let's you and me go foraging and put together a feast. We'll invite Del, and Kan, and Clara and Francisco. What do you say?"

Spritzer frowned. "I don't know about Kan. After I tell her about us, I don't think she'll want to have anything much to do with either of us."

Michel nodded. "Perhaps. But at least *you* go foraging with me, and I'll make *us* a splendid supper after."

Spritzer nodded.

They had finished the crepes and were sitting with their coffee. Michel asked. "Would you like a cognac?"

Spritzer said slyly, "You trying to get me drunk so you can have your way with me?"

"The thought *had* crossed my mind," Michel said with a twinkle in his eye.

"As if I'd need convincing..."

"You're progressing rapidly, I see." Michel got up and held out his arms. "But shall we dance instead?"

"I can't dance," Spritzer said, "I've got two left feet."

"That's okay, I've got two right feet. I'm sure that will even things out."

Spritzer stood and went over to Michel. Michel took Spritzer in his arms and held him close.

As Spritzer laid his head on Michel's shoulder, Michel whispered, "I seem to remember we danced pretty well the night of the grand opening."

"Ah yes, the night you claimed nothing happened between us."

"I was hesitant."

"And now?"

Michel rolled his head back and forth and whispered very softly, "Not now."

The music they were dancing to featured a sultry, wailing sax. It oozed sex. Spritzer stepped up lightly onto the tops of Michel's feet, and let him dance them toward the bedroom. Spritzer was uncertain at first if that was Michel's intention, but when Michel kissed Spritzer like he meant it, Spritzer's doubts were resolved.

* * *

Spritzer stood in Michel's shower the next morning. His head was swirling. He kept asking himself, *Am I ready for this*? He had had his first sex with a man—no, made love to a man. He—Spritzer—was now gay. Or was he? Fuck. He no longer knew what to think.

Last night had been more than he could have ever imagined. He thought *he* was hot in bed, but Michel knew moves even the *Kama Sutra* neglected because of their complexity. He let the water rush over his head and shoulders. Even thinking about Michel and last night was causing him to rise to the occasion once again.

He quickly shut off the water and toweled himself down briskly to alleviate the situation.

"Coffee?" Michel called out from the kitchen as Spritzer dressed.

"Of course," he shouted back. He looked over at the unmade bed and had to laugh as he recalled that night, not all that long ago, when Kan had accused him and Michel of sleeping together—and that right after he'd overheard her telling Michel about her escapade with the grease monkey in Santa Rosa during her rodeo weekend. It had kind of riled him up at the time, but it made him feel less guilty about breaking it off with Kan now that he and Michel really *were* sleeping together.

Spritzer's hair was still wet when he presented himself to Michel, dressed and ready for breakfast. Michel stopped frying bacon, turned to him, and smiled.

"Good morning," Spritzer greeted him.

Michel went over without saying anything and put his arms around Spritzer. He nibbled at his neck, and pulled on a wet strand of his hair with his teeth. "Yum. I love freshly showered hair. Ever so sexy."

"Better not get me started," Spritzer warned, "or we may never get out of here."

Michel gave him a quick kiss and went back to the bacon. Spritzer adjusted himself as he was becoming aroused yet again.

Michel pretended not to notice, but he couldn't suppress a slight smile. "Can you start the toaster, please?"

"Did you get any sleep?" Spritzer asked.

"I did. Slept like kitten. And you?"

"Not so much. Strange bed."

"And strange person," he noted.

"Maybe. But I intend to get used to that." Spritzer smiled. Just then, his phone rang. "It's Kan. I'd better take this." He put his phone on speaker and answered the call. "Yeah?"

"It's me. How ya doin'?"

Spritzer was less than enthusiastic. "Oh, hi. Not so bad. What's up?"

"Haven't seen you in ages. How 'bout some hot dancin' this evening? Thought we might hit up Tony's"

Spritzer looked over to Michel, who nodded.

"Ah...sure. 'Bout eight?"

"Okay," Kan said, perky as a parakeet.

Spritzer hung up. "I've got to see her."

Michel nodded. "You are going to tell her, aren't you?"

"Of course."

"It's the only way if we want to salvage our friendships. If we keep it hidden and she finds out, she'll feel betrayed by both of us, and it will be much worse. Remember, she's my friend too."

* * *

The end of October had arrived with a vengeance. A cold rain was pelting Spritzer's Jeep as he drove to his date with Kan. The wipers barely worked—smudging, more than clearing, the view ahead. He made a mental note to replace them. He welcomed the rain for the vineyard, but as his Jeep's heater cranked out only a few struggling wisps of heat, he continued to shiver in his light jacket. Even though the soft top was up, the wind whistled through the many cracks in the ill-fitting windows.

His Jeep was definitely a summer vehicle, but there could be no thought of a new one with the vineyard's finances being what they were. It was not a night to be out.

Spritzer arrived at Tony's. There were only a few cars parked outside, and Spritzer recognized Kan's. He was absolutely dreading this meeting. While he and Kan had been friends since childhood, later in life she had developed expectations that he did not share. He'd strung her along because he thought at one point that he *might* be interested in more, but soon realized it was only because he was lazy and really didn't want to go looking for someone else. He had been comfortable with her, but he realized now that had been a terrible situation for them to be in. He should have made it clear a long time ago that he was only interested in her friendship. But he doubted she would be able to settle for that now. And then there was the issue that he was now having sex with a man. That was going to be a fun introduction.

He dashed out of the car through the rain and into Tony's. He stood at the door. Nothing was quite as dismal as a nearly empty bar. The music was too loud. The stale stench of lingering cigarette smoke reeked. The dance floor was deserted, and the two waitresses were sitting with nothing to do at the end of the bar, chatting with Tony and toying with their beers.

Spritzer saw Kan seated in "their" booth, but her back was to him, and she hadn't seen him come in. He struggled with the impulse to flee, but he clenched his teeth and headed toward the booth.

"Quite a night out there, huh?" he said in the jolliest tone he could muster, as he slipped into the booth opposite Kan.

"I ordered a pitcher," Kan greeted him, with a discernibly forced smile.

One of the waitresses had pried herself from the bar and came over. "What can I get you kids?"

"Pizza?" Kan asked Spritzer.

He didn't reply immediately. "We get that all time. Maybe we could try something different."

"Wings?" Kan countered.

"Haven't you got anything...more healthy? Something green?" Michel's influence was starting to rub off on him.

"We got, like, a chef salad," the waitress suggested.

"Yeah. That sounds good."

"Well, I want a pizza," Kan protested. "Give me a small pepperoni, with green peppers, mushrooms, and extra cheese."

"You got it." The waitress left to fill the order.

"What was *that* all about?" Kan asked, as she settled back in her bench seat and studied Spritzer's face.

Spritzer wanted to jump right in and spill everything about him and Michel, but he couldn't do it just yet. He kept trying to find a way to soften the blow.

"Hey, buddy, wanna dance?" Kan offered brightly, leaning across the table and taking Spritzer's hand.

Spritzer pulled away from her and hung his head, shaking it slightly. This was agony, but he needed to get things settled right now. "Kan..."

She sat bolt upright. "What? What's going on here? You've been somewhere else ever since you got here. I don't know where you've been, but you certainly haven't been with me."

He slid his hand across the table toward her, but she didn't take it. "Kan..."

She was deathly still. She stared at him with an icy glare. "It's Michel, isn't it?"

Spritzer nodded. "Yes. I am *so* sorry..."

"You fucker. You're gay?"

"No, listen, please."

"Why the fuck should I?"

"Because you were my friend long before everything else. And to me you still are. Please don't let us abandon our friendship."

"Friends don't betray each other, Spritz."

"Then what about the episode with that guy in Santa Rosa? You seem to forget I know all about that."

She nodded a bit sheepishly. "Yeah...well..."

"Kan, don't you see, it's both of us. We both need to be honest about the reality of our situation. We were never a real couple. We played at it, but we weren't. And I believe you know that too."

Kan sat back, raised her eyes to the ceiling, and sighed. After a long moment, she nodded and then started laughing.

Spritzer was startled.

"I can't tell you how relieved I am," she said, collapsing on the table as if to prove her words.

"Really?"

"Absolutely. I've just realized I've been struggling for so long to keep up the charade of us as a couple that I got lost in the myth and started to believe it was true." She reached over and took his hand with genuine feeling. "Friends is *ever* so much better."

"Pepperoni pizza and chef salad," the waitress announced as she plopped down the order.

Spritzer and Kan began to laugh.

* * *

"How did it go with Kan last night?" Michel asked, as he stood at the warehouse door next to Spritzer, watching the ebbing and flowing waves of rain.

"Much better than I expected."

"Good to hear."

"It's too wet to work in the vineyard today," Spritzer said, as they peered up at the still threatening sky. "I should probably head over to my other office. I've been neglecting my work at Vallier lately. I've been slightly preoccupied with other things." He took Michel's hand.

Michel smiled. "Is Kan all right?" he asked, removing his hand from Spritzer's.

"Yes. I believe so. I think she recognized it wasn't working for either of us, and said she was actually relieved."

"Was she surprised you were with a man?" Michel asked.

"Somehow not so surprised. More relieved when she felt the burden of carrying a false relationship being lifted from her."

"That's good. I would hate to lose her as a friend."

Michel turned to leave for his office, but Spritzer reached out. "And what about Nelson?"

Michel turned back. "What about him?"

"Are you going to tell him about us?"

He shrugged. "There's no need to."

"Why not?" Spritzer was becoming a little impatient with what appeared to be Michel's nonchalance concerning Nelson.

"Because there was never anything between us, despite your incorrect assumption."

"And does he know that?"

Michel, ever patient, smiled and patted his cheek. "You're so cute when you're jealous." He turned and left for his office.

CHAPTER EIGHT

Michel was shifting a load of laundry from his washer to his dryer when there was a knock at the front door. He was surprised, as, on this Saturday morning, he wasn't expecting anyone. He was a little hesitant to answer the door as he lived in such an isolated and remote area. But he brushed aside his reservations and opened the door.

"Jean-Claude!" he exclaimed in great surprise, seeing his lover standing before him. Or, as he had determined before coming to California, his ex-lover.

"*Bonjour,* Michel..." Jean-Claude held a stunning bouquet of exotic flowers, which he presented to Michel with a charming bow.

Michel stood in utter shock.

"Aren't you going to ask me in?" Jean-Claude asked in French, and then laughed slightly.

Michel simply shook his head in disbelief. "Yes, yes. Please come in." He stepped back to allow Jean-Claude to enter. "Why didn't you call me first?"

"Wanted to surprise you."

"Are you here on business?" Michel asked, as he went to the kitchen to put the flowers in the sink with a little water until he could arrange them properly in a vase.

"No, not business—pleasure," Jean-Claude called out.

Jean-Claude *was* a handsome devil; Michel had to admit. His mother had been Vietnamese and his father French, so he had beautiful Eurasian features. At forty-three, he still retained a boyish charm and rugged good looks—even though there was gray now flecking the dark hair at his temples. He was a man who knew hard manual labor, and he had a broad chest and strong, laborer's arms, even though he was the owner of a competing vineyard in France.

As Michel returned to find Jean-Claude sitting on the sofa, he asked, "Did you come for the sights? For the art scene? Are you traveling the country?"

"No—I came to see you."

Michel, though happy to see him, was also uncomfortable. In his mind, they had separated permanently, and it was a shock to find that Jean-Claude still seemed to have expectations around their relationship.

"I'm sorry...You made a trip all this way just to see me?"

"Of course. I've missed you terribly." Jean-Claude rose and went over to Michel, putting his hands on his hips. He leaned in to kiss him, but Michel turned his head away and pulled back from his grasp.

Michel stood his ground. "Jean-Claude, it *is* nice to see you, but there must be some misunderstanding on your part. You see, when we parted last year, for me it was a breaking off, not some sort of a trial separation. I thought you understood that."

"But I haven't been able to stop thinking about you, Michel. I've tried, believe me. I've dated other men, but no one comes even close to your class, your style, your intelligence, and wonderful sense of humor—and not to mention the fantastic sex. And it's been driving me crazy. I just had to come and see if you might please reconsider."

Michel was thoughtful. He had to admit Jean-Claude did look mighty good right now, but he also remembered how abusive he could become when thwarted or angry. And, of course, there was Spritzer. Michel was not about to take his new, budding relationship with the American lightly.

He clasped his hands together in front of him to show his resolve. "Jean-Claude, I greatly appreciate your sentiments and interest. However, you must know I am now involved with someone else."

"Someone from here in the States?"

"Yes. My coworker, Spritzer Vallier."

Jean-Claude laughed. "Spritzer? Really? Is that even a real name?"

"A nickname."

"And how old is this Spritzer—twelve?"

"Don't be rude. You see, you are behaving exactly the way you used to. And it was for that very reason I decided to break it off with you. You could be insufferably snide and demeaning—along with your many other unpleasant qualities."

Jean-Claude bowed his head. "I am truly sorry, Michel. I was on a very long flight, and I came straight here from the airport. Forgive me. I am really tired. It won't happen again, I promise."

After a pause, Michel asked, "Where are you staying?"

"I was hoping I could stay with you."

He shook his head. "Absolutely not. This place only has one bedroom, and I don't think you would be comfortable on the couch."

"I understand. Then can you suggest some place nice nearby?"

"There are a number of pleasant B and B's close by along the Russian River." He smiled. "Though many cater to the San Francisco gay community, I feel certain they would welcome you with open arms, and might even give you a hefty discount."

Jean-Claude nodded and smiled, appreciating Michel's wicked humor. "Very funny. There must be something else? No?"

Michel wanted to make one point perfectly clear. "Why do you even want to stay? I can assure you nothing is going to happen between us."

"I understand. But can't we be friends? You know I care for you a great deal. And that can include friendship, no?"

"Perhaps," he said cautiously, still not completely trusting him.

"And my flight back is booked for a week from now. It would cost a fortune to change my ticket. Please, let me visit you then as a friend."

"Very well. I know of a nice B&B in Guerneville I think you might like. I can give you directions."

"That would be nice. And will you have dinner with me this evening?"

Michel considered that. "Perhaps. If you can promise to behave yourself like a gentleman."

"Of course." He gave Michel his most devastating grin.

* * *

Spritzer was surprised to be at the warehouse before Michel on Monday morning. Michel was usually the first one of them at work. Normally, it was Spritzer who was running late, having overslept and dashed through breakfast.

Spritzer heard the large warehouse door slide open. It was a bit early for the workers to be here, so he turned to see who had arrived. He saw Michel approaching, with a strange man walking next to him.

"You're early," Michel called out.

Spritzer was instantly suspicious of this way-too-handsome stranger. "No, actually, it's you who is a little late," he grouched.

Michel chose to ignore his pique. "Did you have a nice weekend?"

Spritzer nodded, but didn't answer his question. "Who's this?"

Jean-Claude was hanging back slightly.

"Oh sorry, how rude of me. This is my friend from France, Jean-Claude."

He stepped forward and firmly shook Spritzer's hand. "*Enchanté*," he offered.

"Howdy." Spritzer stood back and studied this "friend." "Are you just passing through, then?"

Jean-Claude turned to Michel and smiled, as he slipped his arm through Michel's. "Renewing an old acquaintance."

Michel withdrew his arm and turned to Spritzer. "Just for a few days." He seemed to want to make that very clear to Spritzer. "He's staying at the Guerneville B&B."

"Can I speak to you a minute—privately?" Spritzer asked.

"Certainly." Michel turned to Jean-Claude. "Why don't you check out the winery? It has the very latest top-of-the-line equipment. I think you'll be impressed."

Spritzer and Michel walked aside, leaving Jean-Claude to inspect the rest of the winery by himself.

"Is this *the* Jean-Claude? The clown you dumped?"

"Well, he's been very gentlemanly since he's been here. We had a quite civilized dinner last night."

"And what is he doing here? I thought you two broke it off—permanently."

Michel took Spritzer by the shoulders. "Most certainly we did. And you have absolutely nothing to worry about. I've made it perfectly clear that there is to be no rerun of our relationship. I've explained that you and I are together now and he has to accept that fact. And I believe he has."

Spritzer nodded. "Excellent. And I hope he understands that completely."

"Yes, he does." Michel leaned over and gave him a quick kiss on the cheek.

"Very nice facility," Jean-Claude said as he came ambling back to them. "As you say—very state of the art. But, of course, the proof will be in that first sip, will it not?" He looked at Michel and gave him a sly grin.

"It will, indeed—and I expect it to excel," said Spritzer. "I have every faith in Michel."

"That's splendid," Jean-Claude said.

Michel suddenly became businesslike. "I have to run into town. The labels are ready to be picked up at the printers. Anything else we need while I'm there?"

"Want me to go with you?" Jean-Claude asked.

"Why don't you let me give you a tour of the vineyard? It's an impressive layout," Spritzer offered. "Michel won't be that long."

Jean-Claude looked at Michel. It was clear he preferred to go with him. But Michel nodded, indicating he should stay.

"Very well then, lead on," Jean-Claude said, as Michel left for town.

Spritzer kept glancing over at Jean-Claude as they drove out to the vineyard overlook. The man was extremely handsome, and it unsettled him no end. He had a firm, masculine grace that Spritzer could see any woman—or man—would find immediately attractive. He understood now what Michel had seen in him. And he was concerned that with Jean-Claude here, it could easily start up all over again. He didn't know Michel well enough yet to know how firm his resolve might be.

It was a fairly warm day, and Spritzer had the top down. Jean-Claude's hair was long enough to be whipped by the wind. A lock of hair fell over his face, and he deftly pushed it back in place. As he did, he gave Spritzer a wickedly winning smile. Spritzer turned his eyes back on the road.

They soon pulled up at the overlook and stepped out of the Jeep.

"Well, this is it. You can see most of the vineyard from here."

"Very impressive," Jean-Claude said, resting against the front of the Jeep and surveying the extent of the vineyard.

Spritzer walked farther down the lookout and stood gazing over his domain, pointing and naming the various stands of grapes. Jean-Claude had followed and stood close by. "So, are you and Michel enjoying your little fling?" he asked, turning toward Spritzer with his intrepid smile.

Spritzer turned to him but didn't respond immediately. "It's not just a fling, Jean-Claude. Let me make that perfectly clear."

"Really? I see." He studied Spritzer. "Yes, well, I can see why he might find you attractive. A certain youthful charm. In good physical shape. Handsome in an American boy-next-door kind of way. Maybe a little rough around the edges. But not bad. Not bad at all." He put his hand on Spritzer's shoulder and gazed out over the vineyard again.

Spritzer pulled from his touch and looked at him. Jean-Claude returned the gaze.

"So tell me, Spritzer, you ever go to check out the Russian River scene?" He let the question linger with its implications.

"I sometimes go swimming in the summer," Spritzer said. "A lot of the locals do."

"I see. And nothing else?"

"How do you mean?" Spritzer thought he was catching his drift, but wanted to put him on the spot by making him be more explicit.

"Michel was telling me it's somewhat of a hot spot."

"Hot spot?"

"Oh come now, Spritzer. I'm sure you understand my meaning. You can't be that clueless." Jean-Claude shot Spritzer his gorgeous smile, once again. "You're telling me you never sampled any of the area's *other* activities?"

"I'm not into that," Spritzer answered firmly.

"Not under any circumstances?"

"No."

"And you've never been curious? Not even experimented—just a little? Before Michel, that is." He reached out and very gently ran his hand down Spritzer's arm.

Spritzer turned away and headed back toward the Jeep. "I need to get back. I have an appointment with my aunt Del. And Michel should be back any moment now."

Jean-Claude sighed. "As you wish. But too bad—I thought you might be a more curious and adventurous fellow."

* * *

When they got back to the winery, Michel had not yet arrived. They got out of the Jeep.

"What's that over there?" Jean-Claude asked, as he pointed to the Vallier Wine warehouses.

"That's our commercial wine division. That's been the backbone of our family's business for decades."

"Hmm."

"Want to take a look?" Spritzer asked, hoping to unload him on an employee for a tour.

"Why not?"

Spritzer took his walkie-talkie from his belt and called Francisco. "Hey, have you got anybody free who could give a quick tour of Vallier to a guest?"

"Lorne could do it," Francisco replied.

"Okay, thanks. Send him out. I'm outside the new building."

"Okay, ten-four."

"When do you think Michel will be back?" Jean-Claude asked.

"Any minute now."

Lorne emerged from the new building and came over to them.

"Hey, Lorne."

"Hey, Spritz. This guy need a tour?"

Spritzer nodded. "This is a winemaker friend of Michel's, who's visiting from France. Could you give him a look around Vallier?"

"Sure." Spritzer caught Lorne giving Jean-Claude an appreciative look. "This way."

Jean-Claude turned to Spritzer and smiled. Then the two walked toward the Vallier winery.

Spritzer was relieved to be free of the guy and was anxious for Michel to return—which he did shortly. He went over to Michel's truck and, even before he got out, Spritzer said, almost whispering, "He came on to me."

"What?" Michel descended from the truck. "What are you talking about? Who?"

"Jean-Claude made a pass at me."

Michel laughed. "Oh really? Come on. You must be imagining it."

"I am *not*. I know when someone's getting frisky with me."

"Okay then, what did he say?"

"He asked me if I knew about the Russian River scene. And you know what that means."

Michel smiled slightly. "I'm sure he just wanted to know about the sporting activities. He's quite the sportsman, you know."

"Not the kind of sport you're thinking about, I'm sure," Spritzer insisted.

"Really? What else did he say?"

"He asked if I'd sampled any of the other *activities*. Un-huh...un-huh. Know what I mean?"

Michel just stood and looked at him, arms on his hips. "Jean-Claude would never hit on my boyfriend. He promised me he'd behave himself."

"With you, perhaps, but not with me. And then he *touched* my arm. And not just touched it, but slid his hand down, like this." He reached over and demonstrated the action on Michel's arm.

"He likes you. He's just being friendly." Michel turned to go into the winery. But Spritzer followed closely behind.

"And he asked me if I experimented. Yeah. Experimented."

Michel turned to him and sighed. "Where is he now?"

"Lorne's giving him a tour of Vallier."

"Well, when you see him tell him I'm waiting for him in my office."

Spritzer was dumbfounded. "That's it. You're just gonna walk away?" Michel walked on without answering him. "Well, don't be surprised if you find me ravished and bleeding behind some vat," he shouted after the departing Frenchman.

Michel turned before he went inside. "Might be good for you. Loosen you up a bit."

"Ah..." he said in exasperation, and just stood and stared as Michel disappeared into the warehouse.

* * *

Michel was dining with Jean-Claude at his B&B. Most B&Bs didn't serve meals other than breakfast, but this facility had a charming dining room that attracted a lot of locals with its select menu and reasonable prices. They were seated near the fireplace where a cozy fire was warming them nicely, as a cold front had moved in from the northeast and threatened the season's first snow. They were finishing a second bottle of Stag's Leap Artemis and enjoying a dessert of New Orleans–style bread pudding. Jean-Claude had just ordered them each a snifter of Remy Martin XO.

Michel leaned back in his chair and took in the superb ambiance. "This has been very nice."

Jean-Claude smiled. "I thought you might like it here. As you can see, they have an excellent selection of California reds, and I must congratulate you on picking an especially fine one."

"Yes, but I have to say, it's sometimes difficult for we French to acknowledge how good the California wines can be."

"Ah, but you are bringing the French sensibility to a California wine, so I guess you could say it's a perfect marriage."

Michel laughed. "I certainly don't know about 'perfect.' It has not been an easy process I can assure you. And, as dear as he is to me, Spritzer can be awfully stubborn and bullheaded."

Jean-Claude spoke carefully. "But I can see he has his charms."

Michel smiled slightly. "Yes. I meant to ask you about that."

"What?"

"Spritzer tells me you came on to him this morning while I was in town."

With his hands on the table, Jean-Claude leaned back, and let out a hearty laugh. "Really? He said that?"

"And he didn't take it lightly," Michel drilled.

"Oh come now, Michel. You know, as well as I do, that it was just some harmless teasing. I enjoy testing the limits of a person's comfort zone—especially with rivals. Certainly, you know me well enough by now to know how I love to tease."

"That's what I said." Michel looked at Jean-Claude with more intensity than mirth. "But he didn't seem to think so."

Jean-Claude became silent and looked at Michel with a faint smile. "Would you like me to prove to you who my one true love is?"

"No, I would not," Michel said firmly.

Jean-Claude looked out the window that was at Michel's back. "It's snowing."

He turned to look. "So it is. I really can't stay."

Jean-Claude placed his hand on top of Michel's, and smiled. "But, baby, it's cold outside." He burst into song. *"This evening has been so ver-y nice."*

"Okay, okay, I get it. You're a charmer. But charm is not enough for me anymore, Jean-Claude."

"I'll hold your hands—they're cold as ice," he continued.

"Just stop it," Michel said, but couldn't help but laugh.

Jean-Claude pouted. "But, baby, it's cold outside..."

"Please don't ruin such a nice evening. I am not going to stay. I mean it."

Jean-Claude signaled for the check. He leaned in toward Michel. "You're not going to leave before you've enjoyed that excellent, and *very* expensive, XO are you?"

Michel picked up the snifter and took a sip. He inclined his head slightly. "My, that is good."

"I have a fire in my room as well. Come, let's take our cognac, and sit by the fire for a little while longer. It's still quite early." Jean-Claude signed the check and then stood, offering Michel his hand.

Michel stood and picked up his coat but didn't put it on. He lifted his bag to his shoulder. With his free hand, he picked up the snifter. "Half an hour...no more."

"Of course."

Jean-Claude led them through the lobby to his room at the back. He deftly used his keycard to unlock the door and gently ushered Michel into his room. Before closing the door, he lifted the "do not disturb" card from the inside handle and placed it outside. He then closed the door quietly behind them.

* * *

Del's recovery was accelerating steadily now. Her strength and vigor were slowly returning. She no longer needed the walker, but was toddling along quite handily with only a cane. And even though she was not able to go back to her ceramics, she spent most of each day in her studio. There was always inventory to ship for an exhibition or to a gallery, and it made her feel connected to her work, even though it did not take up that much of her time.

She was surprised when Spritzer came to the studio one midmorning.

"Didn't expect to see you today. Any problem?" she asked.

Spritzer stood quietly and was hesitant and shy. Quite unlike the Spritzer she knew so well.

"Ah...well...yes, I need to tell you something."

"Not another disaster I hope."

"Oh no, nothing work related. It's about me."

"Okay." She sat down and gave Spritzer her full attention.

He didn't speak up immediately but finally said, "Remember when you asked me about my future? Specifically, about my future with Kan?"

"I do. Have you two come to a decision? Are there going to be wedding bells?" she asked, brightly.

"Well, not exactly."

"Oh? Trouble in paradise?"

Spritzer smiled. "Life can sure be funny sometimes, huh?"

"I've found that to be so."

"Well, let me start by saying that Kan and I are no longer a couple. Great friends as we have always been, but not in a romantic relationship."

"Oh, I'm sorry to hear that. You always seemed to be so close. What happened?"

"Michel happened," Spritzer added.

"Kan and Michel? Have they become a couple?"

"No, Del. Michel and I have."

Del blinked. Stunned into a momentary silence.

Spritzer nodded. "Yes. You heard correctly."

"So you're gay?"

"Not sure about that. But I find I have really deep feelings for him. Can't explain it. Don't know where it's going or what it means. But what's happened has happened."

"And Kan knows about this?"

"She does. And, to be quite honest, we are both greatly relieved to be free of our old expectations about each other."

"Hmm..."

"I hope I've not upset you," Spritzer said cautiously.

"Not at all. All I've ever want was your happiness, Stevie, you know that."

"Thank you."

"And he makes you happy?"

Spritzer smiled and nodded.

"Just imagine...the two of you...I for sure never saw that coming."

"Crazy, huh?"

"Well, I have to say we certainly are an interesting family."

* * *

It was getting close to Christmas, and it was time to decorate the family home for the traditional Vallier Winery Christmas Day celebration. Del and Clara went to mass Christmas Eve—Spritzer did not, as he was not religious. But Christmas Day was party time. It was Del's favorite day of entertainment. She invited the family, and all of the workers from the vineyard. Del and Clara would spend the entire week before Christmas cooking—even if it was Clara who did most of the cooking while Del pointed her cane at the stacks of Christmas treats and commented on how grand everything looked. For the two of them, preparing for the party was a grand event. They made traditional American Christmas delicacies, but also a Mexican feast for the Hispanic workers and their wives and children. Del believed in pampering her workers and keeping them loyal.

Spritzer had volunteered, as he did yearly, to go up into the mountains to harvest evergreen branches to decorate the great room in preparation for the party. He thought it might be a fun treat for Michel, so he asked him to come along, and Michel readily agreed. Michel suggested they use his truck, as there was more room for the branches in the truck bed than in the back of Spritzer's Jeep.

Michel and Spritzer were driving back down the mountain after gathering a nice load of evergreens. They had spent a lighthearted morning teasing and laughing as they collected the branches. Even though they were inside the cab of the truck, the scent of pine filled the air. Spritzer sniffed his fingers where a residue of pine resin still clung to his fingers. "It's really beginning to smell like Christmas," he said merrily.

"You've been full of chatter and goodwill today." Michel smiled.

He laughed. "I guess I'm relieved that your boyfriend's gone back to France."

Michel turned to look at him. "He's not my boyfriend. You know that."

"But I'm not sure *he* knew that."

"You weren't jealous, were you?" he teased.

Spritzer turned to look at him. "No. Why? Should I be?"

Michel became solemn and kept his eyes on the road ahead. Spritzer could sense something was troubling him. "What?" he asked.

Finally, Michel answered. "*Mon amour*, I need to tell you something." And, again, he kept his eyes focused on the road.

Spritzer tensed. That phrase never boded well. He turned to look at Michel. "Okay, what?"

He shot Spritzer a quick look. "I did something I'm not proud of."

Spritzer didn't respond but just looked straight ahead.

Michel told him about the evening at the B&B—how magical it had been; how the fire danced; how the wine soothed; how Jean-Claude crooned a corny song to him; how seductive the warmth of the cognac was; and, finally, how he had gone back to Jean-Claude's room with him.

Spritzer braced himself for the final chapter of this tale.

"But I want you to know that nothing happened," Michel said. "We sat by the fire in his room, I finished my cognac, and then I left."

Spritzer turned to him. "Is that for real?"

Michel nodded. "Absolutely."

Spritzer didn't respond. Michel reached over and put his hand on top of Spritzer's. "Spritz, talk to me. Tell me what you feel."

Spritzer thought for a moment, then said, "The little boy in me wants to rant, and scream, and throw a tantrum. But the man I am becoming, partly because of your help, wants to look objectively at this like an adult and trust in what you say."

"And which one, do you believe, is going to prevail?" Michel asked gently.

"I'll let you know when I know."

* * *

It was already getting dark as they arrived back at the family home. They unloaded the fragrant greens onto the patio, with easy access to the great room. Del came to the French doors and waved for them to come inside.

"It's snowing up on the mountain," Michel said as they followed Del through the great room, the dining room, and into the kitchen.

"Well, you two deserve a treat after all your effort." She pointed to stacks of Christmas cookies on a series of cooling racks. "Help yourselves, and how about some hot chocolate?" She chortled. "Spritzer could never refuse."

"Me either." Michel beamed. "Can I help?"

"Milk's in the refrigerator. I'll get the cocoa."

Spritzer brought over a pan and turned on a burner. Michel got the milk and poured. Del brought the cocoa, sugar, and a whisk, and together they made the cocoa, laughing and chatting.

Spritzer went over to the cooling racks and piled a plate high with an assortment of cookies. When all was ready, the three of them sat at the large kitchen table and celebrated being together.

Spritzer leaned close to Michel, put his arm around his shoulder, and whispered, "The man I am becoming has won."

Michel gave him a kiss on the cheek. "I thought as much."

CHAPTER NINE

On Christmas morning, Spritzer and Michel got out of bed, shivering, while it was still dark. Michel made coffee while Spritzer showered, and then Michel showered. They dressed and headed straight over to Coeur du Chêne, without breakfast, arriving before Del was even up. Even Clara, who was usually the first to arrive each morning, had still not shown up yet.

Michel and Spritzer had decorated the great room last weekend with garlands of twinkle-lit greens; large red bows; pots of poinsettias; bowls of gold and silver Christmas balls; and decorative candles to be lit just before the guests arrived. They'd installed two Christmas trees and decorated them, and now they were laying and lighting fires in the two fireplaces at either end of the room. It would take some time before the fires heated the whole room.

Del came shuffling into the great hall in her slippers and bathrobe. "My, you two are busy little bees. Or should I say, Christmas fairies?"

They laughed. Spritzer came over and hugged Del. "Merry Christmas, sweet one."

"Merry Christmas, Stevie. And you too, Michel. Had breakfast yet?"

"No, ma'am," Spritzer said.

"Well, come along." She stopped and surveyed the room. "My, it looks just beautiful. You did a great job with the decorations."

"Thanks."

The three of them headed toward the kitchen just as Clara was putting on her apron.

"Breakfast!" Del shouted out.

* * *

The guests started arriving at eleven thirty. Spritzer took on the job of directing the arriving cars to facilitate parking. Michel lit all the candles in the great room and the dining room, then helped Clara put the food out on the serving table.

Del sat in the center of the sofa, hands on her cane, and waited for the guests to arrive, which didn't take long at all. She had an array of envelopes spread out on the table before her, and she would be the center of attention for all of the employees as these envelopes contained Christmas bonuses for everyone at Vallier.

Of course, there were kids everywhere—running, laughing, crying, screaming. And Del had not forgotten them. Michel had been assigned to make sure each child got a present from under one of the two trees— one tree with gifts for boys, and the second tree had gifts for girls. Simple gifts—as the budget was tight—but no one was forgotten.

After the initial scurry of arrivals, the party settled down as people visited the food table and searched for a comfortable place to enjoy their meals. Spritzer was back from his parking duties and Michel, after making sure each child had a present, was sitting with Del after bringing her a plate of food and a glass of champagne.

Kan and Dan came forward to pay their respects, greeting Del and Michel.

"Splendid party as always," Dan said, as he unwound his scarf.

"Nice to see you again, Michel. It's been a while," Kan said, after handing a gift to Del.

"It has, and after you and Dan have some Christmas cheer, come and find me. I need to chat with you about the olive oil. I've had contact with the marketing and distribution folks in France, and I have some paperwork to go over with you. They definitely want to move forward."

"Now, that's the best Christmas present ever. I'll come find you later." She turned to her father. "Come along, Dad, you must be starved."

"Yes, I saw the spread as we came in—most delicious looking. I'm ready."

As they left, Del turned to Michel after reaching for an envelope on the table and handed it to him. "Here, Merry Christmas, my dear."

Michel was unaware of the Vallier bonus tradition, as he opened the envelope. He was shocked to see a quite generous amount of cash. "Oh, Del. No. No. I can't accept this. You shouldn't be doing this with things as tight as they are."

Del put her hand on Michel's hand. "But you deserve it. And it is the holidays."

Michel shook his head, but then he had an idea when he saw there was also an envelope for Spritzer. He leaned forward and gave Del a hug.

"My darling Del, I just want you to know that being here has been so very magical. Even though I am away from my family this Christmas, I feel welcomed and valued here."

"Well, what more could one ask for?" Del smiled.

Nelson came over toting a glass of champagne. "A very merry Christmas, Aunt Del. Charming event, as ever. You never disappoint."

"Thank you, Nelson. Has Santa been good to you, or have you been a naughty boy?"

"Oh, very naughty indeed. My stocking was just stuffed to overflowing with lumps of coal."

Del evidently never ceased to be amused by her brash nephew. "Well, you'll find a modest present in the library where I've left the family's gifts."

"And I have left my gift for you in the kitchen, under Clara's watchful eye—a case of Shafer Hillside Select Cab. I know how much you enjoy that."

"How delightful. You are a charmer."

Nelson turned to Michel. "And will you join me in a glass of Christmas cheer? I shall tell you all about the New Year's goodie I have planned for you."

Michel turned to Del. "Do you need anything?"

"No, dear, I'm fine. You go amuse Nelson."

Michel rose from the sofa to refill his champagne and visit with Nelson. They decided to chat by a French door looking out at the patio, where a few snow flurries suggested the possibility of a white Christmas.

Nelson leaned toward Michel. "How's the new wine coming? I've not had my watchful eye on you for ever so long. Where have you been keeping yourself?"

"The wine's coming well. We've had some growing pains, but eventually it will even out and be everything you and we had hoped for."

"I'm glad to hear that." He put his hand at the base of Michel's back. "And you? I've left a number of messages. But no response."

"As I said, I've been very busy."

"Uh-huh." He leaned in closer. "Well, now I can tell you about your holiday surprise."

"Nelson..." Michel tried to free himself from Nelson's intimacy.

But Nelson leaned in even closer. "I've booked *the* most charming little hotel over the New Year's weekend at Bear Valley. You do ski, do you not?"

"Nelson..." Michel put his hand on Nelson's chest to create some distance.

"Never mind...Even if you don't, it will be a charming weekend. Quaint little shops...divine restaurants...spas and hot springs. Just everything your heart could desire." He leaned in again. "And most especially...me."

Michel was tired of playing nice with Nelson. He forcefully pushed him away. "Nelson, shut up and listen to me." Nelson was stunned. "No. No, I will not go away with you. If you'd stop for just one minute, and stop being such an asshole, you would find out that Spritzer and I are together now. I have absolutely no interest in you romantically. Never have and never will. So just back off."

Nelson stiffened and glowered. "Spritzer? You've got to be kidding me. My dear, have you lost your mind? He's not even gay."

Michel was firm. "No. Not lost my mind, and I'm not kidding you."

"But aside from his skill with wine, he is a total jerk. A boor—a ruffian—a lout."

"I grant you that might be one's first impression of him—it certainly was mine. But underneath he is charming, vulnerable, and a very fine lover."

Nelson took a step backward. "That could be dangerous."

Michel straightened. "I assure you there is nothing to fear from Spritzer."

"No, not from him. From me." Nelson's inner fire flared but briefly. "Do not underestimate me and my power." He then turned and walked forcefully away.

Michel didn't know whether to cringe or laugh. He took a long sip of his champagne. He would have to talk to both Spritzer and Del about this episode to see it they needed to take any precautions in case Nelson decided to turn nasty.

The party was going well. A group of youngsters was singing carols at the piano, and a group of adults was gathered around the second fireplace playing charades. The house was filled with the aroma of spiced cider for the children, and spiced wine for the adults. As the party wore on, the children had, for the most part, quieted down. A few of the younger ones were even napping in their mothers' laps.

Michel saw Kan clearing plates to take to the kitchen. He went over to lend her a hand.

"Oh thanks," Kan said as Michel joined her. "I'm free if you want to chat now."

They took the plates and a few glasses to the kitchen where Spritzer, Lorne, and Clara were cleaning up.

"Hey, guys...you need to take a break. It's your party too." Kan insisted.

Lorne smiled. "Oh, not to worry, I've been celebrating plenty. I'm so full I could burst. Thought it would be good if I moved around a bit, and I don't want Mom to be faced with all the cleaning up by herself."

Clara patted her son on the shoulder. "He's a good boy. Makes his mama proud." She leaned over and pinched his cheek.

"Mo-o-o-m..." he groaned.

Michel went over and took Spritzer by the arm so he could pull him aside. He advised him quietly, "I had a rather nasty little run-in with Nelson."

"Really?"

"Oh yes. He wanted to take me skiing over New Year's, and I told him you and I are together now."

"Well, I bet that was a surprise for ol' coz."

"You might say—and one that he didn't take very well."

Spritzer laughed slightly. "I'm certainly glad you said no."

Michel stood back and stared at him. "I don't know, Spritz. I really don't know why you insist there was ever anything between him and me. You need to let that thought go."

He nodded. "I know."

"Anyway...he was sort of enigmatically threatening at the end of our conversation, and I think we need to be prepared in case he has any ill intentions toward the winery or Del."

"You think he'd hurt Del?" Spritzer sounded alarmed.

"Oh no, not violence, but he might try something financially. He's threatened it before."

"We should speak to Del about that."

"Yes, I agree. Oh, and one more thing. I didn't know we were getting Christmas bonuses."

Spritzer nodded and said, "I don't know if I should accept it this year with everything so tight financially."

"I thought that too."

"Last year I put mine toward one of your expensive sparkling wine toys—the coquard press, I believe it was."

Michel smiled. "I didn't know that. I am very impressed."

"Was thinking of doing something similar this year as well. I don't want to hurt Del's feelings by just returning the money."

"Good idea. I'll do the same. Let's discuss this later and decide where's the best place to use the bonuses this year."

Spritzer nodded.

Michel wanted to give Spritzer a quick kiss on the cheek but thought that might not be appropriate, as Spritzer was not officially out yet. "Gotta go." Michel turned and went over to Kan who was, by now, chatting with Clara and Lorne. "Come, let's go to the library. It'll be quiet there." He took Kan by the hand, and they left.

They moved through the party to the library where it *was* nice and quiet. A fire with a bed of coals kept the room cozy. Michel went over to the desk where he had stored a briefcase. "Let's sit by the fire," he said, as he added a few more logs.

They took the two armchairs fronting the fireplace.

Michel opened his briefcase and removed a page with some sample designs for a new label. "Here, first I wanted to show you these designs for your label that our marketing department came up with." He handed Kan the sheet.

Kan studied them. "Oh, these are nice. And I really like this one." She pointed to a label featuring several tree branches filled with olives in front of a California mission. It was warm, colorful, and enticing.

"Yes, very nice," Michel responded. "Is that the one you want to go with?"

"I think so."

"Then I'll have marketing send you the graphic files you'll need to print them up for your next release."

"Oh, this is exciting."

Michel then reached into his briefcase and took out a folder.

"Here." He handed the bound papers to Kan. "This is a contract for the sale of your olive oil. I've looked it over, and it's pretty standard. However, there are a few points I'd like to go over with you so you understand. And, of course, after you read it through, if you or your attorney have any questions, come back to me, and we'll discuss it."

Kan took the folder and opened it.

Michel turned toward Kan and began. "The first issue, and it's an important one, is about the amount of inventory. In order for this to work for the distributor, you will need to provide at least three thousand cases of oil per year. Is that going to be something you can do?"

"It depends. When would I need to ship that amount?"

"When we talked before, you said you had about fifteen hundred cases in current inventory."

"Yes. And we won't be harvesting again until next fall. And by then I will have greatly increased the harvest since we have this new opportunity."

Michel considered. "Do you have any outstanding domestic orders you need to fill?"

"No, I've already taken care of that."

"Good. Then I suggest you ship your entire inventory to them now. And by the end of next year you can make up the difference, and hopefully have a full three thousand cases to fulfill your obligation for the following year."

"Yes, I expect I can do that. I'll make sure of it."

"And remember, this is only the beginning. As the market for your oil grows, you will need to increase your output. Do you think that will be a problem?"

Kan considered that. "No, I think we can handle the increase, and if we need more olives I know a couple of places where I can buy more."

"Excellent. Now, let's discuss the price. You will be able to get more for your oil in Europe than you do in the US. However, as currency fluctuates with the market, the distributors cannot offer you a fixed price. They will base the price on the Euro, and your payout will depend on the currency exchange between the dollar and the Euro at the time of payment."

"I understand."

"Are you okay with that?"

"Yes. But what about shipping costs? Who pays that?"

"You do. But remember you will be getting substantially more for your oil in Europe, so that should cover the shipping."

Kan looked a little concerned. "Can you recommend a shipper?"

"Yes. We have one we use for all our champagne shipments. They are reliable and reasonably priced."

Kan beamed in delight. "My dad is going to be so pleased and proud."

Michel nodded. "Any other questions?"

"Not now, but let me read through the contract, and if I do, I'll get in touch."

"Good. I'm really excited for you." Michel closed his briefcase. "And when you're ready, sign it and get it back to me. I'll send it on."

They rose from their chairs. Michel had a further thought. "Oh, you know, you might want to consider entering your oil in the New York International Olive Oil Competition. It's the premier event for qualifying olive oil. A win or a prize would add value to the product and be a great marketing tool."

"Never thought of that. Great idea." Kan gave Michel a hug. "Thank you so much for your help. You have no idea what a grand opportunity this is for me. My dad and I are so grateful." Michel smiled. "And I'm sorry I treated you so badly...about Spritz. You know... she said shyly.

"I do."

"And I'm glad it's working out well for the two of you."

"We're still finding our way, but hopefully we'll get there."

"I hope so." She held up the contract. I'll take a look at this and get back to you. I'd better go find Dad."

They left the library.

* * *

The party was nearly over. A few stragglers were chatting with Del before leaving. Dan was lightly snoozing in an easy chair by the far fireplace, waiting for Kan to return so they could leave. Clara was in the dining room, taking the last of the leftover food into the kitchen.

Lorne was drying the plates that Spritzer was washing.

"So, is your place big enough for both of you?" Spritzer asked.

"For now. Robert doesn't have a lot of stuff. But if we're going to start the business we need to create a workspace, and it will be a lot easier if we're both there."

"So you're not moving in together because you've become a couple?" Spritzer teased.

Lorne smiled shyly. "Well, that might be part of it..."

Spritzer studied Lorne. He was not sure if this was the moment, but decided to take the plunge. He wanted to trust his friend and strengthen their closer relationship. "Lorne, I've got something to tell you. Don't laugh, please," he said, a little hesitantly.

"Oh?"

"Yeah, Michel and I have become a couple."

Lorne stopped drying and just stared at Spritzer.

"You...Michel...you mean like lovers?"

Spritzer nodded. "Un-huh."

"Well, I certainly wouldn't laugh—but I have to say I *am* amazed."

Spritzer laughed. "I know, me too."

"But that means you're gay? Right?"

"Not sure about that. All I know right now is that Michel and I are exploring."

"But you two seem so different..." Lorne said. "You guys fought like ninja warriors when he first arrived."

Spritzer laughed. "We did. We s-u-u-re did. But you know, working side by side and seeing each other every day..." He shook his head. "There have been a lot of really difficult times at the winery, and as we worked through those difficulties, it just couldn't help but bring us closer together."

Lorne thought about that. "Yeah, well, a lot of people work through problems together, but that doesn't mean they fall in love. There had to be something else working for you two as well."

"Ah...you mean the spark."

Lorne nodded. "I guess you could call it that."

"Who knows what? Destiny? Fate? One day I hated Michel, the next day I was intrigued by him, and then I found myself in love."

"The mystery...the mystery," Lorne teased.

Clara was wrapping the last of the remaining food or putting it in containers—all bound for the refrigerator or the freezer for Del's lunches or dinners for the next few days.

"And now you two are a...?" Lorne asked, not quite able to define their current relationship.

"A work in progress."

Lorne thought about that. "But what will you do when he goes back to France?"

Spritzer shrugged. "I don't know. What do they say? One day at a time."

* * *

Clara went into the great room to find Del still seated on the sofa. The fires were mostly embers now, and a stillness had settled over the house after the rambunctious party.

"How you doing?" Clara asked, as she leaned over Del. "Tired?"

Del looked up. "A little, but I didn't move around much. Mostly just exhausted by all the activity. It's nice and quiet now."

Clara sat down next to Del. "Don't know how you feel about it, but both Stevie and Lorne are cleaning up in the kitchen, and they seem to be getting on well together. This might be the perfect time to have our talk with them. What do you think?" Del nodded. "Unless you're too tired. I could take you to your room if you'd like to lie down."

"No. Let's do it. But what about Francisco? Will he want to join us?"

"I think he'd rather I did it. He's still embarrassed by the fact that he couldn't father children. And anyway, he's gone over to the winery for a while."

"On Christmas?"

"Said he needed to check an iffy vat. Won't be too long."

"Okay. You want to get them? How's the library?"

"Okay."

Clara helped Del rise from the sofa and walked with her to the library. She then went to the kitchen and over to where Lorne and Spritzer were drying glasses. She put an arm on each of their shoulders. "Might I have a few moments of your gentlemen's time?"

Spritzer laughed at her formality. "Sure, what's up?"

"Come," she directed, and led them to the library.

"Stevie—Lorne, come sit down with us. We'd like to have a little chat with the two of you," Del greeted them as they walked in.

"What's goin' on?" Spritzer asked, as he and Lorne sat with Del and Clara at the library table.

Del and Clara looked at each other, and Del nodded to Clara.

Clara turned to Lorne and put her hand on top of his. "Honey, there's something I need to tell you."

Lorne blanched. "You're not ill, are you?" Clara shook her head. "Is it Dad?"

"No. No. Nothing bad. It's about the family—about your parentage."

"I don't understand—you're my mom, Dad's my dad. What's there to understand?" Looking nervous, Lorne quickly glanced over to Del and Spritzer.

Clara continued, "Honey, your dad and I both love you so very much. You're everything to both of us...but your dad is not your biological father."

Lorne just stared at her, not comprehending.

"Your dad and I tried to have children for several years after we were married, but without any success. And, after consulting with a specialist, we were told he was infertile."

"Dad...?" Clara nodded. "Then who...?"

"We didn't want to adopt. We...I...didn't want some anonymous donor. We made an arrangement."

"It was my dad, wasn't it?" Spritzer spoke up. Clara nodded. "Was it before Mom ran away?"

Clara nodded again. "It was. But that wasn't why she left."

"How do you know?"

Clara hesitated. "Because she told me so."

"Did she know...about you and Dad?"

Clara shook her head. "Your father decided not to tell her. She left for her own reasons."

Lorne turned to Spritzer. "Then we're brothers." He lit up with a smile.

"Half-brothers," Del reminded him.

Spritzer turned to Del. "And you knew about this?"

"I did."

"Then why didn't you tell me?"

"It wasn't my place to do so, honey. Especially since Lorne didn't know yet."

"And why did it take you so long for you to tell me?" Lorne asked.

"Cowardice on your dad's and my parts. And uncertainty about how you'd take it," Clara said, lowering her eyes.

"Does Dad know you're telling me this?" Lorne asked.

"Not today. But we've discussed it, and he left the timing up to me."

Lorne nodded. He was still processing this shocker. "Mom, if you don't mind, I would rather you not tell Dad that you told me about this today."

"Why, honey?"

"I want to talk to him about it myself. I don't want him to stress about how I took the news. And I want him to know I'm okay with it. Think it will be better coming from me."

"If that's what you want."

Spritzer turned to Del. "Did you have any part in this arrangement?"

"No, but Clara was my friend, and I knew all about it," Del replied.

"You didn't think it might damage our family?" Spritzer pressed.

"Your father was very conscientious about his part in the arrangement—and very discreet."

Spritzer was thoughtful. "I wish he'd told me before he died."

Clara added, "He wanted to, but we asked to him wait until we'd told Lorne. Unfortunately, he died before we had the chance."

Lorne smiled and turned to Spritzer. "But hey...glad to have a new brother...half-brother." He reached out and pounded Spritzer on the arm. "Now we can fight like real brothers."

Spritzer smiled. "Just watch it, baby brother."

"No, you watch it."

"Damn..." Spritzer started laughing. "Merry Christmas."

* * *

"Will you go with me?" Lorne asked.

"If you want. But are you sure?" Spritzer asked. "It seems like it should be a son-dad thing."

"But you're my brother now."

"Half-brother."

Lorne shook his head. "No. You're my *brother,* and I'd like you to be there with me."

"Okay, if that's what you want."

Lorne nodded.

They were standing in Lorne's family kitchen. It was a Saturday morning, and they were just finishing mugs of coffee after they'd come back from grocery shopping for Clara. She usually did the shopping herself, but today she was completing the cleanup at Coeur du Chêne after the Christmas party.

After putting their mugs in the kitchen sink, they went out the back door. They headed toward the garage where Francisco was restoring a vintage '58 Corvette—a labor of love he'd been working on for six months.

"Lookin' sharp," Spritzer said, as he leaned in to examine the engine Francisco was working on.

"Just gettin' started really," Francisco said, as he placed the carburetor on his workbench. "It's slow work, but can't tell you how much I enjoy it."

Spritzer stood back to admire the whole car. "What color?"

"Red with the white accent, like the original." He turned from the bench and wiped his hands on the rag he pulled from the back pocket of his jumpsuit.

Lorne stepped forward. "Dad, could I have a word?"

"Sure, what's up, guys? Did you get your mom's shoppin' done?"

"Yeah."

Spritzer could tell Lorne was nervous. He was rubbing his hands together, and looked down, trying to find his words.

"Dad, I wanted to have Spritz here today, because Mom told us both about my biological father at Christmas. And I know Stevie's my half-brother."

"Ah…Okay." Francisco seemed more relieved than upset. "And you're okay with that?"

Lorne nodded. "I am. Mom explained all the circumstances to me."

They stood in silence for a moment.

"But you know it makes no difference how I feel about you," Francisco offered.

Lorne nodded again. He looked up. "My family just got bigger," he said, smiling.

"You could say that."

"But, Dad, there's something else."

"Oh?"

Now Lorne was *really* nervous. "I also wanted to tell you…You see…I ah…need you to understand…that I'm gay."

Francisco rolled his eyes. "So, what else is new?"

Lorne was taken aback. "You knew?"

"How could I not? Never brought any girls home—shunned the prom—couldn't catch a ball if I walked over and placed it in your hand—and then there were the magazines…"

"You found those?" Francisco nodded, blushing. "Then why didn't you say anything?"

"It was your business. Not for me judge…After all…I've had my own little secrets. And, of course, your mother told me," he added, laughing.

"Dad. You are so great." Lorne went over and hugged his father.

"And you knew about this gay thing?" Francisco turned and asked Spritzer.

"Only just learned."

"Sorry 'bout that," Lorne replied. "But then…I guess we all learn something new every day?" He winked at Spritzer.

"Hey, I think this calls for a round of beers, don't you?" Francisco said, marching over to the old refrigerator at the back of the garage.

CHAPTER TEN

2014

Even though it was only late February, the first fragrant hint of spring was in the air. Michel stood looking out over his vegetable garden and could see the first stirrings of new growth. The chives were already sending up their tasty spears. Italian parsley was also showing signs of new life. And, before long, the rest of the perennials would begin to reemerge. He was looking forward to planting his new vegetable crop for the year. That was a nice thing about California—a much-extended growing season. A trip to the nursery would be in order in the next week or two. But a sudden gust of wind whipped up behind him, reminding that spring was not officially here quite yet. He pulled his jacket collar up and turned back toward the house.

His phone rang. It was Spritzer.

"Hey..."

"You gonna be at work soon?" he asked.

"Leaving in five minutes."

"Good. I just got a call from Del. She needs to see us both first thing. I'm on my way to her studio right now."

"About anything specific?"

"She didn't say, but she sounded concerned about something."

"Okay, I'll meet you there."

* * *

Spritzer's Jeep was already parked at Coeur du Chêne when Michel drove up. He parked and went to the studio.

"Good morning." Michel greeted him cheerfully, still exuberant about his garden.

"Oh, Michel, good morning, darling," Del replied. "I'm afraid we have a little problem." She held up a document.

Spritzer came over to Michel and put his arm around his shoulders.

"Can I see?" Michel asked, as he reached out to take a look at the piece of paperwork.

Del continued, "It's Nelson. I don't know what's gotten into him, but he's demanding an audit of the Maison Vallier books—at our expense."

"Can he do that?" Spritzer asked.

"I'm afraid he can. It's in the agreement we signed when he invested more money for Maison Vallier."

Michel sighed. "I think I know what this is about."

"What's that?" Spritzer asked, as he leaned over Michel's shoulder to view the document.

"Remember the Christmas party, and Nelson's little pout, because I wouldn't go away with him over New Year's?"

"He wouldn't..." Del spouted with indignation.

"I'm afraid he would," Spritzer replied. "He has a definite mean streak, our Nelson. Must take after his mother."

"Why his mother?" Michel asked.

Del answered. "Tom's daughter, Christine, was a bit of a wild one. She ran off with Jerome Wayland and her mother's emeralds, in defiance of her father. Tom was, to say the least, not pleased—and that is why he left the Vallier Winery to me instead of to his only child."

"So what's to worry about? The Maison Vallier books should be fine. It's just a nuisance request, isn't it?" Spritzer asked.

"I don't trust him," Michel said. "Who knows what else he might be up to?" He turned to Del. "Maybe you could have a word with him."

"Believe me, I shall."

"What do we need to do about this?" Spritzer waved the document at Del.

"We'll direct him to our accountants. They can deal with this. But I felt you two needed to know what he was up to."

"We'll go see the accountants to find out what our alternatives are, and then get back to you," Spritzer said.

Michel and Spritzer turned to leave. But Michel stopped and added, "After Nelson's threats at Christmas I started a private investigation on him in case something like this should happen. And I may have an idea or two about how we might get him to withdraw his request for the audit."

* * *

As Michel and Spritzer were leaving the studio, Michel stopped him by taking hold of his arm. Spritzer turned to him.

"What?"

"There may be an issue with the audit," he said quietly.

"What's that?"

"I may have not been quite honest with you about some of the expenses we incurred for equipment." He looked at Spritzer with a plea for understanding. "I hid some of the costs. You were always so angry with me about spending. I'm sorry."

Spritzer was stunned. He started to walk away but stopped, shaking his head. He turned back. "How much are we talking about?"

"Maybe one hundred and fifty to two hundred…"

"Thousand?"

"Yes, I'm afraid so."

"And that's going to show up on the full audit?" Michel nodded. "And how did you get around my supervision of the winery expenses?"

"I sneaked the money from other accounts."

"So those accounts are short?" Michel nodded. "Goddamn it." He paused. "Does Del know about this?"

Michel shook his head. "I am so sorry."

"Do you realize the jeopardy you've put us under?"

"What can I do to make this right? I'll do anything," he pleaded.

"We've got to go to the accountants immediately and talk to them about this. See if we can straighten this out before Del formally requests the audit."

* * *

"The bad news is the total is $180,787. The good news is we can fix this before the audit," the accountant, Dillon Marcus, said, as they sat before him in his office. "*If* you can verify the expenses, and come up with the cash to cover the shortfall in the accounts you borrowed this from."

Spritzer turned to Michel. "Do you think Nelson knew about this? Is that why he's requesting this audit?"

Michel muttered, "I may have mentioned something like this to him once in passing when I was particularly angry with you after you refused to upgrade the AC."

"Really? That means his vendetta is personal against you and not Del."

Michel nodded. "So it would seem."

"Then what do you want to do?" Dillon pushed them for an answer.

"I can get the paperwork together to show what I transferred and from which accounts," Michel offered. "And I realize I am personally responsible for the shortfall. But it's going to take me several weeks to liquidate some assets in France and get the money over here."

Dillon shook his head. "No. We don't have that much time. You would be totally exposed if it took that long."

Spritzer was thoughtful. "I'll cover it."

Michel turned to him. "How could you do that?"

"I have an inheritance from my dad. I've salted it away for a rainy day. Guess today we've got gale-force winds. Time to cash it in."

Michel insisted, "I'll pay you back, I promise—every single penny, with interest."

"It's not about me, Michel. It's about Del. She put her trust in you. It was her money you overspent."

"Yes. I will square it with her. You can trust me on that. But right now, it's you who is putting up the money for the shortfall, and I will make sure you get it back."

Spritzer nodded. "I'd appreciate that." He then turned to Michel and asked, "Why would you ever put yourself in such a situation, knowing you would be financially liable at some point?"

"I wanted Maison Vallier to succeed, and I felt you were impeding our chances for success."

Spritzer nodded. "But that's a lot of *your* money you've committed to *our* project, and I don't know if or when we'll be able to pay you back."

"That's on me. I made the error, and I'm willing to pay for that mistake."

* * *

Spritzer and Michel drove back from the accountants in near silence. Spritzer was having a hard time squaring this new, nefarious version of Michel with the morally superior prig he'd first met.

"I just don't understand..." Spritzer said finally.

Michel sighed. "Me either...Not like me at all. It's just that you were so angry with me all the time..."

"So, you're saying it was my fault?" he said defensively.

"Not at all. Forgive me if I gave you that impression. All I'm asking for is your understanding and forgiveness."

"You're going to have to give me some time."

"Of course. Please don't let this jeopardize our relationship," Michel stated.

"Just give me time" was all he'd say.

* * *

Nelson's warehouse was in the lush Napa Valley, just outside of St. Helena. It was here he conducted his wine-distribution business, and from where he hosted his wine-concierge tours. Nelson was enjoying a cappuccino at his desk and contemplating a massage with the charming Alexander later that afternoon when there was a knock at his open door. He looked up to see Michel scowling at him.

"Michel...do come in. Can I offer you a coffee—cappuccino—latte—macchiato?"

"Nelson, what the fuck are you up to with this ridiculous audit?"

"Ah...no coffee then." He smirked. He extended his hand, offering Michel a chair opposite his desk. "You came all this way for that? A phone call would have sufficed." He clasped his hands behind his head and leaned back.

Michel remained standing. "No, a phone call would not have sufficed. I needed to look into your beady, malevolent eyes."

Nelson laughed. "Charming. I always knew you had spunk. Such a tiger."

"Don't patronize me, Nelson. I am deadly serious."

Nelson lost his buoyant demeanor and studied Michel carefully. "Yes. I can see that. And exactly what is it you want?"

"I want you to drop that ridiculous nuisance request for an audit of Maison Vallier."

"Ah, but I can't do that. You see, I have the right, per my agreement, when you requested an additional hefty loan for your little venture."

"But having the right doesn't mean you must exercise it."

Nelson nodded. "Quite true. However, your—how shall I put this—mischievous behavior toward me has inclined me to press it...If you see what I mean." He leaned forward. "I don't like being taken advantage of."

"And how did I take advantage of you?" Michel asked, finally sitting down.

"You led me on. Made me believe you were interested in me...us. But no, you were only interested in getting me to finance your extravagant little champagne adventure."

"Nelson, that is wholly untrue. I never led you on. In your twisted mind, perhaps. But it was never my intention to be anything to you other than a trusted cocreator in Del's vision to create the finest American version of a French champagne."

"Huh..."

"And remember, we are doing this for Del...your beloved aunt...who is considering making you one of her heirs. And since you are so eminently selfish, certainly you must want us to succeed for your own benefit, if not for hers."

Nelson pondered Michel's audacity. "I think we are finished here," he said, standing from his desk. "I am *not* withdrawing my request for the audit. Now please leave."

Michel's eyes narrowed. "Nelson, seriously, I don't think you want to do this."

"Oh?"

"You do *not* want to make me your enemy. You are dealing with a man who can uproot fifty-year-old grapevines with his bare hands. Believe me—you do not want to mess with me."

"Oh...is that a threat. Do I need to call security?"

Michel took a deep breath and let it go slowly. "Nelson, I really didn't want to do this, but you leave me no alternative." He reached into his bag and drew out a large envelope, which he threw on Nelson's desk.

"What's that?"

"Photographs. Copies, of course. I retain the originals."

Nelson tensed, but picked up the envelope and opened it, pulling out a series of photos.

"How old do you suppose he is?" Michel asked.

Nelson looked up. "He's of age, if that's what you're implying, and how did you get these?" he asked hoarsely.

"After your little snit at Christmas, I hired a private detective to track you, thinking I might find something useful with which to defend ourselves if necessary. I had every reason to believe you were capable of some nasty prank or other. And *voilà*—look what I found. And I'm sure

Del would be just *thrilled* to see these, along with all the lurid details transcribed in a five-page report. And oops—there goes the inheritance."

"You are one fucking son of a bitch."

Michel nodded. "And don't you forget it." He turned and left Nelson's office.

* * *

The next week of February was exceptionally mild. The early morning sun quickly evaporated the nighttime mists, and Michel felt the increased warmth through his light jacket—which he could probably shed by midmorning.

He stood in his garden and picked up a handful of earth, which he brought up to his nose. It smelled damp and loamy. He couldn't resist it any longer, and, as it was a Saturday, he decided to head out to the nursery this very morning—luxuriating in thoughts of fat cabbages; tender, sweet carrots; shiny purple eggplants; arrays of juicy, ripe tomatoes; and a panoply of nutrient-rich leafy greens.

After unloading all his nursery purchases and storing them away safely in his enclosed back porch, his first task was to rototill the garden. He called Spritzer.

"Do we have a rototiller at the winery?" Michel asked.

"And a cheery good morning to you as well," Spritzer answered a little sourly.

Michel laughed. "I'm sorry. Yes, good morning. It's just, I got back from the nursery, and I'm so excited to get planting—social niceties just flew right out the window. Forgive me."

"Isn't it a bit early to plant a garden?"

"Not for the cold-loving veggies. They'll just thrive. I'll plant warm-weather plants later. But I want to get started now."

Spritzer paused. "Yeah, we do have one. I'll pick it up and bring it over. Haven't showered yet. Give me an hour or so."

"And I'll fix us some lunch or breakfast—whichever you want."

Spritzer laughed. "That sounds nice. See ya."

"No wait," he added before Spritzer could end the call. "I was just thinking. Remember how we discussed foraging for a meal some time back."

"Yeah."

"Well, this is the perfect time. It's early spring and already the fields are burgeoning with new growth. When you get here, let's gather our lunch. Does that sound fun?"

"Maybe. I don't know…"

"Aw, come on, you'll like it—I promise."

"If you say so. Bye for now."

* * *

Spritzer delivered the rototiller, telling Michel he'd checked that it was filled up with gas and working properly. Even though Michel wanted to get right out there and work on the garden, he wanted, even more, to go foraging with Spritzer. Michel was not certain Spritzer had completely forgiven him for his blunder with hiding the expenses. And he hoped that maybe their day together might help heal any rift left between them.

"What are we looking for?" Spritzer asked, as he carried Michel's forage basket.

They had climbed over the fence around Michel's house and were setting out through the adjacent fallow field.

"Won't really know till we come upon something. I'm more familiar with the wild edibles of France."

"Maybe there won't be anything,"

"Oh, I'm sure there will be." He was carefully examining the ground as they moved slowly through the field. He carried a pair of scissors and a knife in the basket. "And look here." He knelt down. "Field mustard. This will be nice fried up with garlic or in a salad." He dug into the earth around the plants with his knife.

"Is this anything?" Spritzer asked, getting into the spirit of the hunt.

Michel came over and kneeled next to him. "Wild asparagus—very good."

"Yeah, I recognized that." He beamed, and took the knife from Michel and cut enough stalks. "It's probably good to leave some, huh?"

"It is. Need to let the plants reseed, or complete their natural growth cycle in the case of asparagus."

They walked on a bit more, each intently studying the ground.

"Miner's lettuce," Michel announced and kneeled to harvest it.

"This is fun," Spritzer admitted, as he patted Michel on the shoulder.

Michel saw an opening. Standing, he looked over toward Spritzer before he spoke. "Hey, have you forgiven me yet for my terrible mistake with the expenses?"

Spritzer turned and looked at Michel. He nodded. "How can I not? You are just so...you." He paused, then said, "And thank you for repaying me so promptly. I really appreciate that."

"And hopefully it is all behind us now. I met with Del and explained my part in this fiasco, and she has graciously forgiven me," Michel added.

"I'm glad to hear that. Her understanding concerned me the most," Spritzer said.

Michel was much relieved, and they started walking again. He saw some wild onions and pulled up some of those. Nearby was some new spring garlic.

"Oh, I forgot to tell you," Spritzer stated, "Del called me late yesterday afternoon—after you'd gone home—and told me that Nelson has withdrawn his request for the audit."

"Really?" Michel smiled.

"She said he gave no reason, but just backed off with a great deal of apology."

"Well, that certainly is a tremendous relief."

"It sure is. Very puzzling, though. Not like him at all. Wonder what made him change his mind?"

Michel nodded to himself. "I have absolutely no idea. Maybe his conscience got to him."

Spritzer sneered. "Then *that* would be a first."

"The world is often filled with wondrous surprises." Michel had to laugh. They were following the course of a stream. "Ah, look—mint." He gave Spritzer the scissors from the basket, and he cut a nice bunch.

Spritzer spotted some watercress farther along the bank. "I know that. Used to collect that as a kid. Great in a salad. Guess I was a forager and didn't know it." He laughed.

"And here are some baby radishes." Michel pulled one up and took a bite. "Peppery. Need some of these." He stood. "You know, I think we've got enough for a decent lunch."

"Too bad there aren't any wild chickens about. This would make a lovely salad and omelet if we had some eggs."

"Well, I have some nice free-range eggs from the farmers' market at home. Are you ready to go back?"

"Yeah, I'm hungry. Was too lazy to make breakfast this morning."

"Good."

They started back across the field.

Spritzer turned to Michel. "Have you had time to think about what you might want to do with your Christmas bonus?"

"Not really, been too caught up with my stupid financial mess to think about it."

"Then can I make a suggestion?"

"Sure. What you got in mind?"

"I'm really intrigued with Lorne's renewable energy studies. I haven't shown you his master's thesis yet, but it's on renewable energy for commercial wineries."

"Really? Good for him."

"Yeah. And I was thinking I'd like to try a test project using solar or wind, or whatever he thinks would work best for us."

"Interesting. Where would we use it?"

"I was thinking we could start small, and set up an operation to run the irrigation system—as a test, you know. And if that was successful, we could expand as we can afford it. I'd be willing to use my bonus toward it too."

"Do you have a cost yet?"

"Not yet. But Lorne's created a renewable energy business with his friend, Robert, and they're looking for their first job. I'm sure he could spec it out for us. And I know they'd be eager to do the best job possible."

"Yes, I like that. Let's see what the cost is, and if it's reasonable, I'd be happy to use my bonus toward that."

Spritzer beamed and put his arm around Michel as they reached his house. They went inside to put together their foraged lunch.

* * *

Lunch was to be a radically fresh salad, herb omelet, and poached asparagus with a lemon garlic vinaigrette. On his way home from the nursery, Michel had stopped to pick up some bread from one of the specialty bakeries in Guerneville—the only one that had a decent French baguette, he insisted. He whipped up a light, creamy, chipotle dressing for the salad as he heated the baguette and broke apart some Roquefort cheese to top the salad.

Spritzer leaned over Michel's shoulder from behind and picked at the cheese in the salad. Michel slapped his hand. "If you must..." He handed Spritzer a small wedge of cheese to nibble on until the baguette was warmed through.

"I fancy a rather splendid white wine I've been saving," he said, as he opened a 2012 Louis Jadot Pouilly-Fuissé. He poured them each a glass. "*Bonne santé*," he said touching Spritzer's glass and toasting.

"Cheers." Spritzer gave Michel a great smile. "Can I help?"

"Take the salad and I'll bring the rest."

They had just settled down to eat when there was a knock at the door.

"Ooops, who's that?" Michel rose and went to answer the door.

"Curtis and I were driving by, and I wanted to say hi." Kan looked in through the door and saw Spritzer seated at the table. "Oh, I'm sorry, we're interrupting."

"Not at all. Come on in. Have a glass of a very fine Louis Jadot." Michel reached out his hand to Curtis. "Hi, I'm Michel," he offered.

"Curtis Brandeis," the man replied, shaking his hand.

Kan put her arm through Curtis's and smiled. "My new beau. Pretty snappy, huh?"

Michel laughed. "Very. Pleased to meet you."

"One of my rodeo buddies," Kan added.

Curtis had the rough-and-ready appearance common to most rodeo riders. Short, blond hair, and a sun-weathered face, with blue eyes and a winning smile.

"Come on, have some wine and join us. I think we've got enough," Michel said. "We went foraging today, and our lunch is all foraged greens, though I'm sure Spritz would rather have a hot dog."

"Now be fair—I'm learning," Spritzer complained.

They went to the table. Michel gathered two more glasses and place settings. "Sit down. Will you have a taste of our salad?" he asked as he poured the wine.

"Why not?" Kan said. She took a serving of salad for Curtis and herself and tasted it. "Oh my, this is delicious. Can you teach me how to forage? I would really like to do that. I bet we got all kinds of goodies on our land."

"I'm sure you have. I would be happy to teach you."

Michel could see Spritzer was checking out Kan's new fella. He had to smile. Could Spritzer possibly be jealous? But he was more likely just curious and protective, as he and Kan had been such good friends most of their lives.

"The reason I stopped by," Kan said, "was to let you know I've shipped off all the oil this week. I'm really excited to see how sales progress. It will mean such a lot to us if this is successful."

"I have no doubt it will be. Our marketing people are very good at what they do. But don't be impatient. It's probably going to take a while to get you established in the European market."

"And how's everything going with the sparkling wine? See, I remembered—sparkling wine, not champagne."

Michel laughed. "Very well. We've still got a long way to go, but it's all on track."

Kan turned to Spritzer. "I ran into Lorne in town the other day. Did you know he was dating a guy?"

"Yes, I did. Must run in the family."

"What?" Kan asked.

"I've discovered that Lorne is my baby half-brother."

Kan was stunned. "What? No. How is that?"

Spritzer appeared to be amused by her shock, and proceeded to tell the whole tale. After he was finished, he added, "It's all out in the open now. Don't believe I'm breaking any trust by telling you this."

Kan reached over and placed her hand on Spritzer's. "I'm so glad you two are close again. You were such great friends when we were little, and it saddened me when you two drifted apart."

"Life's funny, huh?"

"You know, we've really got to go," Kan said, getting up from the table. "Thanks for the eats and the wine. Been real nice."

Michel rose and led them to the door. He leaned in and whispered to Kan, "Is this one a keeper?" He nodded toward Curtis, who was already walking down the front walk on the way to the car.

"Oh, who knows? But he's fun for now."

Michel laughed. "Take care. We'll chat soon."

After Kan left, and Michel went back to the table. Spritzer had already cleared away most of the lunch, and Michel grabbed the rest.

Spritzer was at the sink, rinsing the plates and putting them in the dishwasher.

"You train up real good," Michel joked. He went over to Spritzer and put his arms around him.

Spritzer said, "You know, I'm sure you want to get out to your garden and start rototilling, but I was wondering if you might want to spend a little quality bedroom time together first." He smiled.

"Hmm. That might be a possibility," Michel said, as he nuzzled Spritzer's neck.

They finished cleaning up and then headed toward the bedroom. Michel flipped on some music.

He did not get any rototilling done that day.

* * *

The physical therapist had just left Del's bedroom. Del was sitting on the side of her bed, pulling on a sweater. Clara came into the room with a load of folded laundry.

"How did the therapy go?" Clara asked.

"Oh, you know...repetitive, boring, and painful."

"But necessary. You want to get back into your studio, don't you?"

"Hum. I don't know. I think it might be time to wind down the ceramics. Haven't I done enough?" She continued to sit on the bed as Clara put the laundry away in Del's chest of drawers and closet.

"Well, that depends..." Clara answered. "Do you want to stop? Or do you need to stop?"

"Bit of both, I expect. I feel torn."

Clara came over and sat next to Del on the bed. "Well, you don't have to decide until you know. But I can't imagine you not wanting to have a go at that old wheel of yours."

Del laughed. "Maybe. We'll see."

"I bet you got years of fine work ahead of you."

Del turned to Clara. "And what about you? We've never talked about it, but do you ever think about retiring? It can't be getting any easier for you with your arthritis."

"Me? Retire?" She sighed. "As long as you need me, I'll be here." She turned and put her hand on top of Del's. "I got lots of gumption left in me. Don't know what I'd do sitting around at home all day. Maybe when Francisco retires...we'll see. Wouldn't mind doing some traveling, you know. Always fancied a cruise around the world. Probably the only way I'd get to see most of it at my age."

"But that's expensive, isn't it?"

"I'm sure it is. But what are dreams for?"

Del was thoughtful. "Feel like a game of chess?"

Clara looked at Del with some surprise. "If you like. Shall I make us some tea?"

"Yes. That would be lovely. I'll set up while you make it."

"Scones or cookies?"

"Something light."

Del went to her chess table by the window overlooking the orchard. She set up the board with the ceramic chess pieces she'd made ten years ago. Clara soon came back with the tea and a plate of *zaleti*—Venetian cornmeal cookies with pine nuts and dried black currants.

Del held out her closed hands to Clara. "Choose for opening." Clara reached out and tapped Del's left hand. She opened it, revealing a white pawn. "White. You go first."

They played, sipped tea, and relaxed, thoroughly enjoying themselves. Then Del asked, "How's Lorne doing?"

"Very well. He and Francisco had a great talk about him being gay, and he seems much more relaxed these days. And Lorne's come to find out that Spritzer is now in a relationship with Michel. Did you know about that?"

"I did."

"My, my, what a world it's become." Clara had a twinkle in her eye as she asked, "You ever have a fling with a woman?"

Del looked quite surprised, but laughed. "Well...might have done. Have you?"

Clara giggled. "Oh no...no one ever asked."

"Really. Well, would you if they did?"

"Not now. Too settled in my ways. Also, there's Francisco...But when I was younger, who knows?"

"Ah yes, age does change one's perspective, does it not?"

Clara nodded. "I bet you were pretty frisky where you were younger. Living in France. A pretty woman like you. Alone. Unattached. An adventurous, free-spirited artist..."

Del smiled and nodded. "I had my time. But, to be quite honest, I'm quite glad it's all behind me. Not that I didn't have some thrilling romances and some quite stunning lovers along the way, but I have to say, it's quite exhausting being constantly driven by one's hormones. I realize now how compulsive we humans are about sex and love. It seems to dominate a major portion of our lives...not to mention books, movies, and pop music. At least now I am free to contemplate other aspects of life without all the *Sturm und Drang* of romance."

"Well, we would hardly survive as a race for very long without it," Clara pointed out.

"True. But you know one of my most memorable experiences of romance was with a man I met who was married and very much attached to his wife. We were passengers on a ship. I was traveling from Marseille to Istanbul on holiday, and he was a concert pianist traveling there for a concert. We were instantly and deeply attracted to each other, and we had an intense romance for three days. But we never consummated our desires—never kissed even. Our only contact was brief touching. A hand on an arm—a brush of shoulders—a placement of a strand of hair behind an ear. But it was intense beyond belief. Our senses were heightened, and our spirits were totally engaged. It was one of the most thrilling romantic experiences I have ever had."

"Did you ever see or hear from him again?"

Del was quiet and thoughtful. "No, never. It was what it was in that moment. And I wouldn't change that for all the wealth of rubies."

Clara thought about that, then nodded.

Del, because of their conversation, had lost interest in playing chess and sat staring out the window into the orchard. "The first buds will start appearing soon. It won't be long before we are canning and making jams again."

"Year after year. Cycle after cycle. Life just rolls along. There are the ups and downs of the daily dramas, but, underneath, the same repeating cycles move our inner realities into the deeper mysteries."

Both women were now lost in their own contemplations. Silence fell over the room as they gazed out the window as the light began to fade into twilight.

PART TWO

CHAPTER ELEVEN

2016

The sun glared as it rose over the top of the ridge overlooking the Vallier Winery. Spritzer shaded his eyes with his hand as he gazed up to where Lorne was pointing.

"You think that would work for you?" Lorne asked.

"I don't know...Electrical windmills are so tall and...out there. Kind of an eyesore, don't you think? I'm afraid we might get a lot of blowback from the community."

"Yes, I can see that," Robert added. "And they can make a lot of noise, and be dangerous to birds—particularly migrating ones. And I see a lot of those this time of year."

Lorne's partner, Robert, had a blond crewcut and a football player's build. Spritzer could see he was used to manual labor and thought him a good compliment to Lorne's more delicate physique.

"We know solar works, but those installations do take up a lot of space," Spritzer said.

"But they're low maintenance, and remember, you've got a lot of free space up on the warehouse roofs. Much less conspicuous."

"True...true." Spritzer was thinking this through.

Meanwhile, Robert was searching through some papers in his briefcase. He pulled out a brochure. "Here. Take a look at this..." He handed it to Spritzer.

"Geothermal? Hmm. That sounds interesting. How would that work?"

"We all know Calistoga is just up the road, and they have the springs and a very active geothermal footprint. We might be able to tap into that. And it's very clean and almost trouble-free once it's established."

"What would we have to do to determine if it could work here?"

"We'd first need to do a geological survey to see if it could be a possibility," Robert said. "I could look into that."

"Yeah, do. I like that idea. And if that won't work, I'm okay with going solar. I'd love Vallier to be totally energy self-sufficient. Or as much as we can manage."

"Okay, we'll get working on it." Lorne put his arm around Spritzer's shoulder as they headed back toward the Maison Vallier offices.

"We miss you at the winery," Spritzer said.

"Thanks, I miss being here. But our client list is growing, and we're going to need to hire some more workers soon ourselves."

"That's great." Spritzer laughed. "And if our sparkling wine falls flat, then I may be coming to you for a job."

"That's not going to happen, and you know that. You and Michel have done a great job."

"We'll see..."

Lorne turned to Spritzer. "Hey, bro, when's Michel leaving?"

Spritzer's mood darkened. "By the end of the year."

"What are you going to do without him? You two going to remain a couple?"

Spritzer shook his head. He avoided thinking too much about that. "I don't know. I really don't."

* * *

"And this is the gyropalette," Michel stated, as he turned to the young man walking beside him. "Traditionally, at this stage in champagne production, the bottles were inserted neck down in riddling racks. The bottles would remain in these racks during the rest of the aging process, and a worker would turn the bottles by hand, an eighth of a turn every day. This would gradually force the sediment into the neck of the bottle where it could later be removed. However, the sediment is instrumental in enhancing the champagne's flavor, so it's necessary to retain it in the bottle for the duration of the aging process."

"That seems very labor-intensive," Darrel, the young man, said.

"Indeed it is, and that is exactly why we have this new device—the gyropalette. It performs the same function, automatically, and in a much shorter period of time and without the need for workers to be involved—but with the same end result."

"This is all very interesting," Darrel said. "I'm sure this is going to make a terrific documentary for my class."

"Are you studying to be a filmmaker?" Michel continued, leading the young student through the warehouse.

"I'd like to. But my parents...well..."

"I understand. But I can tell you from personal experience that you must always follow your dream. Anything else...well..." He shook his head.

"What's that machine over there?" Darrel asked, pointing to the bottling machine.

"Ah yes, the final step. It looks rather formidable, does it not?"

Darrel laughed. "It looks like it could launch itself into space."

Now Michel laughed. "Indeed. But it *is* a rather complex system. Remember I told you about riddling the sediment into the neck of the bottle?"

"Yes."

"Well, that must be removed from the bottle when the long aging process is complete."

"And how is that done without the bubbles escaping?"

"Ah...the machine freezes the neck of the bottle, then the pop-off cap is removed. The frozen plug, containing the sediment, is released and we top the bottle up with what we call the *liqueur d'expedition*. It consists of a mixture of reserve wine, sugar, and brandy. That is how we control the sweetness or dryness of the wine."

"Oh my. Very tricky, I'd imagine."

"That's the art. Each house establishes its own identity, and that is one way they control the signature character of their wine."

"Fascinating."

"Then the cork is placed in the bottle. The wire cap is tightened around the neck, and then the foil cap is wrapped around the top."

"And all of that is done on this machine?"

"It is, indeed."

"Wow. And then it's ready to drink?"

"After it rests a bit more. Then it's ready for shipping."

Darrel turned off his recorder. "Thank you so much for the tour. When is the best time to schedule the shoot?"

Michel began leading Darrel back toward his office. He smiled. "Well, this is a rather special time for us. We are just about to launch our first bottling. We are going to be very busy for the next few weeks. Why don't you give me a call in November? We'll be in a much quieter period then."

"Congratulations on the launch."

"Thanks."

"I will. I'll call later to schedule the shoot. Can I count on both you and Mr. Vallier to be available for on camera interviews?"

"I expect so. But don't leave it too late. My contract is up at the end of the year, and then I'm off back to France."

"Really? You're not here permanently?"

"No, I was hired to get the operation set up and to train Mr. Vallier. He'll run the operation by himself from then on."

As they were about to enter Michel's office, Spritzer came up to them. "Hey, how did the tour go?"

"Very well. You're about to become a movie star," Michel joked.

"Will I be getting the big bucks?"

"It's a documentary for a student film project. I think all *you'll* be getting is screen credit."

"Well…that's something."

Darrel shook their hands. "Thank you so much for your time. I'm off now. I'm sure you got lots to do before the launch."

"Keep in touch," Michel said. He turned back to Spritzer.

Spritzer was rubbing his hands together, and said, "You ready for the big moment?"

"I am."

They walked out of the warehouse and over to the edge of the vineyard, where a table had been set up with a number of bottles of the first release of Maison Vallier. A photo shoot was underway. A photographer had been snapping pictures of the bottles, artfully arranged with autumn leaves and bunches of grapes from the vines. An assistant was holding a reflector, and umbrella lights were positioned to properly light the bottles when the photographer shot a picture.

"We're ready," Spritzer called out to the assembled group.

"Excellent. I think I've got all the shots I need of the product. Now we just need a few of you two holding the bottles," the photographer said.

"And with big smiles, I'd imagine," Michel beamed.

"Indeed."

The photographer got them into place and directed them how to hold the bottles. He went back to the camera and began shooting.

"Spritzer, a little to your left, please, and turn the label more toward me." He did. "That's it. Excellent." The photographer continued snapping away, one shot right after the other. "Michel, bigger smile, please, and turn your head just a little more toward the center. And hold the bottle a little higher." He took a couple dozen shots in all. "That's great. That should do it."

"That didn't take long," Spritzer said.

"Well, you're working with a professional. We know there's nothing more tedious than a long photo shoot." He smiled. "I'll email you the proofs after I've sorted them out."

"Look forward to it, thanks," Michel said.

Spritzer turned to Michel and took him in his arms. "Well. Did you ever think we would actually get to this moment?"

"I sure wondered from time to time."

"I was a bit of an ass, wasn't I?" Spritzer said with a faint smile and a touch of regret in his voice as he broke from the embrace.

"From time to time." Michel paused. "Though I was just the tiniest bit arrogant, as well, I seem to remember."

"But we've both changed a lot, don't you think?"

Michel reached up and put his hand on Spritzer's cheek. "Yes, I think we have."

Spritzer nodded, but suddenly seemed sad again. "Do you think I'm really ready to handle all of this by myself?" He waved his hand toward the winery. "How can I do it without you?"

"You're just nervous about the change, but you'll be fine." Michel shook his head. "We knew this time was coming. My contract's up, and I need to get back to France."

"But what if Del agreed to extend your contract by another year...or even two?"

Michel shook his head again. "No. No. My life is back in France. This has been a grand adventure, but we both knew it was only to be temporary."

"I know. But I don't want this to end—us."

Michel was silent and looked down. "We'll keep in touch. I promise."

Spritzer turned and walked away a few steps. "No. That is not enough. We've come too far—as a couple. How can you consider separating?"

"Are you willing to give up your life here and move to France with me?" Michel asked with a slight challenge in his voice.

Spritzer turned to Michel but couldn't speak. His silence was what spoke the answer.

"I didn't think so. Yet you expect me to give up my life and stay here with you?"

"Impossible, isn't it?" he said sorrowfully.

Michel nodded. "We still have a few months. Let's just enjoy the time we have left."

"So, love doesn't necessarily conquer all, does it?" Spritzer said, despondently.

"Not without a lot of extra help—or unexpected life-changing circumstances."

* * *

Del and Clara were having BLTs at the big table in the kitchen.

"Hello?" a voice rang out, followed by knocking on the outside kitchen door. "Anybody home? Need some help here."

Clara went over and opened the door. "Hello. Come on in, you two."

"We tried the studio, but you weren't there," Michel said.

"Lunchtime." Del gestured to her plate of food, smiling.

Spritzer and Michel came over with a large bucket filled with ice and two bottles of sparkling wine, and a closed case of wine, putting them down on the table.

"What's this?" Del asked, but clearly already guessing the answer.

"Del...it's finally time. The moment we've all worked toward, and waited for—for four years." Spritzer beamed.

Del put her hands together, thumbs against her lips, overcome with emotion, and unable to speak right away. "Oh, Stevie..."

Spritzer pulled a bottle out of the ice bucket and began to remove the foil cap. "Can you believe all these years of hard work and concern have come to this very moment?"

Clara went to the cupboard and took out champagne flutes. She brought them to the table.

"It's just glorious. I can't wait," Del whispered.

Clara laughed and pointed to the carton of wine. "We're not going to drink all that, are we?"

Michel laughed too. "No, that's being shipped to the Prix d'Or. That's our entry. But we wanted you to see a full carton. Nice design on the outside, don't you think?"

"Splendid," Del said.

"Are we all ready? Here goes, then." Spritzer popped the cork.

Everyone responded with an awed "Ah-h-h," like at a firework display.

He poured four glasses of sparkling wine. It was a rich, golden color with a bursting fountain trail of dancing bubbles. He handed a glass to each.

"Del, I think you deserve the first sip. After all, it was your dream that made it all possible," Michel stated.

"And most of my money," Del added, with a twinkle in her eye. She proceeded to take a sip. The others watched her, anxiously awaiting her reaction. Del closed her eyes and savored the wine. Then her face lit up and she said, "Ah, my dears, I'm drinking the stars. My papa would be so proud." She was smiling, but her eyes were tearing up as well.

The other three took their sips. They tasted it—then Michel and Spritzer turned to each other and broke out in great smiles. Spritzer toasted Michel. "You were right about everything. This is magnificent. I'm really so proud of you."

Michel nodded and bowed. Spritzer leaned in and gave him a kiss.

Del had already finished her glass. "More...more!" she said, reaching over the table for a refill. "What else do you have with bacon, lettuce, and tomato sandwiches?"

Spritzer refilled the rest of the now empty glasses.

Del turned to Clara. "How about some music?"

"What would you like?" Clara asked, as she went over to the boom box with a stack of CDs on the side.

"Aznavour," Del stated.

Clara started the music and a ballad began playing. The lyrics were evocative and yearning, harking back to a time when the singer was a young man, and the taste of life was sweet on his tongue.

"Ah, Paris...Let us dance." She held out her arms to Spritzer, who came over and took her in his arms. They began to move across the floor, swaying in time to the music. But, tiring quickly, she took Michel's and Spritzer's hands and brought the two of them together. Then they began to dance. Spritzer held Michel closely to him. They stared into each other's eyes. They glided to the far side of the kitchen.

"We've come a long way," Spritzer said quietly to him.

"Yes, we have."

"You know, I love you, don't you?" He leaned in to try and catch Michel's eye.

He didn't answer. Spritzer gently turned Michel's face toward him, but he couldn't look Spritzer in the eyes.

"There's nothing to be afraid of, you know."

Michel broke away from the dance. "Not now. This is supposed to be Del's moment. Don't ruin it—please."

Spritzer said nothing.

Michel went to Del and gave her a hug. "Are you really happy?"

"Oh, my dear, you have no idea." She took Michel's hand. "We're really going to miss you, you know."

"I know. Me too."

Del leaned in closer and asked softly, "Is Stevie going to be okay managing this whole operation by himself now?"

Michel laughed. "I've trained him well. He'll be fine. And there's always Skype in an emergency."

Del was surprised. "Good heavens...what is that?"

"A form of live Internet chat."

"Oh...sorry. I'm not up with all of that computer stuff so much these days."

"I'll set you up. That way you and I can visit too, whenever you'd like."

"Oh, that would be nice."

Spritzer took out the second bottle of wine. "We finished the first bottle. Anyone want some more?"

"Enough for now," Del said.

"I'll leave this in the fridge, then. And, of course, we can always bring you more."

"We need to sell it more than we need to drink it, don't you think?" Del reminded him.

Spritzer tapped the top of the wine carton. "And that's what this is for. If we do well at the Prix d'Or, we'll be able to establish a good, solid base price. I'm on my way to ship this right now."

Del went over and gave Spritzer a long hug. "I'm so proud of you, Stevie. Can't tell you how happy this makes me."

"I'm so glad." He looked at her and said, "And I'm sorry I was such a spoiled brat at times."

Del laughed and nodded, reaching up and pinching his cheek. "It's all on you now, my boy. Got to be a man now—like your father."

"I know. I won't disappoint. Promise."

"Good."

Spritzer picked up the carton of wine. "Now, I need to go ship this." He turned to Michel. "Ready?"

Michel nodded, took the ice bucket, and they left the kitchen together.

* * *

They had come in separate cars.

"I'd better get back to the office," Michel said. "I've got to pay for my ticket to Paris by this evening to get the best price."

"Whatever..." Spritzer brushed his comment away, as he got into the Jeep after putting the carton in the back.

He drove off with Michel looking after him.

He was headed to the UPS Store in Guerneville. He was still stewing about Michel's leaving, and his mind was not totally focused on the narrow, two-lane county road. As he came around a blind corner, he was faced with a passing car in his lane. He swerved and managed to get to the shoulder without being hit or running into the trees by the side of the road. But he was furious. He brought the Jeep to a halt and bounded out of it. He saw the fleeing car swerve and then strike a black Labrador that had been trotting along the far side of the road. Neither of the two other cars stopped. Spritzer could see that the dog was injured but still alive. He ran over to where the dog lay.

"Hey there, old buddy, let's take a look." He examined the Labrador. It was in shock, and whimpered slightly but didn't seem to be mortally hurt. He saw it had tags on its collar. He could call the owners later, but needed to get the dog to the nearest vet, right now.

He carried the dog over to his Jeep and put it on the front seat, on top of a folded tarp he picked up from the back floor.

Fortunately, the nearest vet was in the next village, not five minutes away. He drove directly to the vet's office. He took the dog inside to get help, then called the owner listed on the dog's tag.

A small child answered. *Oh shit*...What should he say?

"Is your mommy or daddy home?"

"No. Who's this, please?"

Spritzer didn't know what do to. "Do you have any older brothers or sisters?"

"Are you selling something?" the child asked.

"No. But I need to talk to someone older. It's about your family."

"Okay. Just a minute."

"Hello," an older girl answered. "What's this about?"

Spritzer thought quickly. "Hi, can you reach your parents? It's rather important."

"Who is this? Do we know you?"

Spritzer took a deep breath. "No, but I'm calling from the vet's office, and your parents need to call this number." He picked up a card from the front desk and then gave the girl the number.

"Is something wrong with Waldo?" she asked anxiously.

He assumed Waldo was the dog. "Just have them call this office, please. They can explain everything."

The girl seemed flustered. "I—ah...What...Okay." The girl hung up.

Spritzer turned to the office manager. "Thank you. The dog's owners will be calling you. I've gotta go." He turned to leave.

"Wait, you can't leave without paying."

Spritzer whipped back to the desk. "But I'm not the owner. I just found the dog by the side of the road and brought him in."

"Yeah, that's what they all say, then they stiff us on the bill."

Spritzer did not want to argue. He shook his head. "Okay, how much?"

"One hundred twenty-five deposit. Balance when you pick up the dog."

"But it's *not* my dog. I told you already." He opened his wallet and shelled out the money. "Okay, here."

The manager started to print out a receipt, but Spritzer was already running out the front door. He was too flustered and upset to spend any more time in the office. He just had to get out of there.

He got in the Jeep and started it up. After picking up the tarp from the front seat and tossing it into the back, he put the car in gear and then raced off.

* * *

Michel and Spritzer, with Del's blessing, had decided not to release the wine until after the Prix d'Or, as they wanted to set the very best price possible, and they knew that a good placement in the Prix d'Or would greatly increase the value of the wine. However, as the competition was later than they would usually release the wine, they needed to be patient and wait. This put a strain on Del's finances, and it was decided not to have the harvest festival this year.

Michel and Spritzer had been summoned by Del for a meeting. Del and Clara were in the orchard, harvesting the last of the ripe Italian plums. Clara was on a ladder, picking, and Del was standing on the ground, holding up a basket where Clara was tossing the plums. They had already filled two large baskets.

"Can we help?" Spritzer asked.

Clara said, "You can carry those two baskets into the kitchen when you leave."

"What are you going to do with all of those?" Michel queried.

"Jam and chutney," Del answered.

Michel said, "Let me know if I can help. I love canning."

"Thanks for the offer. All hands are welcome." Clara laughed as she descended the ladder.

"What did you want to meet about?" Spritzer asked Del, as he picked up the two baskets of plums. Michel took the third, and they headed toward the kitchen.

Del took Michel's arm. "It's been bothering me that we can't have the harvest festival this year. We've never missed having one since I came home from France all those years ago."

"It's your call, of course," Spritzer said, "but I don't see how we can afford it."

"Then how about a nice little celebration when we release the wine—for the workers and a few select friends?" Del asked. "Even though we're not to have the festival, don't you think we should celebrate our first sparkling wine release in some way?"

"I love the idea," Spritzer offered, "but, to be quite honest, if we celebrate the first release, people are going to expect to taste the wine, and I feel like we need to sell every single bottle we have since it's such a modest release."

"But we can spare *one* case, no? We won't be having that many folks. We can have other drinks, and offer just one glass to each of the guests when we officially release Maison Vallier."

"As you like," he agreed.

"And might I suggest we serve curried chicken pizzas with plum chutney as finger food. No need for a big spread," Michel offered.

"Love it." Del smiled. "And you're definitely welcome to help make the chutney."

"Count me in."

* * *

The Maison Vallier celebration was to be held on the Saturday before the Prix d'Or in the winery warehouse. Del thought it would be nice for the workers' families and guests to see how the wine was made, with Spritzer leading a guided tour for those interested.

"Did you invite Nelson?" Michel asked Del, as he opened out the white tablecloth across the serving table.

"Of course, how could I not? Remember, without his help, we wouldn't even be here."

"I know...but it's just..." He'd never told Del about his discovery of the darker side of Nelson, and he didn't see a reason to do so now. After all, he was their investor and one of Del's heirs. Best to leave it alone, he thought. "Never mind," he finally said.

Clara finished preparing the table for serving the food and wine, and Spritzer and Lorne came over with a large washtub filled with ice and the bottles of Maison Vallier. Then they brought out boxes of rented champagne flutes and placed the glasses on the table.

A number of workers and their families were already at the warehouse, and dozens of kids were running around, enjoying the large echoing space.

Kan and her husband, Reggie Trotter, and their one-year-old girl, Debbie, arrived.

"Hey, guys," Kan called out as she came over and gave Michel, and then Spritzer, a hug. Reggie, holding Debbie in his arms, followed. Reggie was not one of Kan's usual boyish rodeo roughnecks, but a stable, family man—slightly balding and nondescript, but with a pleasant air. He was an insurance provider with a solid business in Guerneville, and he doted on Kan and his daughter. And, for once, Kan seemed truly at peace with her situation.

Michel greeted Reggie and, looking at Debbie, said, "Oh my, look how she's grown. Hi, sweetie." He reached out and tousled her hair, but the child squirmed away.

"She's missing her nap. And she gets squirrely when she's tired," Reggie said.

Kan was examining the wine bottles in the tub when Michel came over to her. "My gosh, you guys really did it. I'm so excited to try the wine. Are we going to get a taste today?"

"You sure are," Michel assured her. "Is your dad coming?"

"He wanted to, but his arthritis is really acting up today, and I insisted he stay home." Kan reached out and took Michel's arm. "I am so going to miss you...When are you going back to France?"

"End of December."

"So, you'll be here for the Christmas party?"

Michel nodded. "Hey, I've been getting great reports about the sales of your oil in Europe."

Kan smiled and nodded. "Yes, indeed. And I'm developing a much larger market here in the US, as well."

"That's great."

"It's because your marketing department has given us a lot of very useful suggestions."

"Excellent."

Just then, there was the roar of an engine at the far end of the warehouse. Everyone turned to see Francisco drive through the open warehouse doors in his now completely restored Corvette.

Spritzer dashed over and stood admiring the finished car. "Man, that is one sweet ride."

"It took longer than I thought it would—but it's finally done," Francisco said, as he stood next to Spritzer, admiring his work.

By now a dozen men and boys were swarming around the car, looking at the engine, sitting in the new leather seats, and dreaming of their own sweet rides.

Michel came over and addressed Francisco. "So, this is what you did on your time off?"

"Better than a mistress. At least that's what Clara says." He laughed.

"So now what? Are you going to grieve, not having this to work on anymore?"

"I think Clara has ideas about me renovating the kitchen."

"Uh-oh...What have you got yourself into now?" Michel teased.

"It's okay. She's been very patient with me while I worked on this. And then there are the occasional classic car shows on weekends. I imagine I'll be checking those out from time to time."

Clara came over and gave Francisco a kiss on the cheek. "Now maybe there'll be space in the garage for me to park." She turned to Michel. "You can't imagine the room renovating a small car can take up."

"So, we have a double celebration today," Michel graciously added.

Clara responded, "Speaking of which...Del's ready to serve the wine. She's a little tired, but wants to say a few words before she goes back to the house."

"Then let's do it," Michel said, grabbing Spritzer by the arm and leading him toward the party table.

Spritzer turned to Michel as they headed back. "Lorne has a little surprise for us."

"Yeah?"

"He's arranged for a quartet from the Gay Men's Chorus to come and serenade Del before we serve the wine."

"Splendid."

They reached the serving table. Clara had placed a chair for Del to sit in until her little welcoming speech. Del was chatting with some of the workers' kids. Nelson was standing beside her, and he gave Michel a cool look as he approached.

Lorne came over to Spritzer. "They're ready. Shall we have the songs first?"

Spritzer nodded. "Sounds good. Do you want to introduce them?"

"Sure."

Michel and Spritzer went over to Del.

"We're going to start now, and we have a little surprise for you," Spritzer told her.

"What's that, honey?"

Spritzer nodded to Lorne who stepped forward. "Before the official welcoming of the new wine, we have a little serenade for the founder of this sparkling event. Del, and ladies and gentlemen, I present to you the Stonewall Quartet from the San Francisco Gay Men's Chorus." He reached his arm out and presented the four men, who stepped forward and began to sing to Del.

They started with the song "Pink Champagne," followed by "I Get a Kick Out of You," and ended with the song "Champagne, Champagne." Their performance was well received by the crowd, and it provided a nice opening to the afternoon.

Del just beamed. "Oh, that was charming. Thank you." She stood and addressed the group. "And welcome, everybody. I am so happy to have you all here this afternoon. It's been such a long, and sometimes frustrating, journey to get to where we are today. But here we are. Of course, none of this could have happened without my darling nephew, Stevie, and our sparkling *Chef de Cave*, Michel Bast. And, I must also add a special thanks to my other nephew, Nelson Wayland, whose invaluable investments helped make my dream become a reality. A big thanks to each one of you.

"But enough from me. I know you are all dying to taste the fruits of our labors. And so, without further ado, I officially announce the first release of the Maison Vallier Grand Reserve Wayland Demi-Sec Sparkling Wine."

Spritzer, Michel, and Clara were standing by, and at the end of Del's speech they popped the first corks and began pouring the wine for the guests.

Then Spritzer shouted out to the crowd as he poured, "Please wait to taste the wine until everyone is served, and then we'll have a toast."

They kept opening bottles until all of the guests had a full glass.

And then Spritzer turned to the audience and announced, "And now we toast. To Del's wonderful vision—may the dream always inspire the reality."

Then each guest turned to their neighbor, smiled, and clinked their glasses.

Spritzer turned to Michel and touched his glass with his, "To you."

"To us," Michel responded.

Nelson wandered his way over to Spritzer and Michel. He tipped his glass of sparkling wine toward them.

"Very sporty," Nelson said.

"And what exactly does that mean?" Spritzer asked. "Are you judging horses now?"

Nelson chuckled. "No, I just meant that I think you'll have a sporting chance at the Prix d'Or."

"So, you like our modest effort?" Michel asked.

Nelson smiled. "Come now, I don't for a moment believe that you think this delightful wine is modest."

"That means you like it then?"

"I know we've had our differences," Nelson said, "but I have to give praise where and when praise is due. And I fully acknowledge your fine accomplishment." He nodded. "Michel...Spritzer, all the best of luck at the competition. I look forward to seeing the results."

CHAPTER TWELVE

It was the early morning of the Prix d'Or, and the Marconi Conference Center in San Francisco bustled with activity as the tablecloth-covered presentation tables were being prepared by the center's staff for the International Wine Competition later that morning.

At the champagne and sparkling wine table, two Prix d'Or judges were conferring, trying to solve a puzzle. They had been checking each entry as the cartons of entered wine were being placed on the tables.

"Did you check all of the boxes?" the first official asked.

"Every single one," the second answered. "And also the intake paperwork."

They double-checked all the boxes on the table.

"I don't think it ever arrived," the first said.

"But their entry paperwork is in order?"

"Yes. Absolutely."

"What do we do in a case like this?"

"Where is the entry from?"

"Sonoma."

The first official thought for a moment. "Let's give them a break. Let me give them a call. Perhaps they could get here with their entry before the judging begins." He pulled out his phone and dialed.

* * *

Spritzer stood in front of the long mirror in Michel's bedroom. He was dressed in a suit and tie—a very rare occurrence for him. *I look ridiculous,* he thought, examining his reflection from every angle. *What imbecile dreamed up this ridiculous outfit?* He pulled at the too-tight collar at his neck.

He turned toward the bathroom where Michel was finishing shaving. He shouted, "I said we'd pick up Lorne on our way out."

Michel shouted back, "You don't have to shout, I can hear you just fine."

"I wasn't shouting," Spritzer shouted. His phone rang. He didn't recognize the caller ID. "Hello."

"Hello, this is Dalton Wibner at the Prix d'Or."

"Yes, sir..."

"I have you listed as the contact for the Maison Vallier Winery."

"Yes, Steven Vallier..."

"For some reason, we can't find your entry for the sparkling wine competition. You did send it in, didn't you?

As he listened, his expression changed from mildly anxious to outright terror.

"Yes...yes, of course."

"Well, as far as we can see, it never arrived."

"Oh my God. What can be done?"

"As your paperwork is all in order, if you can be here by ten o'clock with a carton of your wine, we can still fit you into the competition. Do you think you can do that?"

"Absolutely, we'll do our very best. Thanks so much for letting me know." He hung up and raced to the bathroom door. "That was the Prix d'Or. They can't find our carton of wine."

Michel stopped drying his hair and turned to Spritzer. "What the fuck?"

Then Spritzer remembered. He'd never sent it. He slammed his hand to his head. "Dumb, dumb, dumb," he chanted. "And it's all my fault."

"What?" Michel cried out.

"But they said if we could get a carton of wine there by ten, we could still be in the judging," he said, forestalling having to tell Michel why he was responsible for this mix-up.

Michel glanced at his watch. "How much time do we have?"

"Two hours."

"Okay, let's go. Let's go." He quickly finished dressing, ran to the living room, carrying his shoes, and grabbed his bag.

Spritzer dashed out of the house to his Jeep. He tore away the tarp, and found the carton of wine he had forgotten to ship after the accident with the dog. He jumped into the driver's seat and opened the passenger door for Michel. He scrambled in, and they sped off as he put on his shoes.

Spritzer headed toward the entrance of the 101 Freeway to San Francisco. Michel turned to him. "Where are you going? We've got to go get the wine first."

Spritzer glanced over at him. "No, I've already got it."

"What?"

"I never shipped it. It's in the back." He turned his head toward the back of the Jeep.

Michel was too stunned at first to respond. But he turned to where Spritzer indicated and saw the carton. He lifted it up, placing it on the floor in front of him. He opened the carton and said, "Ice. We've got to get ice to chill some of the wine. It'll be a disaster if we don't."

"I've got a work bucket in the back. We can use that."

"Then stop at the first store that sells ice, and I'll chill it while you drive."

They stopped at a gas station and bought two bags of ice. Michel began chilling the wine.

"Oh shit," Spritzer said. "I forgot to pick up Lorne. Can you call him and tell him what's happened?"

Michel glowered at Spritzer, but took out his phone and called.

"Your jackass of a half-brother forgot to ship the wine to the competition. And he's asked me to tell you he's also forgotten to pick you up. So sorry." He ended the call and glared out the front window.

* * *

They drove in silence for a while, tension rising in the Jeep.

"Do you care to tell me exactly why you forgot to ship our entry?" Michel asked carefully, not wanting to stir up a heated argument just now.

Spritzer reminded him of the incident with the injured dog, and how it had diverted him from his errand to send the wine. That mollified Michel somewhat, as he could understand how Spritzer might have been upset and forgetful after the accident.

They remained silent until they neared Sausalito.

"Shit..." Spritzer said.

"What now?"

"I've got to get gas."

"Why didn't you get it when we got the ice?"

He turned to Michel. "Come on, give me a personal break. Think I might be under a little stress here?"

Michel nodded.

Spritzer sped off the freeway and headed toward the first gas station he could find. He filled the tank and got back into the car. Traffic was reduced to a crawl as they headed toward the next Sausalito freeway entrance—tourists dashing in front of cars as they bounded from boutique to café.

"What's the time?" Spritzer asked.

"Nine fifteen. Are we going to make it?"

"Don't know. Ah...here we go, a break." Spritzer accelerated past a double-parked car that had been slowing the traffic, and they were soon crossing the Golden Gate Bridge.

Finally, the Jeep shuddered to a bouncing stop in front of the conference center. Michel threw open the door. He grabbed the bucket and tore off toward the entrance.

Spritzer called after him, "Ask for Dalton Wibner. I'll park and bring the rest of the wine."

* * *

Michel ran into the exhibition hall where the competition was being held.

"Mr. Bibner?" he called out.

"Wibner...Dalton Wibner," a man said, rather coolly. "How can I help you?"

"I've got the Maison Vallier sparkling wine. Are we still in time?"

"Ah yes," Wibner said, softening slightly. "Bring it over here." He saw Michel's bucket with the four bottles. "However, you do realize we require a full carton of twelve bottles."

"Yes, the rest is coming. My associate is parking. He's bringing the rest."

"Very well, then."

Michel placed the bucket on the table. He then stood back as Dalton prepared their bottles for the competition. As it was a blind tasting, each bottle had a sleeve slipped over it to hide the identity of the winery from the judges.

Spritzer rushed up with the carton with the other eight bottles. "Here." He handed the carton to the second official. "Are we okay?" He turned first to Michel and then to Wibner.

Wibner nodded.

Spritzer went over and fell into Michel's arms. "I'm so sorry. I can't believe I almost blew our best chance. What a fool I am." He began to cry. "Can you forgive me?"

Michel began to laugh. "Come on. Come on. It's nothing. We're here. We're okay, and I completely understand about the oversight."

Michel led Spritzer to the chairs laid out in rows for the participants, wine merchants, and press. Michel saw Nelson at the back of the room, deep in conversation with other merchants and wholesalers.

The judging started at eleven. The sparkling wines were at the very end of the tasting. The judges started with the reds, moved on to the whites, and then the rosés and dessert wines before finally judging the sparkling category.

Spritzer and Michel had a catalogue of the wines being judged, and they studied their competition. Fortunately, the homegrown wines were in a different category from the European, African, Australian, and South American wines. Even Spritzer knew they were not yet able to compete with the best of the French champagnes.

After the judges had sampled all the wines, they retired to make their decisions. It was now well after one o'clock. There was an announcement that the awards would be presented at three.

Spritzer turned to Michel. "Want some lunch?"

He hesitated. "I'm not sure I could eat anything right now."

"Why? Are you nervous?"

"A little. Aren't you?"

"Yes, I'm nervous, but the nervous energy makes me hungry."

"Why don't you go grab a burger or something?"

"Sure you don't want to come with me?"

He shook his head. Spritzer headed out.

Michel was studying the catalogue when a hand tapped him on the shoulder. He turned to look. It was Nelson.

"Greetings. I see you finally made it. There was a flurry of activity before you arrived, with the judges about to pull your entry."

Michel answered coolly, "Yes, there was a slight mix-up with the wine, but all is now well."

Nelson sat down next to him. "How reassuring."

Michel turned forward and again consulted the catalogue.

"So, you'll be heading back to *la belle France* soon, *n'est-ce pas?*"

"Yes, Nelson, I will."

"So, you and Spritzer, then? What? A long-distance relationship? A parting of the ways? What do you two have to look forward to?"

Michel sighed. "Nelson, I honestly don't know. All I know is that I am heading home. My contract with Del is complete. My connection with Maison Vallier is severed, and I expect to get on with the rest of my life. And, most certainly, I can say unequivocally that my relationship with you is finally, irrevocably, and most gratefully ended." He glared at Nelson.

Nelson nodded. He stood, turned, and walked away. He'd only taken a few paces when he turned back and said, "Good luck with the wine. I certainly hope you haven't let Del down."

Michel answered coolly, "You've tasted it. You know its quality."

"But I may be biased. Let's just wait and see what the judges think."

* * *

Just before three, Spritzer returned. He was carrying a small white paper bag. "Here." He offered the bag to Michel. "I thought you might like to have something to eat, so I brought you a croque-monsieur. It sounded appropriately French, so I figured you might like it."

Michel smiled. "That's very nice. And yes, they are quite delicious. Thank you."

"Any news yet?"

"Not yet."

Just then, the judges began filing onto the stage and one went to the microphone.

Spritzer's phone rang. "Oh shit, it's Francisco. I told him I'd call when we got here, and I totally forgot. I'd better get this." Spritzer answered the phone and went out into the hallway to take the call. "Oh good, Lorne told you about our snafu. Sorry, I didn't call earlier, but we got caught up in our little emergency...The judges have just come out with their decisions. We should know any minute now."

Francisco had a question about a part for one of the forklifts, and he and Spritzer were discussing that when Michel came charging out into the hall and over to Spritzer. He grabbed Spritzer by the shoulders and spun him around.

"We won! We won a silver medal in the US sparkling wine division."

"Really?" Spritzer shouted.

"We won. Come." He took Spritzer's phone and shouted to Francisco. "We won. We won. It's a second, but we won." He handed the phone back to Spritzer. "Say good-bye. Come." But then he had a thought and grabbed the phone again. "Francisco, don't tell Del just yet. We want to surprise her." He gave the phone back to Spritzer.

Spritzer said good-bye as Michel led him back into the hall. They raced over to see their medal laid out on the table in front of their bottle.

The judges were still placing medals, and a judge came over and placed a second certificate in front of their bottle. It was an honorable mention in their class in the worldwide competition.

Spritzer and Michel looked at each other in disbelief.

"We got a silver in the US and an honorable mention in the worldwide. Can you believe it?" Michel shouted, grabbing hold of Spritzer and shaking him. "This is unheard of."

As the awards were posted on the electric signboard at the front of the hall, Spritzer and Michel were immediately surrounded by a swarm of press and merchants.

A reporter thrust his microphone at Michel. "This is a first. A new sparkling wine winning a medal in its first release. How do you feel about that?"

"Great!" Spritzer blurted out.

"*Formidable.*" Michel beamed.

A second reporter leaned in and asked, "Do you have a press release you can give me about your wine?"

Spritzer was breathless with the attention. "No, not yet. I'm afraid we were unprepared. We never expected such a success and so much attention. Sorry." He reached into his jacket pocket and took out a bunch of business cards that he began handing out. "But here's our card. Call us and we'll send you whatever you need."

A third reporter asked, "How large is your first release?"

Michel answered. "About five thousand cases."

The reporters were surprised.

"That's exceptionally small," one of the reporters commented.

"What is your retail price going to be?" one of the merchants asked.

Spritzer stammered. "Well...it's not clear...We've not set a price yet."

"We've been waiting for the results of the competition," Michel answered.

"Are you the Cellar Master?" the first reporter asked.

"*Chef de Cave,*" Michel insisted.

"I'd like an interview if I may. I'd like to ask some more detailed questions. Do you have a moment now?"

"Certainly."

The reporter led Michel to the chairs where they could sit and conduct the interview.

Several merchants pushed forward, as the other reporters headed out to interview other winners.

One handed Spritzer a card. "I'd like to buy a hundred cases."

A second merchant added, "And me." He handed Spritzer his card as well.

Another merchant said, "I'm up in Sonoma next week. May I stop by? I'd like to talk about a long-term commitment.

Suddenly Nelson appeared, elbowing his way through the admirers. "Well, well, well. Ya done good, kids."

"Nelson, I didn't know you were going to be here?" Spritzer said.

Another merchant interrupted Nelson. "Mr. Vallier, I'd like to place an order too."

Nelson turned to all the merchants, lifting his hands up in the air to stop them. "Ladies, gentlemen. I am so sorry, but this release is already completely sold out. However, you may contact Wayland Distributors to place your orders."

The merchants were disappointed, but at least now knew where to order.

Spritzer, however, was not sure what was going on. "What?"

"Come with me, dear boy." Nelson led Spritzer away from the crowd.

"What are you doing? We haven't sold anything yet."

"Oh yes, you have."

"Oh yeah, to whom?"

"Why, to me, of course. I'll buy your entire release for...let's say twenty dollars a bottle. Is that acceptable?"

Spritzer was speechless.

"Of course, we'll need to make up some additional labels to stick on the bottles, touting your prizes. Very impressive, dear boy. I never knew you had it in you." Nelson took out his checkbook and began writing out a check. "Here's a deposit...the balance upon delivery. After all, I believe in keeping it all in the family, don't you?"

"Wait, don't we need some kind of contract or something?" Spritzer said. It was all moving so fast and he needed to speak to Michel about this first.

"And why would we need that? It's a straightforward transaction. You have wine to sell—I buy it."

"I'm sorry. That's an excellent offer, but I want to confer with Michel about this first before we accept."

"As you wish. However, my offer will expire in ten minutes."

Spritzer dashed over to Michel, who was still chatting with the reporter.

"Excuse me," Spritzer said, as he pulled Michel away.

"I'll be right back," he said to the reporter as Spritzer led him aside.

"What? I was right in the middle of a very good interview."

"Sorry. But Nelson has just offered to buy the whole release for twenty a bottle. I didn't want to say yes without talking to you first."

"Twenty, eh?"

"That's a great price, but do you think we could get more? A lot of merchants gave me their cards and wanted to buy a hundred cases or more."

"Did Nelson want a contract?"

"He said not."

"Then I think you should accept his offer. Since you aren't obliged to sell other releases to him, it would give you time to see how sales go at that price and maybe next year you could set an even higher price. With the win today, I'm sure many offers will come in and you can consider them for next year. It's good to keep your options open."

"Okay, let's do it, then."

* * *

Spritzer treated Michel to a celebratory dinner after the competition at his favorite Italian restaurant in Little Italy. However, as their sparkling wine wasn't on the menu yet, they treated themselves to a fine bottle of Italian prosecco. As happy as Spritzer was with the win at the competition, he was also sad, as he realized it was getting ever closer to Michel's time of departure.

They were a little later getting away from San Francisco than they'd anticipated, so when they got back to Coeur du Chêne, it was nearly ten o'clock.

"Are we too late to go see Del?" Michel asked.

"Don't think it will matter. I know she's going to want to celebrate with us," Spritzer insisted.

They went inside. As they walked quietly through the house, Spritzer slipped the medal from around his neck and then knocked gently on Del's bedroom door. She didn't answer.

Spritzer opened the door and peeked in. Del was in her bed, a book on her lap. She was asleep against a bank of pillows with the bedside light still on.

They tiptoed over to her bed. Michel picked up the book, and Spritzer leaned in and gave Del a kiss on her forehead.

Del opened her eyes. "Oh, you're back. Sorry, I dozed off. I was hoping you'd come to see me. How did it go?"

Spritzer leaned over and put the medal around her neck.

"What's this?"

"We won a second-place medal for the US and an honorable mention for worldwide."

Del's face lit up. She picked up the medal and looked at it.

"And here, take a look at this." Spritzer handed her the check for the sale of the wine. "The entire release is sold out! Nelson is paying us twenty dollars a bottle. Now you can make all your payments, pay down some debt, and we'll have enough to keep us going into the next year."

Del leaned back against her pillows and smiled. She reached out and took each of their hands. "You did it...you two together. I'm so very proud."

Spritzer added. "And I promise you...next year...first place."

"So...you've become a *Chef de Cave,* have you?" she said, addressing Spritzer. "Ready to run Maison Vallier all by yourself now?"

Spritzer glanced over to Michel. "If he'll let me."

Michel smiled, but answered honestly. "He certainly knows how to run the operation, and I've been training him on how to create each year's cuvée, but only time will tell if he has the palate and the skill to maintain the character that's been established."

"I've tried hard to learn."

Del looked at Spritzer. "I have faith in him."

* * *

As it was a cold late-December night, Spritzer and Michel were curled up together in front of Michel's fireplace, where the embers of the evening's fire were turning to ash and giving out the last of their warmth. Michel was resting against an upholstered chair with the seat cushion slipped down for him to lean against. Spritzer was stretched out on the floor with his head in Michel's lap. Michel stroked Spritzer's hair.

"What time do you need to be at the airport?" Spritzer asked.

"Two."

They remained silent a few more moments. Then Michel shifted, indicating he wanted to stand.

"I need to finish my packing," he said. "Maybe you could run the dishwasher. I want to leave the house as nice as I found it."

But before he could rise, Spritzer turned, supported himself with his elbow, and faced Michel. "Not just yet. Let's stay here a little longer. I can help you finish your packing in the morning."

"It's not just that," he said.

"What then?" Spritzer sounded alarmed.

Michel was thoughtful. He was struggling to say what must be said. "Spritz, these past few years have been wonderful." He paused. "But I really didn't want this to happen."

"Why?"

"We're so different. It could never work in the long term."

"I don't believe that," Spritzer said, taking hold of Michel's hand.

He pulled away. "But I thought you understood this was just for a limited time. It's a different kind of relationship when you know you must part eventually. My contract is up, and I need to go home. You know that. And you've known that from the beginning."

"No. Stay. Someday, part of the winery will be mine. It could be ours. You could do everything here that you do in France. No...More. It's all new here. Wide open possibilities. It's exciting."

"Do you really think we could make it together as a couple—over the long haul?" Michel asked gently.

"Why not?"

"I think I know myself, and I think I know you. At the base, we are both fundamentally different. I know it's painful right now, but I think it's really for the best if we part."

Spritzer thought for a moment. "You're afraid, aren't you?" Michel didn't answer. "You're afraid of loving me—of loving anyone."

"I am not afraid. But I've not had the best track record with men truly willing to commit to a relationship. And honestly, Spritz, do you really know if you're even gay?"

"What does it matter? I do love you. I do commit to you. What else could you want?"

Michel shook his head. "Let's just make a clean break of it. Okay? I haven't got anything more to say."

Spritzer looked deeply into Michel's eyes. "It's you. You're the one who's changed me."

"Spritz, please." He shook his head, stood, and then headed to the bedroom to finish his packing.

* * *

Michel insisted he did *not* want Spritzer to go with him inside the airport. As he explained, Spritzer didn't have a ticket, he would not be allowed through security, and he wouldn't be able to accompany Michel to the gate. He had rationalized it very well, but that was not his real reason for not wanting Spritzer to join him. He hated good-byes and did not want to create an emotional spectacle.

So Spritzer dropped Michel off at the curb, and they made their hasty farewells—hugging, quick kisses on the cheek, and a parting wish for a *bon voyage*. Spritzer got back in the car, but, instead of driving away, he went to the parking garage. Once he had parked, he went to the observation deck where he could watch Michel's Air France plane take off. It was pointless, of course, but he waved good-bye as Michel's plane taxied from the terminal and took off down the runway.

* * *

2017

After Michel left, Spritzer was totally in charge of Maison Vallier. He'd promoted Francisco to run Vallier Winery. And while he took his new responsibility seriously, he was also lost in a fog—his days a series of poignant vignettes:

* * *

Standing at the loading dock, he looked out over the vineyard in the gray light. A light drizzle was falling. Suddenly, a gust of wind gave him a piercing chill. He'd been remembering when he and Michel were T-budding in the blazing sun...

At his desk, he picked up the silver frame with the photo of Michel and him holding a bottle of the first release—huge smiles on their faces. That strand of hair he found so attractive had fallen across Michel's forehead...

Spritzer drove by Michel's house. He stopped outside. A child's truck was on the front lawn. New curtains were in the windows. A single tennis shoe was on the front step. This house no longer belonged to his absent friend. He drove away...

Spritzer and dozens of workers were picking grapes by hand for the next harvest. And, as he worked, he still couldn't break the habit of wanting to turn to Michel and tell him his latest brilliant idea, or exchange a simple smile...

Spritzer was pressing the grapes in Michel's famous coquard press. He went over to the vat that was to contain the first pressing. Hanging on the side of the vat was the chalk slate from the previous season, still bearing Michel's handwriting. He started to wipe it clean to put in the new information, but he couldn't bring himself to erase it. He stood looking at it for a few moments, but then, finally, he took his sleeve and wiped the slate clean.

* * *

Spritzer got out of his Jeep in front of Coeur du Chêne. He took an ice bucket with the first bottle of the second release out of the passenger seat, along with two champagne flutes. This release would be substantially larger than the first, and he had already presold the entire inventory at an even better price than the year before. The press and reviews had been fantastic and demand was high. He walked through the arbor to Del's studio and went inside.

Del was packing a box with a few of her ceramic works. It made Spritzer sad to see the almost empty shelves. The potter's wheel was clean and unused—as it had been for far too many months now.

Spritzer said brightly, "Well, here it is. Number one of number two."

"What?" Del asked, looking up from her packing.

"First bottle of the second release. Are you ready to try it?"

Del's face brightened. "Oh, my goodness. I can't wait. But I've got to sit, dear."

Spritzer put the ice bucket and glasses on her worktable and then escorted her to the sofa. She was still using a cane, and had yet to regain her full strength and mobility after the fall.

Spritzer went back to the table and carefully opened the bottle with the satisfying fizzy release as he slowly edged the cork out of the bottle to avoid spillage. He filled the two glasses and then went over to the sofa and sat down next to Del, after handing her a glass.

She looked at him, smiling, and they clinked glasses. "To Maison Vallier and a successful second release," she said.

Spritzer nodded. They both carefully tasted the new wine.

Del turned to him. "It's even better than the first. Isn't it?"

"Yes. I believe it is."

Del lowered her eyes, thoughtfully. "We miss him, don't we," she said softly.

Tears welled up in Spritzer's eyes. "If it wasn't for him..." But he couldn't say any more.

They looked at each other, and Del reached over and patted Spritzer's hand affectionately. "I've been wanting to talk to you but, oh dear, it's been so difficult...I've really not been able to work since the fall. But you know that."

"But you're improving, aren't you?"

Del shook her head. "No, Stevie. The fall was three years ago. I'm never going to get back to the shape I was in before. It's finished. I'm tired, and I've made a decision."

"Yes?"

"I'm going to settle my affairs now with a living trust. That way there will be no need for probate when I go. I want you to have your inheritance now."

Spritzer took her hand. "Del..."

"Wait, hear me out. It's not quite what you might expect."

Spritzer suddenly felt uneasy. What did she have in mind?

Del continued, "I'm leaving half of the jug winery to Nelson..."

"What?"

"Wait. Wait. Not quite half. Forty-nine percent to him and fifty-one percent to you. I want you to have the control." She laughed. "It will do him good to have to sell jug wine with all his uppity ways."

They both found that profoundly amusing.

"Oh, is he going to be pissed. I'm sure he was hoping to get the champagne winery all for himself," Spritzer said.

"Sparkling wine."

He nodded and smiled. "Yes..."

"And Stevie, honey, I'm leaving all of the Maison Vallier winery to you—"

"Del..."

"—and Michel. He's become family, don't you think?"

Spritzer was too shocked to speak.

"Well, fifty-one percent to Michel, and forty-nine percent to you."

His mind was reeling. He still couldn't speak, as he tried to assimilate this news with all its implications.

Del smiled as she said, "Think you can handle it?"

"I...I...but...but..."

"But, Stevie, there is still one thing that displeases me very much."

"Oh my...what's that?"

"Your behavior lately has been far too sullen. I think something needs to be done about that." She got up and went over to her desk. She opened a drawer, took out an envelope, and returned, sitting down again. "First, I think Michel needs to sample this year's release. Secondly, someone is going to have to tell him about the trust. And, lastly, don't you think it's time you took a real vacation?"

She handed the envelope to Spritzer. He opened it and took out a confirmation for a flight on Air France to Paris.

"What...?"

"First class. I think you deserve it."

"Holy cow...are you serious?"

"Absolutely."

"But, Del, why don't you come with me? Wouldn't it be wonderful for you to go back to France? Then you could tell Michel yourself. I'm sure he would appreciate that."

Del laughed. "I believe on an international flight you're allowed to check one old bag for free. Do you think I might qualify?"

"Del..."

"Didn't think so. No. You need to do this alone. And besides, honey, I don't feel up for a trip right now. It would be much better for you two to have some time together alone. Oh, and make sure the wine is good and cold when you serve it to him."

* * *

Spritzer drove through the Champagne countryside in a rental car. All around him, the hills were covered in vines. Every square meter that could be cultivated was. He'd never seen anything quite like it before. Beside him on the passenger seat was a bucket of ice with a bottle of the new release. Up ahead he saw a sign for the Domaine Bast estate. He suddenly became unexpectedly nervous at seeing Michel again after a year.

He drove up to the winery, got out of the car, and studied the surroundings. It was a beautiful setting, and he looked for the tasting room, but didn't see one. A worker was passing by and Spritzer called out. "Hello. Hello. Can you help me?"

The worker came over. "*Monsieur*?"

"Do you speak English?"

"A leettle."

Spritzer began talking too loud, the way people tend to do when they think someone can't understand them. "I'm looking for Michel Bast."

The worker laughed. "Ah...he is in ah...Zer es ah...*competition*...ah..." He struggled to find more words.

"I understand."

"*Pour le champagne*...you know to go?"

Spritzer unfolded his map. "I have a map. Where?"

The worker pointed to a town not far away. "*Ici...ah*...beeg...beeg...ah *hotel de ville*."

Spritzer was puzzled. "A hotel?"

The worker was flustered. "*No...ah...comment*...city hall, I think you say. *Oui...oui*."

Spritzer understood. "Ah, yes. I understand. *Merci*." He started toward the car, but stopped and turned back to the worker.

"At what time? *A quelle heure?*" He remembered Michel using that phrase.

"*Treize*." The worker held up ten fingers, then three.

"Thirteen?" Then he remembered France was on the twenty-four-hour clock—one o'clock his time. He checked his watch. It was already twelve thirty. He dashed to the car, got in, and sped off.

It was not difficult finding the city hall. It was the single most imposing building in the village square. Parking was not going to be easy, as this appeared to be a very prestigious event and there were many attendees. But he had a small car and found a place he could squeeze into—though it may not have been a legal parking space.

Spritzer dashed over to the entrance and went inside. It was clear where the competition was being held, and he went into the hall. He stood and looked around. It was a very impressive location. The hall was very old—probably sixteenth or seventeenth century. The judges wore black robes and formal hats. Each judge had a large, ceremonial gold chain around his neck, at the end of which was a gold cup. He wondered if was it to be used in the tasting of the wines or whether it was merely ceremonial. The dark, wood-paneled room was lit with candle chandeliers and candelabras on the presentation tables.

Spritzer looked around. He saw Michel at a table across the room. He was preparing several bottles of his chateau's wine for the competition. He didn't see Spritzer.

Spritzer suddenly got an idea, and rushed out of the building and back to his car. He opened the passenger door and took out his bottle of wine. He dashed back to the city hall and ran up to the registration table. He waved his bottle at the young man attending at the table.

"*Entrée, por favor,*" Spritzer blurted out.

The registrar laughed and handed Spritzer a card to fill out along with a numbered card for his bottle. "I speak English. Here, please fill this out. It's a little late, but they might still accept your entry."

"I just got off the plane from San Francisco. Sorry, I'm late."

The registrar nodded, then took the bottle, placed a sleeve over it, and went over to put it near the end of the sparkling wine table. Spritzer stood at the registration table and filled out the entry form, struggling with the instructions in French. When the registrar returned, Spritzer handed him the form.

"Is that okay? My French—not so good."

The registrar examined it, made a few changes, then nodded. "Yes, sir. This is fine. Good luck."

Spritzer stayed at the back of the hall. He didn't want Michel to see him just yet, although part of him wanted to rush into his arms. He found it sweet to prolong the anticipation. But, after a while, he couldn't stand the suspense anymore, and he went back to the registrar and asked, "What time will the results be announced?"

"About 15:00," he said.

"Three o'clock. Thank you."

Spritzer went outside and decided to get a bite to eat, as he'd not had anything since he landed in Paris. He found a small café, sat down, and took a deep breath.

A waiter came over. "*Monsieur?*"

Spritzer looked around and pointed to a glass of red wine at an adjoining table. "And..." He mimed eating a sandwich. "Ham...cheese...*fromage.*" He remembered that word as well.

"*Oui, Monsieur.*"

After he'd eaten, Spritzer was too nervous to sit quietly and wait. He paid his bill and left the café. He wandered around the town until it was almost time for the announcements, and then headed back to the city hall.

As he returned, the judges were already presenting the awards. He continued to hang back. The winning wines had their sleeves removed, and a certificate was placed in front of the winning bottles. Medals for first, second, and third places were hung around the neck of each winning bottle. Honorable mentions received only a certificate.

There were different judges for each category so the awards were presented expeditiously. Spritzer was gratified to see that Michel's champagne had won a gold medal. Michel went up to the table to accept the award. He was quickly surrounded by a crowd of well-wishers and other vintners. It was clear he had done this before, as his house was a consistent winner at these events.

Spritzer watched, as Michel glanced at the end of the table. The last of the awards at the champagne table were being presented. Michel froze. Then he went to over to where Spritzer's bottle was receiving an honorable mention certificate. He picked up the bottle and studied the familiar label. He put the bottle down and turned, scanning the room. Then Michel saw him standing at the back of the room, smiling his wonderful quirky grin. But Michel didn't move. Instead, Spritzer started walking toward Michel, his arms open to receive him. But, on his way over, he got another idea. Instead, he picked up two champagne flutes from a table. He walked over to his bottle and filled the two glasses. He then turned to Michel.

Michel smiled broadly. "Hello, you."

Spritzer handed him a glass. "Thought you might like to try a really superior second release sparkling wine from across the pond."

Michel held the glass up to the light. "Looks promising." He held the glass up to his nose. "The aroma is promising." He then closed his eyes as he took a sip. He savored the taste. "And it more than lives up to that promise."

"Hi," Spritzer, said simply.

They looked at each other for a long time before speaking.

"I've missed you so much," Michel finally stated. "More than I ever thought I could."

"Really? Me too."

Michel was almost unable to speak again. "I never thought..." He began to shake. "Look, I'm trembling."

"I'll take care of that." Spritzer put his glass down and took Michel in his arms, holding him silently for a long moment. "Oh, that is so good."

Finally, Michel broke away, and, holding up his glass to Spritzer, said, "A toast to us. May the blending of our two very different natures produce the perfect cuvée."

Spritzer picked up his glass, and they clinked and drank.

"Ah, it's wonderful. You should be very proud," Michel said.

"I'm glad you like it. Because I have some very interesting news for you from Del."

"How nice. Can't tell you how much I've missed her. Is she well?"

"Not good. Not bad—but improving slowly."

Michel leaned against Spritzer and put his arm around his shoulder. "So, what is it Del needs to tell me that she couldn't call, Skype, or email me?"

"It's about the future of the vineyard...and about us. I think you and I are going to need to find a way to live together in two different places," Spritzer said, with his slyest smile. "We have a lot to talk about."

ABOUT THE AUTHOR

Jon McDonald lives in Santa Fe, New Mexico. He has seven published novels, a memoir, and three children's books. His short stories have appeared in a number of prestigious publications. He considers himself a genre-bending author—he loves to take an established literary genre, play with it, and turn it on its head. He has lived abroad and traveled extensively.

Facebook: https://www.facebook.com/Jon-McDonald-146587072143639
Website: www.jonmcdonaldauthor.com
E-mail jonauthor@gmail.com

ALSO BY JON MCDONALD

Gotta Dance with the One Who Brung Ya

The Seed

NINESTAR PRESS, LLC

www.ninestarpress.com

www.ingramcontent.com/pod-product-compliance
Lightning Source LLC
Chambersburg PA
CBHW050039180626
46810CB00002B/805